THE FISHERMAN RETURNS

by
J T Owens

THE FISHERMAN RETURNS
Copyright © 2024 by Red Lodge Publications
All rights reserved.

The Characters and events portrayed in this book are ficticious. Any similarity to real persons, living or dead is coincidental and not intended by the author.

No part of this book may be used or reproduced in any manner whatsoever without written permission except in the case of brief quotations embodied in critical articles or reviews.

For more information visit:
htps://jtowensauthor.co.uk
First Edition: April 2024

CONTENT

Preface 4
1. Pedro Batista - Oporto 1975 5
2. Póvoa de Varzim Northern Portugal Summer 1978 . 18
3. Póvoa do Varzim - The same evening 32
4. London, England – the following day 48
5. London, Heathrow Airport - The next day 60
6. The Fisherman Returns 75
7. A Farmhouse near Viana do Castelo Northern Portugal . 90
8. Captive again 104
9. News comes to Oporto 111
10. The search for Laura 126
11. Helga's Spite 134
12. The Farmhouse – the following morning 143
13. A Package Arrives 154
14. The Angel at João's Apartment 162
15. Night stalking at the Farmhouse 170
16. Luis examines his Plan 183
17. Dos Santos goes on a Mission 195
18. Deception 204
19. Countdown 218
20. Police Headquarters - Póvoa de Varzim 227
21. Luis goes into Action 233
22. Sunday Morning - Póvoa de Varzim
    The Feast of Nossa Senhora da Assunção 239
23. The Farmhouse - Sunday Lunch 250
24. Denouement 257

Epilogue 267

PREFACE

In April 1932, Antonio de Oliveira Salazar became the Presidente do Conselho, Prime Minister of Portugal. There followed over 40 years of dictatorship for Portugal. It was not brought to an end until 1975. Throughout that time the PIDE, the Policia International e de Defesa do Esta-do, Portugal's political and security police rigidly enforced Article 8 of the constitution which stated: *"special laws shall govern the exercise of the freedom of expression, education, meeting and of association."*

Their prime target was the infant Communist movement, one of whose strongest branches was in the north of Portugal. The PIDE, like all security police, had their own very special methods of interrogation.

'*The Fisherman Returns*' follows the aftermath of one such interrogation and its widespread consequences for those both directly and indirectly involved. Those conse-quences reached a British family, a few years after the fall of the dictatorship, and the breakup of the PIDE. It was the family of a British Sanctum agent who had been indirectly involved in that interrogation. J T Owens

CHAPTER I
PEDRO BATISTA - OPORTO 1975

It was early afternoon and the heat of an Oporto July day had reached its peak. Inside the clinic room where Pedro Batista lay fitfully sleeping, the air was oppressive. A strong smell of disinfectant clung to the dark green curtains and crumpled bedcovers. An old-fashioned fan had been placed by one of the nurses on a table near the bed. It hummed unevenly and gave only the merest whisper of air. Batista twitched as a fly flew from the ceiling and landed on his cheek.

A heavily built man, wearing a beige cotton suit, stood in the corner near the window. He wiped away the beads of sweat oozing from beneath his bushy grey hair and trickling down his face. He drew close to the small gap at the bottom of the one window and took in a breath of fresh air. Then he tapped the wooden blocks that had been screwed into the frame to act as stoppers. From out of his pocket, he drew a penknife and fumbled with it until he found the screwdriver. Stooping slightly, he undid some of the screws and pushing at the blocks managed to open the window wider. The noise woke Batista who groaned and gazed in panic around the room:

"Leonid! Leonid, where are you?"

"I am here, where I have been all day." The man crossed the room and stood at the foot of the bed where he could be seen.

"I suddenly felt so afraid." Batista drew in a long breath and closed his eyes. Tears trickled through the closed lids and onto the pillow, but he made no attempt to wipe them away: "I am so afraid of dying, Leonid, I don't want to die."

"What are you talking about? Who says you are going to die, eh? Has one of those stupid nurses said anything to you?" The voice was deep, but the tone was gentle.

"There are some things you don't have to be told."

"Is that so!" Leonid laughed and walked around the bed until he stood next to Batista.

"I thought you always needed to be told everything at least twice before you even heard it. Then told twice more before you thought about it. Then you would have to go and find out for yourself if it were true. And now you are telling me that there are things you don't need to be told."

"That was in the old days, Leonid, when everything was going right for us."

"What old days were those? I don't remember a time when things ever went right for us. Nothing has gone right since I came to this god forsaken country of yours."

"Whatever you think of it, it's my home." Batista began coughing violently and spat out blood into the bowl next to his side.

Leonid sat on the bed and raised him up, propping him against his arm and shoulder. He wiped Batista's mouth and face and then took the bowl to empty the contents down the small sink. He brought a dampened towel back to the bed and ran it over the feverish man's head.

"If you hadn't wanted to stay here and trust your own people, I **would** have had you back in Moscow where they really know how to look after the sick.

They'd have made you well again. We'd have had none of this, if you'd only listened to me."

"Perhaps," Batista rested his head against Leonid's arm. "Perhaps you were right. I should have gone back with you after the PIDE released me. There might still have been time then."

"*The Policia International e de Defesa do Estado!* The PIDE!" Leonid almost spat the words out, "it's ironic, isn't it? My country is condemned for the atrocities of its secret police. But they are like fairy godmothers compared with the Portuguese PIDE! How many liberals in England or America protest about what has been done in Portugal in the name of liberal democracy? How many?"

"Not now!" Batista smiled faintly, "I have not the strength to listen to one of your speeches." He held on to Leonid's hand for support. "You never miss the chance of preaching, do you? If you had been born here instead of Moscow, you would have made a fine priest."

They sat in silence for a while, gradually Batista's breathing became easier and the unhealthy flush that had spread across his thin face faded.

"Have you ever believed in God?" Batista asked.

"How can you, who know me better than anyone else, ask such a question? I have never believed in a God of any sort. I know there is no God. There is only man and man's achievements. But I'll tell you what God is: God is a useful tool, nothing more, nothing less. Religion is still the opium of the people, as Marx knew it was.

"Look at what goes on here in Portugal the poor give their money to the Catholic church. The priests make the sign of the cross over them and say: '*Go away my children, your reward will be in heaven.*' Huh! In heaven! What is this heaven? Have you ever met someone who has been to heaven?

"I tell you, Pedro, all we know is what we actually have. And that, my friend, is this life! Those who live should enjoy this life not wait for the promise of heaven just to keep them quiet! Heaven and God are words that have hung like chains around the necks of the poor and the peasants for centuries.

Salazar and Caetano knew exactly how to play with words. Your degenerate old Kings and Queens also knew the use of God. None of them was stupid enough to be-lieve in him, but he was so useful."

Batista listened to Leonid patiently: "My parents were good Catholics; I was brought up a Catholic. I was taught by the Jesuit Fathers. At one time, my mother thought I might even become a priest."

"Then, my friend, fortunately you grew up and grew wise, eh? You found out the real truth from me."

"Communism is fine, when you are strong and healthy." Batista said, "but what about people like I am now? What about the sick and the dying? What happens to a good Communist when he dies? Is this life all there is? Was everything over for me once the PIDE got me? Was that the beginning of the end for me?"

"What good does all this do, Pedro?" Leonid sighed. "It makes me angry, and I don't want to get angry. We'll wait till you're well before we fight again."

Batista became drowsy and dozed. Leonid leaned back against the metal bedstead and looked at the flies as some ran across the ceiling and others circled above the bed.

A young nurse came into the room, she looked at Leonid cradling the sick man in his arms and went over to them: "I need to check his pulse and temperature," she said. "Dr Fonseca will be here soon. I think he'd like to have a word with you." She waited for a response, but Leonid remained silent. As she reached out for Batista's wrist, he started violently and clutched at Leonid's arm.

"It's all right, Pedro, it's only a nurse." Leonid reassured him.

The nurse took Batista's pulse as she waited for the thermometer to register. She looked at his wasted face and body and shook her head. Batista saw the look on her face and turned away for comfort to Leonid. When she was satisfied, she got his chart from the foot of the bed and marked in the new readings. Then she left the room.

"I've been dreaming a lot recently." Batista said. "Every time I close my eyes, I think I'm back in the detention centre. Do you think I will ever be able to forget?"

"It's over a year since you got out, still early days to forget what happened to you. But the memories will fade in time." Leonid rose and walked to the foot of the bed and glanced at the chart. He saw that the lines had shot up sharply again.

The door opened and Dr Fonseca, out of sight of the bed, beckoned to Leonid. Batista, sensing the signal, tried to raise himself: "Don't go!"

"Pedro, I told you I won't leave you. I'm just going to see Dr Fonseca for a while. I'll be back soon."

Fonseca waited in the corridor as Leonid closed the door. They walked together to his office. The sun streamed in through the window making the room feel like a hothouse. Fonseca lowered the blinds and sat down in a highback swivel chair. He indicated for Leonid to sit as well. Nervously he tapped his fingers on the desk, then leaned forward peering closely at Leonid.

"So, my friend, you must prepare yourself. I have done all that I can. It is just a matter of time now."

Leonid clenched his fists on the desk that stood between them, and half rose from his seat: "I don't believe you! Why! Why now? After all this time!"

"Protesting will do no good. I've told you the truth right from the start…"

"You told me nothing! Why should I believe you now?"

"Sit down," Fonseca turned in his chair towards a small cabinet and opened its door. He took out a crystal decanter of brandy and two glasses. Pouring out the drinks, he pushed one across the desk towards Leonid. "Drink. It may not be vodka, but it will help to put out your anger."

Leonid sat down and took the glass. He drank it in one gulp and pushed it back across the table. Fonseca smiled and poured him another.

"That's better, my friend, it is better to be blunt." Fonseca spoke calmly. "And I did tell you this when you first brought Pedro here. I told you that there was little to be done. Those PIDE knew how to do their work. I am just amazed he survived so long. Surely, you must have known this?"

"Why? You don't want to see something happening that you dread; the mind won't accept it." Leonid twisted the crystal glass between his fingers, watching the rainbow colours dance around the room. "Do you know, Fonseca, Pedro has been talking about God. Does that please you?"

"Should it?"

"You're a good Catholic, aren't you?"

"I'm neither Catholic nor pagan. I don't care very much either way. I just try to keep the living going as long as possible and with as little suffering as possible."

"Your fellow countrymen are Catholics. Salazar was a Catholic." He leaned forward. "And I tell you this, if he was a Christian, then I'm glad I'm a Communist. Your dictators and that Blue Army of Fatima maintained their wealth and power by invoking the name of God, and" he paused, "with a little help from the PIDE."

"Save your political dogma for the masses, Leonid, I'm too old and too set in my ways to be impressed. Maybe Portugal has suffered from dictatorships but don't tell me that your masters back in Moscow are any better. You and

Pedro are idealists. But was Stalin so different from Hitler? Are your masters, who worship at Lenin's tomb, so different from ours who bend their knees at the shrine of Fatima? What do you think they both ask for? I'll tell you what it is: they both ask for power. So, where's the difference?"

"It isn't the same, Fonseca, and you know it. We are fighting to build a new world. Here they are striving to prop up a corrupt old regime. Pedro knew that and that is why they never really broke him."

"He's broken now, Leonid, and you must learn to face it. It won't be easy, that's why I have told you now." He watched the other man for a while, and he leaned forward. "Will you leave Portugal once he's dead?"

"Leave! No, I shall not leave. I will stay here and work for both of us. I will make sure he does not go unavenged. I suppose that sounds melodramatic to a doctor like you, doesn't it?"

"I don't know about being melodramatic, but I would say it is more like madness to try to take on the machinery of government. That's what it would be surely. The PIDE and their successors are the cogs of government."

"It's not them that I have in mind. They are no better than animals and what revenge is there in killing an animal that has savaged you? It's the master you want."

Fonseca waited for him to go on, he didn't understand what Leonid meant. Leonid's eyebrows knitted together as he held back waves of anger and grief. After a while he grew more composed.

"Did you know that the Americans and the British had agents working here to help to support your dictatorships?" Fonseca shook his head. "Well, they did! They were very worried that the infant Communist movement here in the north of Portugal would undermine the stability of the dictatorships. Of course, that could not have been tolerated."

"I don't see why. What did it have to do with the US or England?" Fonseca was genuinely surprised.

"A great deal. America can't tolerate the thought of communism getting a hold anywhere. It is a threat to their own security, in their minds anyway. So, the policy was, and still is, to crush any left-wing movements wherever they arise. This country of yours and Spain were two areas they were determined to keep free of Soviet influence."

Fonseca shook his head: "Leonid, are you human? Or are you just a talking robot made to look human. Just press a button and you shoot out the same old speeches all the time."

"You don't like hearing the truth. What I have said is the truth."

"What has all this to do with your desire to avenge Pedro?"

"It's got everything to do with it. The PIDE were animals," he paused and nodded his head slightly, "but there was a British agent working here for years. I got to know a great deal about him. He wasn't an animal, but he slipped Pedro into the hands of beasts. Then he slunk away like a guilty man. He didn't stay to watch the feast. That would have turned his stomach."

"Is this man still here?"

"No, he returned to England."

"So how will…"

"I have my ideas. I need time to plan, but then I shall have all the time I need, once Pedro has gone." He paused and looked into Fonseca's eyes as if searching for a denial of the truth. "How long does he have?"

"Very little time. This new infection is not responding to the drugs. Unless it does, he could be dead within days. Maybe it will be easier for you and for him if you stayed here at the clinic. Would you like that?" For answer, Leonid nodded.

By the time Leonid returned to Batista's room, a young nurse had tidied it and given him a drink. His brown eyes looked anxious when he saw the door open: "Leonid, I don't like being alone! I'm glad you're back."

"Not even with the pretty nurses?" Leonid teased. "You'll not have much time on your own from now on, they're going to make up a bed for me. I'll be staying with you until you are well enough to leave. But I must go and phone Dos Santos now to let him know."

"Why should they let you stay?" Batista felt a wave of suspicion pass over him and he shivered: "This cough I have is serious, isn't it? Tell me the truth!"

"I told you all you need to know, Pedro. Have I ever done anything that would be harmful to you?" Batista shook his head. "Well, Pedro, trust me now to do what is best for you and for me. I must phone, I won't be long. Is there anything I can get you?"

"I just want you back here again soon. There are phones in the corridor."

Leonid had to get out of the room before he was overcome with anger and grief. The sight of Batista's emaciated face was too much for him, so soon after hearing Fonseca's prognosis.

As Batista had told him, there was a phone in the corridor, but Leonid felt the need to get away from the cloying heat of the clinic. He took the lift to the ground floor and went out into the busy street. For a second, he was bewildered by the noise of the traffic and the rush of ordinary people going about their lives. He felt almost angry that life was continuing all around him. Why didn't people stop and tell him how sorry they were? Why didn't they even glance at him in sympathy? He walked slowly to the post office at the corner of the street and rang Dos Santos' number.

When a woman's voice answered, he demanded to speak to Dos Santos. She told him that Dos Santos was not there. He was in Viana do Castelo and would not be due back until the evening.

"Just give him a message." Leonid said. "Tell him things look bad with Pedro. I'm staying at the hospital with him. It'll make it easier for him and for me. Also, and this is important, tell him to go through all our dossiers on the one called 'O Pescador', the 'Fisherman'. When I see Dos Santos next, I want to be reminded about everything we have on record about this agent and his network. Tell him to wire through to Moscow to get information about the present whereabouts of the Fisherman, his recent activity, and details about his family."

"Anything else?"

"No, I'll see you all when I can."

He left the post office and looked at his watch. It had already been twenty minutes, but the thought of going back and being with Batista whilst he still felt upset worried him. He knew he had to pretend things were going to be all right and he was not sure he could do that.

He crossed the road and went into a shop where he bought some pyjamas and slippers. Afterwards he bought other things that would be needed for his stay. Then, he walked slowly back to the clinic and returned to the sickroom.

"You've been gone a long time. They've made your bed up in the corner near the window." Pedro glanced at the bags Leonid was carrying. Then he looked at him reproachfully, "you've been out."

"I had things to do for arranging to stay here. The call was important I didn't want to risk doing it from here. A phone box is always safer, you know that."

"So, what did you ask him to do?"

"Get out the files on 'O Pescador'."

"Why!" Batista tried to sit up and began to cough.

"Because, my friend, when you are well again, we will start work on this particular devil we call 'The Fisherman'."

"I don't want to think about that man ever again. It was because of him I am lying here now."

"All the more reason why we must think of him again. We are going to make him pay. Pay for what he did to you – to us."

"But why now, why so suddenly? You always said that a good comrade understands personalities and when to strike. I remember that. You said that once business became tangled with emotion, then judgement would fail. I thought it was very wise." He smiled. "Do you know afterwards I never thought of our enemies as human but only as wooden puppets who needed their strings cut. So why this talk of 'making him pay'?" He waited for a response.

Instead of replying, Leonid unwrapped his pyjamas taking out the pins that attached them to the cardboard. He smoothed them out and lay them on the bed.

"Did you hear what I said, Leonid? It is no joke what I'm saying. There is so much work left to do here. To get involved with The Fisherman again would be foolish, feeling as angry as we both do. You said feelings were a luxury and anger is surely a luxury."

"Well, my friend, this is one luxury I can afford. To hell with wisdom and theory, I owe this one for you and for me. Later, we can go about our other work."

Batista took the newspaper that Leonid had tossed onto his bed and looked at the front page. He didn't feel strong enough to argue any more.

It was a mere three days later that Leonid sent a wire through to Moscow. On receiving the message, officers in the *Komitet Gosudarstvennoy Bezopasnosti* (KGB), within the Lubyanka, removed the files on Pedro Fernando Costa Batista from the 'Active Agents' list. The files were placed in the section labelled: 'Deceased'.

Leonid's spymaster, Malyshkin, remained impassive when he heard the news. He had never liked the emotional, highly strung Batista. He regarded him as a hindrance to the efficient working of Leonid Paustovsky, whom he had trained himself years before. Then, Leonid had been young and eager to do his bidding. Now, perhaps, he would do so again. Malyshkin thought carefully about the message he would send back to Oporto. After a while, he dictated it to his secretary:

"I have closed the file on Comrade Batista. I extend my sympathy to all of his comrades. I shall be sending a replacement. Her name is Helga Kaufmann. She will join you immediately. More details will follow."

Leonid read the message carefully twice. At one time any message from Malyshkin would have been a source of inspiration. That had not been the case since Batista had been allowed to rot in the PIDE detention centre. Then there had been no help or advice coming from Moscow. Leonid crumpled the message in his hand and threw it into the bin.

After Batista's funeral, Leonid drove along the coast road leading north from Oporto. For an hour he drove, almost mechanically, reliving the events of the last week, the last year, the last 16 years. How easy it was, he thought, to '*close the file*' on a dead agent when you are thousands of miles away in the Lubyanka.

At one time he too could have closed the file on a dead agent. He had done so more than once. But for the rest of his life, he could never close the file on Pedro Batista. That agent had become the sole purpose of his existence for the last 16 years. He had grown to love him more passionately and more tenderly than he thought it was possible for him to love anyone.

Together they have been fulfilled; as a team they could not have been bettered. Together, even the disasters and mistakes had been bearable. Now, as he drove towards Dos Santos' quinta, he felt alone and naked. He saw the world as an alien place where he was without friend or ideal.

His car passed through the dusty villages, passed the carts laden down with seaweed; passed the huts where the peasants rested out of the sun. The images so vivid and bright flashed unnoticed by him. At one time, Batista would have ranted about the poverty and the filth and stirred his own feelings of injustice. Now as he drove all alone, there was only one thought that kept returning to him. Gradually, the thought became a new sense of purpose. As he reached Viana Do Castello, Leonid smiled to himself.

"Well, Harry Randall, O Pescador, The Fisherman, by whatever name you are now known, we are going to do battle once more. Only this time there will be more at stake for both of us than just an ideal. It may take me one year or it may take five – but we will meet again, and you will know what you have done. And you will know the meaning of suffering too."

CHAPTER 2
PÓVOA DE VARZIM
NORTHERN PORTUGAL
SUMMER 1978

Luis spat into the dry dust at his feet, then he moved into the retreating piece of shade offered by the stone wall surrounding the hotel grounds. From behind the wall, he could hear the shrieks of bathers in the swimming pool and the splash of water as another well-oiled tanned body dived into the clear blue pool.

A thin green lizard ran along the stonework of the wall and darted nervously into a minute crack, as Luis kicked the ground with impatience. Along the road came a heavily laden donkey cart, the beast trotted unsure of its footing on the smooth tarmac surface. Luis rubbed his hand across the stubble on his chin, as he peered up the pathway leading to the side entrance of the hotel.

He decided that he must do something more active, standing in the shade or sun was a barren occupation. He walked to the end of the path and looked up towards the hotel. As he did so, a woman appeared on the steps of the entrance and began walking down the path towards him. She moved swiftly and was almost too close to him before he was able to bend down, quickly pretending to adjust the straps of his worn sandals. The woman brushed past without even noticing him. Then he saw her quite clearly.

He glanced at the small photo from his pocket. Then he went over the description of the woman that he had been given that morning: slim, about 30, shoulder length blonde hair, blue eyes. Yes, this was the one! He gave a toothy grin as he watched her take the road towards town. After counting to twenty, he followed, keeping her always within sight. He muttered under his breath: 'keep on walking, Mrs Laura Bayliss, just keep walking'.

Laura picked her way along the dusty road. There was no pavement, and the cars and taxis came perilously close on several occasions. The grit worked its way under the soles of her feet and every now and again she was forced to shake it from her sandals. Whenever this happened, Luis stopped and picked absentmindedly at his teeth.

Laura began to wonder why she had listened to the waiter, the previous evening, when he had told her she really must go to the bullfight.

"You have seen nothing of Portugal," he had said. "Until you have seen our special bullfights, you will not understand us. Ours are for the artist - not for the blood lover who goes to the Spanish fights."

When she had asked him just how they were different, he told her she must find out for herself. No one else in the family wanted to come with her, so she had decided to venture there on her own.

She paused for a few moments and wiped the sweat from her forehead and fanned herself with her sunhat. Then she walked, more slowly this time, towards the pinkish orange stadium where the bullfight was to be held. That was the praça do touros, the place of the bulls. The closer she got to it, the more vivid its colouring appeared compared with the cream-coloured houses.

Soon she was able to hear the noise of a tinny little band and above it the tones of a loudspeaker crackling into life. After a while, a harsh rasping man's voice shouted out something and she heard the crowd shout and cheer. She glanced at her watch and saw the fight was due to start in under five minutes. The hotel receptionist had given her times and directions. She had meant to set out earlier but, as usual, the children had demanded her attention.

She reached the sandy enclosure that surrounded the stadium. Several horseboxes were parked nearby, some of their ramps were still up. The horses inside were restless and they kicked at the sides, impatient to be out.

An old peasant woman, dressed in thick black and grey linen, sat on a wooden orange-box surrounded by piles of cardboard sunhats which she was trying to sell to passers-by. She called out to Laura and held out a hat. Laura shook her head; the old woman mimicked her then said something to the group of urchins standing nearby. They all turned and laughed. Laura blushed and turned quickly towards the ticket office, where there was only a small queue waiting. When it was her turn, she edged timidly forward.

"Falle Inglese?" She asked hopefully as she clasped her bag and tossed back her hair. There was no immediate response. Then slowly, an amused grin spread across the face of the old man in the ticket office as he shook his head. He was evidently enjoying her difficulty. The person behind her in the queue made some comment which made both the ticket seller and several others laugh. Laura thought she would try out her French:

"Est ce que vous avez une ... une chaise sans soleil?"

The man's grin grew even wider as he shrugged his shoulders and raised his hands in mock despair. Luis, standing a few places behind her, was amused at her predicament. 'She will be an easy one to deal with', he thought.

At last, Laura decided to resort to mime, so pointing up at the sun she said: "Nao" repeatedly and emphatically. Instant understanding spread across the ticket seller's face.

"Ah! Sombra! Sombra!" He said waiting for her to agree.

"Yes, that's right sim, sim!" She smiled, "Quanto costa?"

"Quarto cent escudos", he said holding up a ticket.

Laura wanted to ask whether he had any for 350 escudos since 400 would take all the money she had with her. However, after the commotion and even getting this far, she decided she would take the ticket being held out towards her.

There were several entrances to the stadium, so she took the nearest. She found herself in a dark passageway leading directly beneath the stadium itself. When she emerged into the strong sunlight again, her eyes were dazzled by the intensity of the light. She looked at the rows of seats in dismay. A policeman standing nearby, took her ticket and pointed out an empty space. It was right next to the wooden barricade.

She stepped gingerly along the narrow concrete ledges that served both as steps and seating, wishing she'd had the sense to bring something to sit on. Nearly everyone else had a neat little cushion to soften the harshness of the solid concrete. Eventually, she pushed her way to the space and sat down.

The noise and the heat were overpowering. She fanned herself with the pink straw sunhat and noticed everyone else was wearing a little cardboard hat like the ones being sold by the old woman. Two children giggled at her and nudged each other with amusement.

The wooden barricade, next to her, juddered and a sweet sickly smell rose up into the hot air. She peered through a gap in one of the slats and saw a man dressed all in black sitting astride a pole. He was shouting and waving his arms at someone behind him. The sound of cattle bellowing came from somewhere near the man and dust penetrated through the gap.

She turned away and looked into the ring. It was empty but already the sand and sawdust, so smooth in places, appeared to have been trampled over in a straight line from the other side of the ring. She wondered if she had missed the opening parade.

A small boy staggered along the rows of seats. He was bent double under the weight of a tray laden with ice and bottles of coke and lemonade. He stopped in front of her, but Laura shook her head. She would dearly have loved a drink, but she had no more money left. The boy pulled a face and moved away further up the bank of expectant onlookers.

It was then that Luis caught sight of her again. He had scanned the rows of people for some time without being able to see her. He dreaded the consequences of reporting that he had lost her. But as the boy moved away, he saw the sunhat. A feeling of relief flooded over him as he roughly began pushing his way in her direction. He sat down heavily beside her, pushing her closer to the barricade as he did so. The music from the band stopped quite abruptly and the gate at the far end of the ring opened.

Slowly, a horseman rode out into the sun. He was a young man, resplendent in a bronze silk 18th century riding coat adorned with thick lace cuffs. He wore a black tricorn hat which he doffed to the crowd, as his horse performed intricate dressage across the arena. His black leather boots shone, and the silver spurs glinted in the sun. He urged the horse into a canter, then reined it in where there was an area of shade. He sat still, very upright and alert, the horse tightly controlled and motionless as a statue.

Suddenly, from right next to where Laura was sitting, there was the noise of a large gate being hauled open and the thundering sound of hooves. A huge black form threw itself out of the run and into the freedom of the arena. The bull stopped abruptly, looked around and sniffed the sand. The crowd whistled and stamped their feet. A man dressed like a Spanish matador, in a suit of lights, vaulted into the ring and flourished a cloak in front of the bewildered beast. The bull charged half-heartedly. The man repeated the moves several times but with little enthusiasm.

The horseman watched everything that took place, then he signalled that the bull should be left alone. Almost imperceptibly, he spurred the horse to the side of the ring where he was handed a lance decorated with bronze silk ribbons. The bull suddenly saw the movement of the chestnut stallion. He tossed back his head and charged directly at him. When he was within just a few feet, the horseman guided his mount to one side and the bull slithered past. The stallion was turned to face the bull who charged again and yet again. After several charges, the horseman raised his lance high above his head in a gesture of defiance, his voice rasping out: "HoHa! HoHa!" tauntingly at the bull. Some in the crowd joined in the taunts.

Laura watched both horrified and spellbound as the horse was urged into a gallop straight towards the bull who, at the same time, began his own charge at horse and man. At the moment of almost certain impact, the horse swerved violently to one side. The rider leaned out of the saddle and thrust the lance deep into the bull's neck.

The crowd roared a deep hoarse sound of triumph, as if they each had individually achieved success. The bull tossed its head and neck in torment with searing pain, as the sharp barbed point tore into his flesh. The barb held firmly in place, only increasing the beast's impotent rage. He rushed in fury and panic from one side of the ring to the other, hurling himself against the gate through which only a few brief minutes earlier he had arrived.

As the blood began to ooze from the wound, Laura wished she had never come. Everything was too much for her – too much heat, too much fear, too much abhorrence. She looked at her watch, only twenty minutes had passed since she had sat down. She wished she had listened to

Tom and not try to prove how independent she could be. She realised proving a point was only worth it if you didn't have to suffer the consequences. She decided that as soon as this bull left the ring, she would swallow her pride and return to the safe irritations of Tom and the children.

The horseman 'played' the bull. More barbs were thrust into its neck. A shrill fanfare blasted out from the tinny band. Then a man twirled a cloak to distract the bull and the horseman slipped away as unobtrusively as he had entered. The bull held the arena alone, even now his anger, pride and defiance were still apparent.

At the call of a trumpet, some young men dressed in tight black trousers and scarlet jackets assembled behind the barrier in front of Laura.

"Bravo forcados! Bravo!" The crowd shouted.

The 'forcados' huddled around one of the men who seem to be their leader. The trumpet sounded again and this time the men vaulted into the ring. The voice on the loudspeaker blared out an announcement. The crowd shouted approval and the men acknowledged the cheers. The leader put on a stocking cap and the others lined up behind him. Forgetting the previous mood, Laura was curious to know what was going to happen next, but she had no one to ask.

The bull's attention was caught by the line of men. He sniffed the sand and snorted, as the men stamped their feet and strode in defiance towards him. The forcado leader swaggered nearer and nearer, hands on hips, chest thrust out and head held high. When the line of men was within ten feet, the bull charged.

Involuntarily, Laura gasped and reached out to touch Luis's arm. He shrugged her away, too intent on the action himself. The leader of the men stood his ground, then vaulted onto the lowered head of the bull, seizing the creature by its leather-cased, blunted horns. The bull's head was twisted and wrenched, by the leader, in an attempt to bring the charge to a halt.

The other forcados slithered around the animal, one of them taking hold of his tail, the others clawing at his sides. The charge stopped. It seemed they had succeeded. Gradually, man by man they released their hold until only one remained. He was the one holding the bull's tail. The creature's humiliation was complete.

Laura watched with disgust as the old man sitting next to her whistled and hooted his approval. Then the barricade shook again, and the gate was opened. This time a small group of bellowing, skinny, long–horn, brown oxen were driven in. They had large cowbells round their necks which swung and tinkled as they trotted round the ring. They were poked and prodded by the tall man in black whom Laura had noticed earlier.

The bull looked up when he heard the oxen, his nostrils twitched, his flanks heaved from the exertion. The blood was already congealing on his neck, and he was exhausted. Slowly, he edged his way close to the nearest oxen and then, along with them, was herded out of the ring.

Laura hastily gathered her bag and got up. Luis deliberately sat forward blocking her path. She tapped his shoulder and indicated that she wanted to pass. At first, he didn't even look up; then he pretended not to understand what she wanted. She tried to push her way past as gently as possible. But as she would learn very soon, it was no good trying to be gentle where Luis was concerned.

He spoke harshly to her in Portuguese and made an appeal to others sitting around him. They jeered at her and prodded her, seeming to agree with whatever Luis had said. She began to feel embarrassed and angry but not knowing the language proved an insurmountable barrier.

Luis turned away from her and started up a conversation with another old man sitting just behind him. Once again, she tried to push past, this time Luis ignored all her efforts and did not even bother to look at her. Behind, she was hemmed in by a large family party; in front there was no room to get by and next to her was the barricade.

She noticed that a second horseman was about to enter the ring. So reluctantly, she sat down wishing she was not such a timid person. She glanced at Luis and saw a rather self-satisfied smirk cross his face. She decided to sit through the whole performance, rather than face the embarrassment of a scene.

The next horseman was dressed in peacock blue silk and rode a fine grey stallion. His style was neither so skilful nor as exciting as the first rider. He planted fewer barbs and took no unnecessary risks with his horse.

After the third bull had left the ring, Laura found she had grown almost immune to the routine. The initial shock and its impact were lost. Even the gratuitous cruelty passed her by. The tinny little band struck up a tune and the boy with the drinks appeared again from the pit beneath the stadium. She watched him staggering beneath the enormous weight while several people bought drinks from him.

Laura, self-conscious at the best of times, felt isolated by language from everyone around her. She opened her bag and pulled out a Portuguese – English dictionary. It gave all sorts of phrases that she knew she'd never need to use about how to change your disc brakes and tell a doctor you were suffering from appendicitis. Eventually, she found what she was looking for. Turning to Luis she spoke hesitatingly:

"O fim?" She waited for him to reply. Instead, he shrugged his shoulders.

She showed him the page in the book and pointed to the words. He pulled out a crumpled programme from his pocket and pointed to the number six on the cover. Then he held up six fingers and counted down three. She understood what he was implying, so she nodded. He looked back at the programme hoping she wouldn't attempt to leave the stadium again before the fight finished.

Something told him she was not going to present the problem for him that he had imagined. He had been told all Englishwomen were formidable, but this one was going to be easy. Dos Santos need not have worried.

From just below where they were sitting, the tall thin man in black who oversaw the oxen stepped out into the ring. He looked around at the crowd until he caught sight of Luis. He beckoned for him to lean forward and then spoke rapidly nodding frequently in the direction of Laura. Luis grunted and replied before the man re-entered the bull run. At last, Luis knew what had to be done and he began planning his next move.

The first horseman returned to the ring and the second half of the performance began.

"You like the cavaliero?" Luis asked Laura without turning to her. She was completely taken aback; she hadn't expected him to know any English at all. Yet he spoke it with a marked American accent.

"It's very different from Spanish bullfighting. But it's still rather brutal." She waited for an answer but there was none. She wondered whether he had exhausted his total supply of English words, so she sat back and watched the fight.

After what she calculated would be the final horseman had entered, Luis leaned over to her and coughed. His breath was heavy with the smell of garlic, and she drew away from him. Luis didn't notice her reaction and he pointed to the bottom photo on the front cover and tapped it: "He is, how you say, very good. Muito bom! Fine cavaleiro. He has no fear and is a great horseman."

Laura did not think that any of this was 'muito bom' but she did not say so. In fact, she thought this particular rider had been callous in his disregard for his stallion's safety.

Maybe the bull's horns were cased in leather, but the sheer weight of the bull would have crushed the horse's slender flanks into a pulp.

"You like to meet him?" Luis asked.

"Oh yes." Laura heard herself saying and wondering why on earth she was agreeing. The last thing she wanted was to prolong her day there.

"After the fight, I will take you to him."

Laura kicked herself for her timidity and stupidity. She knew just what Tom would say. This was so typical of her, getting into conversations with strangers then involved in something that she didn't really want at all. She knew she'd have to extricate herself.

"It... it's very kind of you, but I don't think I can today. I must get back to the hotel to see my children."

"Yes, yes you come to meet him. Not take too long. You come, I insist." The way he said it, made her think it was less of an invitation and more of a command.

The final performance drove the crowd into a frenzy. Unlike the five previous animals, the final bull spotted the horse and its rider straightaway. He charged directly at them. The crowd gasped and a woman screamed realising the danger. The bull was massive, by far the largest of the day. His enormous legs were thick and strong; his belly slim and curving; his haunches supple. For one fleeting moment, the horseman looked alarmed, then he spurred his horse out of the line of attack. This bull was not fooled by the manoeuvre, he pursued relentlessly.

Man, horse, and bull twisted, turned, and jostled together. The crowd were wild with excitement. This was what they had hoped to see. Luis sat forward, engrossed in the performance, almost forgetting the reason for his presence.

It was like being at some Roman scene of brutality where there was thrill at the prospect of death or injury, Laura thought. She could not look. She felt sick and was disgusted by the whole event. A loud roar made her look back into the ring. One barb had already been implanted in the magnificent beast's neck. He panted and looked up at the people, then at the ground, his neck muscles twitching convulsively.

"HoHa! HoHa! Touro HoHa!" The crowd and the horseman shouted repeatedly goading the animal still more. The performance went on and more barbs were stuck. The horse's flanks were streaked with blood and sweat from the pricking of the sharp rowels in the horseman's spurs. Laura thought she was going to faint. The rest of the so-called performance went by in a blur, Laura's eyes were tightly closed.

"Muito Bom! Muito Bom!" Luis shouted and stamped his feet. Laura began to dislike the vile creature sitting next to her who had prevented her escape.

A fat, waddling man made his way over to the horseman, nodding his approval. Flowers, cushions, hats, and money showered into the ring after the bull left with the scraggy oxen. The crowd's roar was deafening, and Luis stood up clapping and whistling through his broken teeth. He pulled Laura to her feet next to him.

The horseman leapt from his horse into the ring and acknowledged the cheers. Eventually he left, allowing others to remove the objects that now littered the mangled sawdust and sand.

The stadium emptied with extraordinary speed. People poured down through the narrow openings to disappear into the pit. Luis motioned Laura to sit still. Then he leaned over the barrier and called out to the fat man who was mopping his bald head. He nodded in reply to whatever was said, and he nodded to Laura.

"Now, you come with me. Everything is arranged. Mr Dos Santos has agreed I can take you to meet Ricardo."

"I really don't think I can now. Perhaps, my husband and our children can meet him sometime later."

"No, that will not be possible. You come, now." Laura looked around the stadium, it was practically deserted. Already, men and ragged boys were clearing litter away. The little boy selling drinks had returned to collect the empty bottles. Luis took her arm firmly and urged her towards the steps:

"Vindes! Vindes, senhora!"

The sudden darkness in the pit, made her move with caution down the steps and through the passageway. They went through a maze of corridors until they arrived at a small room. Luis opened the door and pushed her in. Without warning, the door was closed behind her, leaving her in a dimly lit room. There was an assortment of bundles in one corner and some old chairs in another. The air was musty, and she began to feel cold.

The minutes ticked away, and she waited feeling increasingly foolish at being in such a predicament. She went over to the door and turned the handle. It was locked. She leaned against it but still it did not budge.

The realisation of her situation made her heart pound, and she flushed in panic. She clutched her hat and bag for reassurance and looked around the room for some other way out. But there were no windows and only the one locked door. She tried the handle again praying that she'd been wrong. The door held fast. She knocked and called out and listened. The silence and the increasing cold made her shiver. Her skin grew pimply with goose flesh.

She vowed when she got out of this scrape, there would be no more 'soppy behaviour' as Tom called it. At that moment, she wouldn't have minded if Tom had come bursting through the door and hurled abuse at her – just so long as he came through the door. She sat on one of the chairs and waited.

The ticking of her watch grew loud, then faded, as her attention wavered. The minutes became an hour and still she sat, and no one came. At last, a scuffling sound behind the door alerted her to the fact someone was there. The key turned in the lock and she saw the silhouette, in the doorway, of the fat man who had been in the ring.

"Please, I think I should like to go straight back to my hotel now. I don't think I'll bother to…"

"Senhora Bayliss, be quiet. You will do as you're told. And now you are to come with me." He walked over to her and tied her hands behind her back. In the struggle, she dropped her bag and hat. A fat, clammy hand covered her mouth and her nose, and she thought she would suffocate.

"Luis! Come here and help." The fat man called out.

Laura saw the old man, who had been sitting next to her, come over. He grinned and clamped a dirty handkerchief soaked in ether over her nose and mouth. The smell nauseated her, and she retched. Slowly, she lost consciousness.

Luis and Dos Santos carried her out into the enclosure behind the stadium. Luis held her, as Dos Santos lowered the ramp on one of the horseboxes. Then between them, they took her into the back and threw her onto the straw. The chestnut stallion tethered inside, kicked out violently and almost struck Laura's side.

"You stay here in the back. Keep an eye on things." Dos Santos said. Luis opened his mouth to protest. "I've got to drive, haven't I? Someone must be here with her." Dos Santos chuckled. "Why are you worried? I wouldn't mind the chance, one attractive, unconscious woman. What's the matter with you, Luis?" He laughed and went down the ramp. Luis heard the bolts being shot to. Sometime later, the engine crackled into life and the box moved slowly away from the bullring.

CHAPTER 3
PÓVOA DO VARZIM - THE SAME EVENING

Tom heard the dinner gong and swore to himself. He twisted his glass of whiskey and watched the liquid roll around leaving transparent tide marks. An hour earlier, he had just been annoyed with Laura for being late and leaving him to look after the children that much longer. Now, he was vaguely uneasy. He had argued with her in the past and she would storm out of the house and walk around the block in a fit of pique. Even at the worst though, she had only ever been away for an hour or so. Besides, that was in England. He looked at his watch and saw it was eight forty. She was over three hours late.

"Daddy, I'm hungry, can't we go and eat now?" Jenny peered up into her father's face and gave a smile that was guaranteed to get her way.

"I'm hungry too" Philip muttered, "let's not wait for mum any longer."

Tom drank the rest of the whiskey in one gulp: "Quite right, we'll go on in. She can join us later when she condescends to return."

The children cheered and tore ahead of him into the dining room to their usual table near the window. The waiter brought the menu and the children's squabbled over what they were going to have.

"Any wine or minerals, sir?" The waiter asked, Tom nodded and ordered a lager.

"I want some orange juice." Philip said.

"So do I." Jenny looked at her father. Tom smiled and nodded again to the waiter.

The sunset's rays filled the whole room with a rich glow which was reflected in the mirrors and through the small fountain in the middle of the seating area. As the enormous orange globe approached the horizon, it seemed to flatten out almost like the mushroom cloud from an atomic bomb. When it disappeared, the sky was flecked with an incredible palette of colours.

"Doesn't the sky look lovely?" Jenny said looking out of the window. "It's never like this at home. I wish we lived here and didn't ever have to go home. Grandpa told me that I wouldn't like it here, but he was wrong, wasn't he?"

"Why didn't Grandpa want us to come?" Philip asked.

"Just because he wasn't coming with us, I expect." Tom replied, but he'd also wondered why Laura's father had made such a fuss. It was as much to irritate Harry, as anything else, that had made him insist on coming to Portugal. They had never got on and the passing years had only served to increase their dislike rather than soften it. Just before they left, Harry had calmed down and said perhaps he was 'just being over cautious'. Over cautious, what on earth had he meant? As Tom sat there, he wondered if, after all, Harry had known something.

The meal dragged on longer than usual with no Laura to give a hand at disciplining the children. By the time they had reached the sweet course it was already 9:30. Thoughts about what could have happened to Laura went through his mind in a bizarre framework. He considered the possibility of an accident with one of the crazy local taxi drivers. Then he dismissed the idea. He was still engrossed in his thoughts when a woman's voice brought him back to reality.

He turned to see who had spoken to him and saw the attractive German woman at the table next to theirs was smiling at him. He smiled back and said, 'good evening'. He was about to say something more when he was distracted by a tug at his sleeve.

"Daddy? Philip and me don't want any pudding. It's only grapes or melon, same as usual. Mummy bought some for us this morning, remember? We've got them upstairs. Can we go and listen to the piano player instead?" Tom hesitated.

He knew that what they both really wanted to do was play hide and seek through the lounge. He had gone beyond worrying about whether they would be a nuisance to anyone else. So, he nodded. In a flash they were away almost knocking over an unsuspecting waiter emerging from the kitchens.

Tom remained at the table and waited for his coffee. He was aware that the German woman was looking at him, so he wasn't surprised when she spoke.

"Why don't you bring your coffee here and keep me company?" Tom smiled and joined her.

"So, we both seem to be alone tonight."

"Yes, my friend has gone on one of those mystery evening coach trips. Your wife has gone too, hasn't she?"

"No ... at least... I suppose she could have done that. What time did the coach leave?"

"At six thirty, I think. I am sure I saw your wife get on the coach." She paused. "Didn't she tell you? The people at the desk were trying to persuade more people to go to make the trip worthwhile."

"That's it then! I bet you're right. Just what the stupid woman would go and do!"

"I'm sorry, I do not understand! You seem angry, yes?"

"Angry? Well, I am. You see I got lumbered with the kids this afternoon. She went out to enjoy herself. I couldn't think where she had gone this evening. I suppose she thought that since she had the afternoon off, she might as well make a day of it, typical of her."

They sat and chatted for a while, then walked together into the lounge. The children were sitting near the piano player. They were red-faced and breathless. When Jenny caught sight of them, she rushed over: "Is Mummy back yet? It's ever so late."

"This lady said she saw your mother get on the evening coach trip. That's why she is not back."

"I think Mum's being really mean. She never misses our bedtime!" Philip looked miserable and sorry for himself.

"I took your advice." Tom said looking at the woman.

"My advice?"

"Yes, you told me yesterday that these bullfights were no good at all. You said they were a waste of money. I told you that Laura was going, and you said I'd be a fool to go with her. Remember?" For reply, she smiled and nodded.

"Me and Philip want to go to bed now, are you going to come up and read to us?" Jenny asked.

"Not this time of night. Anyway, that's your mother's job. She can do it tomorrow to make up for today. Go up and wash and put yourselves to bed."

"Then you'll come up and see us." Jenny said, not so much as a question but more as a statement of fact.

The two children ran for the lift. The German woman took Tom's arm and laughed: "Your little girl is quite possessive over her Daddy. That is a very English trait, I believe. By the way, I do not think you know my name. It is Greta. I know yours already, it's Tom, isn't it? I heard your wife call you several times."

"Would you like a drink?" He asked.

"Yes, very much. But not before you put your children to bed."

"In that case, I think I just go over to the desk to see if they know whether Laura was on the coach. Her father would have my guts for garters if I let anything happen to his precious daughter." Greta put her hand on his arm and smiled.

"Why don't you enjoy your little bit of freedom? I told you I'm almost certain I saw her get on the coach. And as for her daddy, he should know better, shouldn't he?"

"Tom hesitated for a moment and laughed: "you're right, of course. To hell with her!"

"Why don't we go for a short walk. It's a warm evening."

"All right then, why not?" He paused and looked at his watch, "I'll go and settle the kids down. I meet you back here in, say ten minutes."

By the time he got his jacket from his room, he felt sure the children would be asleep. He opened their door quietly and peeped around. They were both sleeping; their clothes scattered in disarray over the floor, bedside lights still on. He went in carefully so as not to wake them; picked up the clothes and threw them onto a chair. He switched off the light and, breathing a sigh of relief, closed the door behind him.

As he headed towards the lift, it occurred to him that he should check to see if Laura's coat was still in the wardrobe. He returned to the room and opened the wardrobe – the coat was still there. He thought it strange that she hadn't taken it with her. Since they arrived in Northern Portugal, there had frequently been high winds from the Atlantic blowing in from the sea in the evenings. The evening air was chill and sharp when these winds blew, and Laura hated to be cold. True there was no wind now, but Laura ever the pessimist, always prepared herself for the worst eventuality. He decided to placate his own conscience, he ought to check at the reception desk, despite what Greta said.

As he came out of the lift, he caught sight of Greta talking to one of the receptionists in the entrance hall. She stepped back, when she saw Tom, and said something rapidly to the porter. Then she walked towards Tom smiling.

"I have been asking about your wife, while you were away. I told you there was no need to worry." She took his arm and snuggled close to him, "I was not the only one who saw her leaving on the coach. Come on, Tom, let's go and enjoy ourselves, shall we?" She looked flirtatiously into his eyes. The look was not wasted on Tom who was never one to miss a chance.

They crossed the main road and stumbled onto the uneven sandy beach. Clouds flitted across the sky occasionally masking the moonlight which lit their way. Their prog-ress was slow. After some distance, she stopped to remove her sandals, leaning against Tom for support. He slipped his arm around her waist and pulled her close to him. She did not resist or pull away. Tom, his mind racing ahead, began to look for somewhere out of sight of the road.

As they walked, the lights of the town faded behind the nearby sand dunes. He guided her towards the dunes and kissed her, his body finely tuned for her response. He an-ticipated an eager and stimulating desire equal to his own. The reality was quite different, she did not encourage or even yield to him.

"It's beginning to get cold, Tom, I think perhaps it is time to return to the hotel." She pushed him gently but firmly away. The walk had served its purpose and she saw no rea-son to play whore as well as distraction. At the same time, she could not afford to arouse his suspicions by dismissing him completely. She inwardly cursed Leonid for having made her take on this role. It was not what she had been trained for, it was degrading. She was no honey trap.

Tom, however, oblivious to her apparent change of mood felt no lessening in his own arousal. She had been acting as if she wanted it as much as he did. She had suggested the walk. Most women were only too eager for his attention. He wasn't going to let this one get away with just a kiss, a cuddle, and a goodbye. As she moved away, he pushed her firmly to the ground. The sand was soft, cold, and slippery and she could not find a firm surface to help push herself up again.

"Come on now, Greta, don't tell me that this isn't what you've been wanting all day." He tugged at the straps of her dress until her breasts were uncovered. She was a strong woman, but the sand held her as efficiently as any net. The more she struggled, the more she dug a deep pit for them both. She felt his movements becoming harder and more insistent, his hands roaming roughly over every part of her body.

Later, using her real name and in her real role, she would find this episode a useful tool to torment others. But at that moment, she was angry with herself for her weakness. This was not what she had spent months in Moscow being trained for.

When he had finished, she lay beside him, drained of all energy. How long they had lain there she was not sure. It was car headlights sweeping across their part of the beach that jarred her back to reality. She pushed Tom away and hurriedly dressed.

"Worried about your reputation?" He asked reaching out to fondle her again. She shrugged him away. "What's that for? You enjoyed it, didn't you? You certainly seemed to."

"I wouldn't say that. But, as your English saying goes, 'enough is enough'. That is what you say, isn't it?"

"Enough is never enough, Helga my sweet. Can't say I've ever known the meaning of the word 'enough'. With Laura there isn't any, let alone enough!" He laughed. "Pity she couldn't have watched us just now. It might have done her good. That's what you Germans like, isn't it?" He reached out to stop her moving away. "I said that's what Germans like, isn't it?"

"What?" Her mind was now racing ahead to what she had to do next.

"Doing it in groups." He smiled when he saw the look on her face. "Well maybe you don't, but I rather like the idea."

"Are you coming?" She asked. "I must get back to the hotel."

They walked back across the sand without talking. As they reached the hotel drive, an empty coach speeded away. She ran up the steps and into the lobby, without looking back.

"Greta!" he called hoping to arrange to see her the next day. But she had gone. 'So typical of women', he thought.

As he went up in the lift, he braced himself for the little-girl-hurt act he expected from Laura. Then he remembered his own grievances for the day which far outweighed any of hers. He planned his comments as he tried the door handle, expecting it to open. But the door held fast. He muttered under his breath and fumbled with the key. The room was in darkness. At first, he stumbled round the room in the dark, hoping not to wake her if she had already gone to sleep. He felt too tired for a row. After knocking his arm on the table, he switched on the light. The room was empty, the bed unruffled.

"Come on, Laura, I know you are here somewhere. Where are you?"

There was no reply. He opened the door of the bathroom, no one there. A wave of panic swept through him quite unexpectedly. He sat down, lit a cigarette, then he went over to the balcony. He heard the waves breaking on the rocks in the distance and felt the cold breeze blowing in from the sea with the advent of high tide. The phone rang, Tom threw himself at full stretch across the bed and grabbed it.

A man's heavily accented voice spoke softly:

"Mr Bayliss, don't interrupt what I have to say until I have finished. We have your wife. She is alive and, so far, she is unhurt. Do nothing until you are told what to do. We will be in touch again." The other end was put down, but Tom lay there holding the phone in disbelief.

A few seconds later, the receiver crackled into life again. It was the reception desk: "Sim? O que deseja?"

"Sorry… I forgot to put the receiver down." Tom replaced it. His hands were shaking.

He could not believe what he'd just heard. It was like something you would see in a television drama, but not something that actually happened in real life. Was it some dreadful practical joke? In the pit of his stomach, he knew it wasn't. He rang reception and asked to be put through to Greta's room. There was no answer from her. He debated whether he should phone the police, but the ominous words 'so far' came back to him.

The dark night sky began to lighten, and his intense feeling of heaviness also began to lift a little. He stood on the balcony watching the fishing boats plough through the sea which was now running high and fast. Already a few donkey carts were travelling along the road towards town. They were heavily laden with piles of fresh seaweed.

Along the strand of beach in front of the hotel, several peasant women were dragging the seaweed, they had just pulled out of the sea, towards their carts. Others still standing waist deep in the sea, were casting their spiked ropes into the waves. He watched as they hauled on the ropes and as the children ran forward to help. Within an hour, they would all be herded away from the hotel area to go further along the beach, so that the rich tourists would not be made to feel uncomfortable.

It was now almost 6 o'clock. Tom washed and shaved and went downstairs, he'd made up his mind what had to be done. The young man at the reception desk did not or could not speak English. After a few futile attempts, Tom lost his temper demanding to see the Manager. A middle-aged man stepped out of the side office and came over to the desk.

"Please, Mr Bayliss, do not make so much noise. It is still very early; I do not wish for other guests to be disturbed."

"By the time I've finished with you and your bloody hotel, more than just the guests will be disturbed." Tom said sharply.

To avoid a public scene, the Manager took Tom to his office. He ordered coffee for them both and tried to calm him. However, when he heard the story of Laura's disappearance and the phone call, he too was visibly alarmed. Anything of this nature, he assessed, could quickly ruin the hotel's reputation.

"Why did you not report this to me last night?" He asked.

Tom could not even explain this to himself. He couldn't explain that he thought it might have been a hoax or even Laura's way of getting back at him. He also could not mention that he had been with a woman until the early hours of the morning.

The Manager tapped his fingers nervously along his highly polished desk. The damned English always bought trouble for him. If it wasn't the food, it was the language; if it was neither of those it was their ill-mannered children! This, however, was far more serious. On impulse, he reached for the phone and seconds later was speaking in rapid Portuguese. Tom made out his own and Laura's names, but nothing more. The Manager finished his conversation and gave a sickly smile.

"I have a friend in the police, a discreet man, you understand. I have reported the matter to him. Please do not worry any longer. If there is anything you need for yourself, or your children, just ask. I shall do all I can for you." He paused, "there is just one thing I would like in return, Mr Bayliss. Please do not mention what has happened to the other guests. You understand? It would spoil their holiday." He smiled again.

"You mean it would spoil your bloody business." Tom snapped in reply. He found the next two hours among the most difficult in his life. Jenny and Philip were expecting to find their mother. He muddled his way through a badly thought-out story explaining how their mummy had gone for a little holiday on her own for a while. Neither really thought she would do such a thing, but they were too young to argue - too young to feel the real enormity of everything. That would come later, much later.

After breakfast, Tom told the children to go and play in the swimming pool. He watched them for a while then breathed a sigh of relief when he saw them rush over to play with some other English children whose parents were also staying at the hotel. He spoke to the mother of one of the children and told her what had happened. Her husband, seeing the alarmed expression on her face, came over. When he heard, he too was shocked. Tom felt easier when he had shared the story. It was like shifting the guilt away from himself.

"We'll keep an eye on your kids." The man said. Tom was surprised, he wasn't sure that if their positions were reversed, he would have been quite so forthcoming. "I hope the matter is cleared up soon, for their sake. I tell you, if it isn't, I'd take the kids home to your own people as soon as possible. They won't benefit from an experience like this." The man seemed genuinely concerned and Tom nodded agreement. He told the children he wouldn't be long, then returned to his room.

He felt he needed to be alone to think. As he reached the door, he heard a noise coming from inside. It was too early for the cleaners. He drew closer and distinctly heard drawers being opened and closed. He jerked the door open. A small, dark, uniformed man jumped up in alarm and reached for his gun belt. When he caught sight of Tom, his face relaxed and he straightened up.

"Ah, Senhor Bayliss, you should not have done that! I might have shot you."

"Who the hell are you?" Tom shouted. "How do you know me?"

The man came over and closed the door. "Please do not shout, Mr Bayliss. The Manager described you to me. I came as soon as I was told about the terrible event. I am head of the local police here in Póvoa." He paused to let the significance of his importance dawn on Tom. "You were not here, but I needed to act quickly. So, I am looking through your things for some clue as to your wife's disappearance. Please not to shout again, it will only cause alarm."

"I suppose you have shares in the hotel too." Tom said sarcastically.

The little man sat on the bed and took off his hat. The rim had imprinted a fine red line across his brow which he rubbed vigorously. "As I said, my name is Chief Lopes. I am assistant to the head of police in the Oporto Guarda Nacional Republicana but head of the local Póvoa police. That is why I am here." He straightened his shoulders with evident pride, as he introduced himself.

"I see, so the big boss from Oporto didn't think the matter important enough to handle the case." Chief Lopes looked hurt. "I suppose foreign women, British women, disappear in this damned backwater of yours with great regularity, do they?" Tom shook a finger in Lopes' direction. "You just wait till the British press here about this!"

Lopes' English was not all that he pretended it to be. Nor was he the most perceptive of men. But even within the framework of these limitations, he could see that Tom was not delighted with his presence. He set about trying to rectify the situation. A good result in this case might even mean promotion to Lisbon.

"Senhor Bayliss, I am the acknowledged expert on missing persons. Also, I have a superb understanding of the English language. It was obvious to all that I was the one best officer for this case."

"Humble little jerk, aren't you?" Tom muttered.

Lopes took out his notebook and poised himself for writing. He coughed:

"I wish to ask some questions."

Tom slumped onto the bed and lit a cigarette: "Okay, fire away then." He saw the look of puzzlement spread across the man's face. "Go on."

"How long have you been married?"

"14 years."

"Ah!" Lopes began scribbling. "How old is your wife?"

"Look in her bloody passport." Tom sighed, "she's 34."

"How many children?"

"Two." He was beginning to really dislike Lopes and his questions. "We also live in London, own a range Rover and a boat. My wife sits alone on her backside all day doing sod all. No, that's not strictly true. She goes to the hairdresser once a week; to the beauty salon once a week; gives coffee mornings for the church once a month. Shopping exhausts her. She also loves her daddy, and her daddy loves her. And now, Chief Lopes, hear this! This is the exciting bit for your ears. We have sex once in a blue moon. Satisfied with all that are you? Well, I'm not."

Lopes' face registered the astonishment that he felt. This was not at all what he had expected, not at all what should have happened. He chewed the tip of his pen while trying to assess how he should respond. Maybe, he thought, this man is in shock and that is why he behaves in this way. He decided to remain impassive.

"I have the following description of your wife, please listen to check it is correct: 5'2" tall, slim with long honey," he peered at the paper, "yes, honey blonde hair, grey-blue eyes. She was wearing a black and red sundress and black flat sandals. She had a red straw sunhat and a shoulder bag." When he'd finished, he looked over at Tom.

Tom said nothing for some time, he heard Lopes cough: "Oh, you are waiting for a response, are you?" He asked. "I'd say it was excellent. I'd be sure to know her anywhere from a description like that. A vivid lifelike image I'd say!" Lopes smiled, failing to register the sarcasm in Tom's voice.

"Also, Senhor Bayliss, we have it from, as you would say, a reliable source that she was last seen entering the praça do touros for the fight yesterday. Several people saw her there. Then …" He shrugged his shoulders. "Then nothing."

"Well, Chief Lopes, all I can say is that you bloody well better have something more than 'nothing' to report when dear daddy gets to hear of this."

The little policeman stood up, straightened his uniform jacket, and smoothed down his hair before putting on his hat. He put his notebook away.

"Your wife, Mrs Bayliss, she did not report that she might go off somewhere for a few days. She had no friends here or …"

"Look, Lopes, do you think if I had any clue at all, however slight, I'd not follow the lead myself? I didn't phone myself up, you know! I know no more than I've told you."

Lopes walked to the door feeling uncomfortable. According to the textbook on English people that he had read, all Englishmen were polite and reserved. This Englishmen did not fit into that category at all. He drew his shoulders back and tried to reassemble something of his dented dignity: "I shall, of course, keep you informed of all the progress that we make."

When he was alone, Tom kicked himself for the way he had behaved. He stepped out onto the balcony and looked down to the swimming pool directly below. Jenny and Philip were playing and screaming their heads off. He scanned the other bodies lying tanning themselves to see if he could see Greta. There was no sign of her.

He wrote a short note and went down to reception to get it put aside for Greta when she returned. She would have had no idea of Laura's disappearance. He gave the note to the man behind the desk.

The man looked at the name and, shaking his head, handed it back to him: "This lady - she is gone."

"That's right! Just see she gets it when she comes back." Tom said.

The man screwed up his nose and shook his head: "No, Senhor, the lady, she will not be back."

"She will, I know she will, so put it in her pigeonhole." Tom said.

"The lady has left the hotel, gone away." The man raised both hands to demonstrate.

"Give me that book." Tom reached over for the counter for the guestbook. As he did so, the Manager came over and remonstrated with him.

Tom said: "I want to leave a note for Greta Peltz, she is a guest here; only this cretin doesn't seem to understand that." The Manager took the book and then looked at Tom.

"He is right, Frau Peltz left this morning at 5 o'clock. Very early. See for yourself." He showed Tom the entry.

Feeling drained of emotion suddenly, Tom walked over to the terrace bar, near the pool. He ordered a large whiskey. Then he tore up the note, which he had written, and put the pieces into a heavy stoneware ashtray on the table in front of him. He considered what he should do next.

CHAPTER 4
LONDON, ENGLAND – THE FOLLOWING DAY

Harry Randall was a big man. He got pleasure from keeping his body in trim. He had just returned from his usual morning three-mile jog around the park, when he caught sight of Elizabeth. She was standing in the doorway of their house looking anxiously up the road. He knew straightaway that something was seriously wrong. He quickened his pace, and she ran to meet him.

"Harry! Thank God you're back!" She stumbled to him and clasped his shoulders. "It's Laura, she's missing."

Before she had spoken, Harry had known what she was going to say. Still, he braced himself when he heard the word 'missing'. Years of training kept him under control, he didn't betray the waves of fear that crept over him. Instead, he put his arm around his wife and led her back to the house. She began sobbing silently, tears rolling heedlessly down her cheek.

"Come on now, Beth, tell me exactly what's happened."

"Tom phoned about half an hour ago. He said that Laura disappeared after going to a bullfight. Then he'd received a phone call telling him that she was being held somewhere and that he was to do nothing. The local police were informed, and they've been investigating." She stopped and looked at him, waiting to be told that it wasn't true. "Harry, what are we going to do?"

Harry didn't answer, he hadn't even heard the question. When he'd first known that the plan for Laura's holiday was to go to Portugal, he feared that something might happen. It was too soon for him, or his family, to return to that area. If they ever could have safely returned after his history with the country.

He had tried to warn Tom as discreetly as possible. He talked about old enemies in Oporto in the wine trade. Tom had laughed and made some sarcastic comment about Harry having 'old enemies' everywhere. So perhaps, he'd commented they'd better not go outside of the house. As the months passed and the holiday approached, Harry realised the more he voiced his opposition, the more Tom was going to be contrary. He said nothing more. But the silent tack had also failed and they had gone. Harry decided that if anything happened to Laura, he would never forgive Tom.

"Harry, please, you've not heard a word I said." His wife's face was white and anxious, her hands clasped nervously together. "What are we going to do? Should we go out there? Should Tom and the children come home? What do you think?"

Harry thought very carefully, he knew his wife would be completely guided by him. Whatever he said went, as far as she was concerned. She had invested him with some power of supreme wisdom. At that moment, he wished he possessed such a trait. He knew, however, that Tom and the children had to leave Portugal. The children were in danger there and Tom's presence served no valuable purpose at all. Harry regretted that the local police had been involved, that would only complicate the issue.

"Look, Beth, you'll have to trust me. Leave it all to me, eh? Tom and the kids must come home. I know the locals; I'll go out and try to help from that end."

Once he'd spoken, Beth's face relaxed, an enormous burden lifted from her. It had been like Superman flying to the rescue. Harry noted the change in her, and his confidence reached an even lower level. If she knew the reality of the situation, the shock would be beyond her fragile nature's ability to cope.

"They can all come and stay here with me." Beth said. "Tom can go to work from our house if he wants to. The children can even go to school from here if they need to. But I'm sure everything will be settled long before the school holidays are over." She smiled and got up. "I'll go and make us a cup of coffee, dear. I think we both need one after the shock."

While she was gone, Harry ran through a plan of what he had to do and do quickly. There were so many things that needed to be organised before he could go to Portugal. But first, the children had to be got home.

"Beth," he called out, "I'm going to phone Tom now at the hotel. I'll tell him to catch a flight back here tomorrow morning. Can you have everything ready by then?" She came back with the coffee and nodded. Now there was something practical to be done, she felt better.

An hour later, the first steps in the arrangements had been made. Tom agreed to return home. He had been persuaded he must inform Lopes, before doing so. He had also been persuaded that he must be discreet. Harry was amazed at his own ability to talk dispassionately to Tom. He was equally amazed at the way Tom agreed to everything so readily.

"They'll arrive at Heathrow tomorrow afternoon at about 4 o'clock. That should give you time, Beth, to get organised with shopping and everything, shouldn't it?" He glanced at the clock, it was already 10:30. Fortunately, he wasn't expected at Sanctum until the afternoon. He should have been checking information this morning, so his absence wouldn't have been noticed.

"Take my advice, Beth, go to the hairdressers, as you'd planned before all this happened," he said. "It'll help to take your mind off things. Then go and stock up for the freezer. You don't need to be running around shopping every two minutes with those hungry kids here. Take the car. I've got arrangements to make if I'm to go out to Oporto. I'll contact our Consulate to enable Tom to leave the country. Otherwise, the police will insist he stays."

As she sat under the hairdryer, Beth ruminated over all that had taken place that morning. She had the feeling that Harry knew more than he'd said. She mused to herself that although she had been married to him for 37 years, she still didn't really know him. She didn't even know exactly what his work entailed. She knew it was something to do with the government and the overseeing of trade negotiations. That was as far as she bothered to enquire. Somehow, she did not see Harry as a bone fide trade official, but her suspicions never led her to find out more. And she pondered, how could he just phone up the British Consulate? But Harry had never encouraged her to ask questions. So, she didn't ask them.

Elizabeth Randall had been brought up in that fading upper-class system where wives were expected to take care of the running of the home and the upbringing of the children. The lifestyle had suited her temperament and she would never betray it. She had tried to instil the same attitudes into Laura, sending her to her old school and encouraging her in the same tradition. She sighed - life was not the same now as when she'd been a girl and Laura's views were undoubtedly different from her own. Beth dreaded that Laura might even take the unprecedented step of divorcing Tom. Although she pretended not to know what was going on, she understood very well what the situation was.

The hairdryer became unbearably hot, so she switched it on to cooler. Then she planned what she would need to buy. She took a conscious decision not to think about Laura again, until she was forced to.

Harry acted swiftly and decisively, he went to the information library as he was supposed to, but instead of reading the files that already been laid out for him on General Fernando Dos Santos Costa, he asked for the files on Pedro Batista and Leonid Paustovsky. The woman behind the desk peered at him when he made the request. Like all good civil servants, she disliked changes and Miss Robotham disliked change more than most.

"Where's the chitty needed for those files, Mr Randall?" She asked primly.

"Come on now, Miss Robotham, ease the rules a bit. I was the one who wrote ninety percent of what's in those files, remember?"

"That's not the point", she was not impressed "I still need a chitty."

"What is the point, Ms Robotham," Harry snarled at her, "is that I need those files urgently. If you like, I can phone Sir George. But if I do, I'll tell him how bloody uncooperative you've been. But have it your way." He reached across her, calling her bluff, and picked up the phone.

"No, don't do that. I'll get them for you, though I want you to know that I don't like this irregularity. It's not the sort of thing that gives us a good name." Harry smiled and watched her disappear behind the tall rows of metal cabinets.

Miss Robotham returned quickly carrying the files. She handed them to him and observed as he moved to the desk near the window. Harry started at the beginning of each file to remind himself of the details. It was painful reading. Every snippet of information had cost him dearly. It had also cost one of his agents his life. How easy it was to forget the dangers of being a 'live' operative from the cosy security of Sanctum.

Harry was surprised to see how sparse the information was that had been gathered in the years since he'd left. He had left with undignified haste on Sir George's orders and against his own better judgement. It was not until he read the last entry in Batista's file that Harry understood everything clearly. He closed the files and returned them to Miss Robotham. Then he headed for Sanctum itself.

Before going to Sir George, he went first to Monty Fairbrother. He and Monty had joined Sanctum in the same month. Going on first operations in North Africa together, they had later operated in Germany. This was where Monty had been wounded in a badly thought-out transaction near the Polish border. It was only Harry's quick thinking that had saved his life. Not a debt that he'd ever been able to repay. Now that time had come. Harry breezed in with an air of quiet confidence, he winked at Monty indicating they should go into the back office. Monty was intrigued.

"I need your help, old boy. I need a new identity to get me into Oporto." Monty's eyebrows rose almost imperceptibly but rise they did. "Also, I want a plane ticket for Oporto. And I need the latest radio equipment you've got; at least three receiver/transmitters. I need a couple of Smith & Wesson 19 Combat Magnums and a model 27. I'll need a good supply of ·357 Magnum Super Vel ammo. Also" he grinned, "any other goodies that will keep an old hand like me from getting into trouble. And, before you ask, I haven't got a requisition order."

"I guessed that The identity will be no problem, the plane ticket too no problem. I'll get a diplomatic bag pass to see the bag through Customs. Don't want you setting off any alarms, do we! As for the rest…"

"Monty, I need them all - everything - like I've never needed anything from you in the past. You'll have to trust me. I won't let you get into any kind of mess. I'll square it with George, but I can't wait for his wheels to start turning. Understand?"

"I'll ask no questions and tell no tales, Harry. But square it if you can. I don't want to lose the pension." He grinned. "Everything will be ready tonight. I leave it in your locker in the old brown suitcase routine, remember?" Harry nodded and clapped a hand on Monty's shoulder. Then, he went to see George.

~✧~

Harry was still musing over his rather disagreeable encounter with Sir George Cattermole as he and Beth waited for Tom's and the children's flight arrival to be announced. Beth had regained some of her old vigour and composure now she had a sense of purpose. She hated inactivity and a feeling of uselessness, now she had something positive to focus on. It was Beth who heard the announcement; Harry was not really listening.

"That's it, Harry, British Airways flight from Oporto." She smiled. "How many times did I wait here for you in the old days, longing for your flight call to come up. I expect they'll be tired; you always were."

They waited patiently for Tom and the children to appear. Harry saw them first. The children were clinging on to Tom who was unusually pale and harassed-looking. Beth rushed forward and gathered the children to her protectively and led them out to the car park.

Harry was relieved she was there to look after them. He walked over to Tom and took one of the cases. They looked at each other without saying anything for a few seconds. Tom had prepared exactly what he was going to say, but now when it came to it, he was at a loss for words.

"No need to say anything, Tom," Harry said. "It's not a good time to start blathering in front of Beth and the children. God knows what they've got ahead of them anyway."

He walked with Tom and headed to where the car was parked. Tom was relieved to be back; he couldn't deny it. One more night in the hotel with all the gossip and stares and he'd have gone crazy.

During supper, Jenny and Philip were quiet. They had lost their energy and gaiety on the way home. Philip had cut his hand and though it was only a small scratch compared with other injuries he had before; this time he cried and asked repeatedly for his mother. His crying had set Jenny off too. So, the homecoming had been tearful, despite Beth's best efforts.

Tom was irritable and snapped at the children for not eating. Beth was beginning to crumble under the effort and strain. She saw Harry looking at her, his face showing the concern he felt both for her and the situation. She tried to smile but didn't succeed.

"I'll put the children to bed, you'd like that wouldn't you?" She said to Jenny and Philip. Jenny nodded and got off her chair. She was sucking her thumb in a way that she hadn't done since she was very small. Philip slid off his chair and took his grandmother's hand. Jenny held the other hand and together the three left the room.

For some time, Harry said nothing, then he got up and poured a whiskey for them both. It was then that the grilling began, as Tom knew it would. He had prepared a series of set answers in his mind, but it was one thing to have set answers to questions which were already prepared. It was quite another to try to make use of those same answers for Harry's expert interrogation. The first muddle came over why he hadn't gone to the bullfight with Laura.

"I thought she'd prefer to go alone." Tom mumbled.

"What, Laura?" Harry's tone expressed surprise. "She was the last person to go to a bullfight on her own. Had you quarrelled or something?"

"Not really, she was just very keen to go, after some chap told her how amazing they were. I didn't think it was suitable for Jenny and Philip. So, I stayed behind with them, besides I'd been told that these Portuguese fights weren't worth going to."

"Who told you that?"

"One of the other guests."

"Tom, I asked who told you? Be more precise?"

"I can't remember, I think there was a general discussion."

"All right, then let's drop it. What about after-dinner then, why on earth didn't you check with reception to see whether she had really gone on the coach trip?"

"I was told she had already been seen getting onto the couch."

"By whom?"

"I told you …"

"Who told you, Tom?" Harry's voice had become harsh and lost its previously friendly tone. "It was the same person who told you not to bother to go to the bullfight, wasn't it?" He stared at Tom in a disconcerting way.

"Look here, Harry, I don't have to answer these bloody questions. You're not the police and I'm not a criminal. Cut it out!"

"I think you'd agree, Tom, that it is preferable to get your story right with your father-in-law before talking to the police. Because that, my lad, is what you're going to have to do sooner rather than later. But have it your way if you insist." He rose from his chair and walked to the door.

"No, Harry, don't go. Let's start again." Tom held out his glass for a refill and watched Harry as he took it and filled it again. "I was told not to bother to go to the fight by a woman called Greta Peltz. She is a perfectly ordinary German tourist who was quite knowledgeable about Portugal.

She told me quite a bit about the place. We'd become quite friendly by the pool."

"Did she talk to the other guests?"

"No, not much, she was with some rather fat Portuguese man, at least, I think he was Portuguese. I never actually spoke to him."

"So, this Peltz woman singled you out, did she?"

"Not really."

"Who else did she talk to then?"

"I don't know!"

"It was this same woman who told you that Laura got on the coach, wasn't it?" Tom nodded. "I suppose it was also this Peltz woman who so conveniently occupied you until the next morning, when you reported the matter to the Manager."

"No, Harry, we parted later that evening."

"How much later?"

"About one or two in the morning, I suppose, I don't remember." He looked at Harry. "You know what it's like on holiday, Harry. A woman like that was just asking for it. You know what it's like." Harry shook his head and pursed his lips.

"No, Tom, I don't know what it's like, as you say. You see I love Beth and I had hoped that you loved Laura. But it's increasingly obvious you couldn't give a damn about her or the children. That German bitch must have laughed her head off at her luck in having found a dupe like you. Christ, what a fool I've been to hope you and Laura could make a go of things!"

"A dupe? What do you mean by that, Harry?"

"She deliberately got you out of the way while Laura was taken, can't you even understand that?"

"But why? Why should anyone want to take Laura anywhere?"

"Maybe one day you'll understand, but I doubt if you would, even if it was spelt out letter by letter. I warned you before you went on this bloody holiday, not to go. Then I warned you to take special care of Laura and the children." He slammed one fist into the palm of the other hand. "I wish I'd been firmer about it, and none of this would have happened."

Tom didn't understand, it was as if Harry actually knew what had happened to Laura, had even known that this type of thing might happen. But why? He watched Harry pace around the room, deep in thought. Harry was right, Tom thought, he didn't understand what was going on. He wasn't even sure that he believed what had already happened. Harry stopped pacing and came and sat down opposite him again.

"There's absolutely no point in your going back to Oporto. You could do no good at all. You'd better stay here with Beth and the children, until there is some news." He held up his hand to stop Tom from interrupting. "All right, it's a bit inconvenient for you. It'll mean you have further to travel to work, but that is a minor inconvenience. Forget yourself and think of Beth and the children. And before you ask some inane question, I'll be abroad. I've got good friends in Portugal. You'll have to trust me, won't you? For someone as inept and emotionally shallow as yourself, I expect that will be a relief." Without waiting for a reply, Harry left the room and went upstairs. He didn't want to be in the same room as Tom a minute longer than was necessary.

Tom sat for a while without moving. His first reaction was annoyance at having been spoken to in that way. The second reaction was relief that it was over. His final feeling was one of something close to jubilation. The weight had been taken from his shoulders and pinned firmly onto that pompous old man's back. It would be irritating staying here in the house, but at least he wouldn't have to worry about the cooking and caring for the kids. Perhaps, things would be all right after all. He went over to the sideboard and poured himself a very large whiskey and settled down to read the paper.

CHAPTER 5
LONDON, HEATHROW AIRPORT - THE NEXT DAY

Heathrow was crowded with holidaymakers anxiously looking at altered flight times and getting their baggage weighed in. As promised, Monty had organised things for his luggage. So, after the delivery of his cases for the diplomatic bag, all Harry needed to do was wait to be allocated a seat. He had queued for some time before he got to the desk. He asked for a seat in the no smoking section and was told there were none left.

"Then ask someone to change." He smiled at the woman.

"I'm sorry, sir, I can't do that." She wasn't rude but Harry detected the firmness in her tones that was intended to keep him in his place. Under normal circumstances, he would have taken up the challenge, but he couldn't afford to draw attention to himself. Instead of arguing, he took the ticket handed to him and went to the departure lounge.

The room was full, every seat was taken and bags littered the floor. Small children and babies wailed restlessly in the heat and inertia. He walked over to the window to see what preparations were being made outside. Twenty minutes to take-off, so he positioned himself near the exit door ready to move at the signal. Half an hour went by, and they were all still waiting in the departure lounge. Harry felt restless and agitated, every minute seemed an age, he wanted above everything else to be doing something constructive.

His attention was diverted from his own troubles by a sudden urgent tugging at his trouser leg. He looked down and saw a small girl of about just over a year, he guessed, desperately using his legs for support. She was attempting to stand up. His first instinct was to move her away, but when she turned her face towards him and smiled, he put his hand out to steady her instead. The child slapped his knees in triumph having achieved an upright position.

"I'm so sorry," the young woman, whom he assumed must be the child's mother, took the little girl's hand. "She just slipped away from me in all this crush."

"You weren't any trouble, were you, young lady?" Harry said to the child.

The loudspeaker crackled into life announcing their flight number and requesting passengers to board the plane. Instantly, there was a mass rush towards the exit. In the scramble, the young mother grew flustered trying to gather up a large teddy bear, a small boy, and the little girl. Her large holdall dropped to the floor. Harry waited to see if one of the hostesses or another passenger would help, but they didn't. He found himself pushing against the flow of people towards the helpless little group.

"Come on, look sharp," he said to the little boy, "can't keep the pilot waiting, can we?"

He took the little boy's hand and picking up the holdall began walking to the door after the retreating queue. The boy, seemingly puzzled, turned to look at his mother. Harry also turned and winked at her and smiled. They were the last to board the plane and their progress was slow. People were standing in the gangway stuffing hand luggage under seats and coats onto ledges. Eventually the mother and children found their seats. Harry held the bag, while the boy scrambled to the inside seat near the porthole. The mother sat in the middle with the little girl on her knee. Another passenger had the gangway seat. He was a large red-faced man wearing a flamboyant blazer. Harry sensed his irritation as the little family settled themselves in.

"My God! Some trip this is going to be!" The man said in a loud American accent. "Why do people bring whiny kids on trips like this? It ruins it for everyone." He looked at Harry for support.

"I'll see the children don't bother you." The mother said flushing with embarrassment.

"Stewardess!" the man shouted, "I want to move, I paid good bucks for this flight, and I want to enjoy it." A tall slim stewardess edged her way to where they were and rapidly assessed the situation.

"I don't really think we could ask one of the other passengers to …"

"I'll change seats with this person," Harry heard himself saying. "It's no smoking down here, that suits me just fine."

"Great, thanks Buddy!" The American said, scrambling to his feet and taking Harry's seat ticket. "Good luck, old fella." He pushed past the stewardess and loped down the gangway.

"That was very helpful, sir," the stewardess said. "We always have one of them!" She leaned over to the mother, "I'm so sorry for the rumpus, you must've found it unpleasant." She moved away to deal with other problems and Harry sat down.

"Can't think why anyone would prefer to sit with all that smoke billowing around." Harry said.

The little boy leaned forward to look at him and grinned. Harry winked back. In truth, he thought, he would value the distractions that the family would provide during the flight. They would keep his mind from thinking too much of Laura and what might lie ahead.

Take-off was delayed still further, and the sun streamed in through the porthole making it rather too warm. At last, the engine started up and the plane taxied to the runway. Once airborne, the hum of the engines and the warmth of the plane made Harry drift off. His mind went over the conversation he'd had with Sir George Cattermole what seemed only hours earlier.

He had not wasted time planning or developing any subtle reasons. He'd made up his mind to go to Portugal within minutes of hearing Tom's story. He also knew he could not expect the Department's cooperation in the plan. So, not for the first time in his long career with M16, he decided to act without sanction.

As the plane flew over the green fields of England, in almost a reverie, he went over the conversation he'd had in Cattermole's office.

~❖~

"Harry, I didn't expect you today. What's this, an early briefing?" Sir George reassured himself that it was Monday, not Tuesday, when his heads of department briefed him every week.

Harry had replied "No, Sir George, you've not lost a day. I've done the report for you though and asked Goddard to bring it in tomorrow." He saw Sir George's eyebrows rise a fraction. "The reason I came was to ask if I could have a week or two off. There are some things I'd really like to do."

Cattermole pondered for a while; this was so unlike Harry who was a man of meticulous routine. But since he had not taken any leave since before Christmas, he suggested why not wait for the following month and then take a whole month off.

"I really need it now, Sir George, not next month. In fact, I'd like to take it from tomorrow. That's why I've asked

Goddard to bring over the report." Harry realised he had made a mistake, the minute he saw the look of surprise change into one of suspicion. Unfortunately, the urgency of Laura's plight had forced him to throw his usual caution to the wind.

"Any special reason, Harry Not health problems, I hope?" Cattermole didn't look up at him but fiddled with a little mound of paper clips on his desk. He hoped Harry would have sufficient judgement to be truthful. However, having worked in the field with him in previous years, he thought his hopes were likely to be dashed. He also knew that if that were to be the case, things might become unpleasant.

"Nothing really special, Sir George, only I've been invited to join some friends in France for a short break. They have a small villa in Menton and have extra space for the next couple of weeks. I thought it would be nice to take Beth. You know she's been slightly under stress recently."

Cattermole got up from his desk and went over to a large metal filing cabinet. Before opening it, he turned to look at Harry: "You know I've got a dossier on you in here. I think I can tell you more about yourself in two minutes than even you know. So, before I make us both feel uncomfortable, why don't you tell me your real reason."

"Real reason, Sir George?" Harry feigned surprise.

"Harry, you disappoint me. If you are the best we can do after years of training, and you are supposed to be the best, then God help England. At least you should be able to lie convincingly, not give pathetic excuses like a recalcitrant schoolboy."

"I don't think what I said sounds like a pathetic excuse."

"Harry, don't insult my intelligence. Are you going to tell me your real reason for the sudden need to leave the country, or do I have to waste time trying to guess?"

"It's nothing whatever to do with Sanctum business. It's personal. No one from Century House needs to be involved at all."

"One thing you must have learned during your long service with us, Harry, is that there is no such thing as 'personal'. Anything you do, or think, or feel is Sanctum business."

"No need to preach to me, Sir George," Harry was annoyed. "I shall be retiring soon, and I know as much about what goes on here as you do, perhaps more."

"Right then, so what is it?"

"I told you, it's …"

"If you say personal again, Harry, so help me I'll pulverise you."

Harry debated with himself for a while. He knew quite well that it would be impossible to carry out his plans if Sir George Cattermole became really difficult. He braced himself and decided to test his reaction, before coming totally clean.

"I've got to go back to Portugal, Sir George. I need to go as soon as possible and alone. And I am going, sir, you can be certain about that."

Cattermole had expected many reasons for Harry's request and strange behaviour, but he recoiled from what he heard. After all, as he recalled, it had not been that long since Harry had been forced to make a speedy withdrawal from Oporto. A withdrawal that had saved his life and secured the future of Sanctum's network. Now here he was saying he was going back. It didn't make sense.

"It's almost four years to the day, Harry, that you got out of there by the skin of your teeth with Leonid's men at your heels. And you couldn't blame him for chasing you. After all you shattered his little cell that had taken a decade to build up. Also, he never forgave you for handing Batista over to the PIDE. Leonid remained there you know, and he still wants your scalp on his belt. Have you forgotten that? So why the hell rush into treacherous waters now? Anyway, I'm not sure I can allow it…"

"I must go, Sir George, it's not choice but necessity. I'd prefer to have your blessing, but I'll go without it if needs be."

"Why all the drama, Harry? Sounds like something out of a bad detective novel. All this talk of 'got to go' and 'necessity'. Do Sanctum and DP1 mean so much to you?"

"Laura's been kidnapped in Portugal. She and her family were there on holiday, much against my advice. I'm pretty sure Leonid's men have her."

Cattermole gave a sharp intake of breath. He said nothing for a while, all the time his mind was searching for a way to prevent the action Harry proposed. It wasn't that he was worried about Harry. There was the new network that had been meticulously built up since Harry's departure. Also, the Americans, now involved in the area, wouldn't like it if there was yet another cock-up implicating Western Intelligence groups.

As against that, he knew Harry would act regardless of threats or disciplining. Perhaps, he surmised, it might be better to allow him to go after all and keep him on a short reign. For the moment, Cattermole decided to keep his options open.

"Harry, you can't be personally involved on a mission, you know that as well as I do. You'll endanger your life, Laura's life, and our new men out there. Why not let me send someone out whom you can trust? It would be strategically more sensible."

"I won't endanger the new men, Sir George, you should know me better than that. I'll use one or two of my own group, from the old days; the ones whose cover wasn't blown. There are a couple whom I can rely on. If you send messages to your new network to keep out of my way for a while, then no one will be any the wiser." Harry had waited for some reaction to cross Cattermole's face.

"It's too big a risk, Harry, you still know too much that would be of inestimable value to Leonid's group. None of the replacements there know half as much as you, even now. That's why Laura's been taken, to draw you back. She will be their little Judas goat. You'd only play right into Leonid's hands. It's my responsibility to save you and Laura from yourself."

"It's not for any secrets or information that Leonid wants me back. It's purely personal."

"Don't be so bloody daft, Harry. Why now, after all this time?"

"One singularly good reason, I should think – Pedro Batista died a few months ago."

"How do you know?"

"I know, that's enough, isn't it? You and I also know why he died. That's even more pertinent to this whole business."

"And you still let Laura go to Portugal?"

"I didn't know he'd died, at the time. As I said before, I tried my damnedest to prevent them going."

Cattermole had moved across to his desk and, speaking to his secretary on the intercom, requested a specific file. There was silence while they waited for it to be brought to the office. Harry sat in one of the large leather chairs and ran his hands over its arms. He watched Cattermole pace slowly round the room.

He was a tall thin man who had never been muscular or athletic. He looked more like a professor of philosophy then head of DP1, one of the major departments in the Current Intelligence Group of MI6. His department was responsible for intelligence work in Western Europe. Cattermole treated it as if it was his special fiefdom. It was totally precious to him, and he guarded its reputation closely.

Although only a part of Sanctum's work, in Cattermole's eyes nothing was more important than DP1. He prided himself on the fact that, since he had taken over the Department, more information came out of Western Europe than all the other DP's put together.

He had his eye on one day actually heading Sanctum itself and of influencing the policy of the JIC. But time was running out for him. Younger, more thrusting men seemed to threaten on all sides. He was determined not to be forced into any foolish action now that might bring his ambitions tumbling round his ears.

There was a knock on the door and a middle-aged secretary came in. She smiled at Harry and handed the buff-coloured file to Cattermole. Then she left the room as discreetly as she had entered. Harry was amused by the atmosphere in the building; it was quite different from the way he and Goddard ran their own office. He watched Sir George thumb his way through the file slowly and steadily.

"Harry, I'd forgotten just how much damage you inflicted on the whole Soviet system not only in Portugal, but throughout the entire Iberian Peninsula. When you cracked Leonid's cell, a whole series of domino reactions were felt throughout much of northern Portugal. They reached right across the border into Spain and into the Basque area. Leonid was the lynchpin for operations, supplying delicate information from Moscow direct to a chain of other cells." He closed the file. "We know he's back in business again now, but we haven't managed to find out exactly where he's operating from, nor what he's really up to. The work is much more subtle these days, our friends in the KGB don't use the old crude stir up trouble methods, they used to."

"I do know all this, Sir George, I happen to still work for DP1, remember?" Harry's impatience was growing, he didn't need a history lesson, he wanted a response. At the best of times, he disliked being patronised. This was not the best of times.

Cattermole tapped the top of his desk for some time. As he read the file, a thought occurred to him: if Harry was successful and unearthed Leonid then he, Sir George Cattermole, would cash in on the credit. If on the other hand, Harry failed and had been working alone, what would be lost. There would be one dead Harry and one dead Laura. Neither might even be noticed by JIC. He made up his mind but decided not to let Harry know just yet.

"So, you think you can work alone, do you?"

"Yes, at least, I can work with one particular person whom I trust. You needn't worry about your new network out there. I won't even need an angel. In fact, I'd rather not have one." He laughed, "the angels you sent out in the past were more of a bloody hindrance than a help."

"All right then, Harry, I'll write you up for two week's leave. As long as you know the risks of running after a Judas goat. Even if she happens to be your daughter. Two weeks, not a day longer. If you and Laura aren't out by then, well your imagination can fill in the rest. Certainly, there wouldn't be a job here for you. But that would be the least of your worries. After two weeks, I shall order the new network to go in and finish the job."

"What would be the point of that?"

"Sorry to sound an opportunist, Harry, particularly because of the circumstances, but I have to think of DP1 as well. My reasoning is that two week's investigation by you will have stirred up a hornets' nest out there. Agents get careless in such circumstances and my new network deserve to get the pickings."

Harry sat and evaluated what he'd just heard. There was certainly no sentiment expressed, but he hadn't really expected any. If he was honest, there was precious little sentiment in his own life, except where Laura, Beth and the children were concerned. Yes, he thought, it was a reasonable offer. He just prayed that two weeks would be long enough.

"It's a deal, Sir George, I accept."

"Fine." Cattermole rubbed his hands together, congratulating himself that he had salvaged a potential gem out of what might have been disaster. And he had possibly turned it into what might turn out to be a very worthwhile exercise.

"Go to field HQ for a briefing on current events in the Peninsular. Go to Monty for equipment and papers." He caught sight of the faint smile that crossed Harry's face. "You bastard, Harry, I suppose you've already done it."

Harry didn't reply, instead he got up. As Sir George Cattermole reached out to shake his hand, he felt a slight tremor in Harry's hand.

"You sure about this, Harry?"

"Yes, quite sure. It's not fear that's making me tremble, it's just that this is my first field operation for a while. The prospect is as exciting as the very first one I did in North Africa years ago."

"Well, this isn't your first assignment, and it's been some time since you were in the field. In that time, changes in operational technique have been made – there's fresh political intrigue, unrest, propaganda. Leonid has resuscitated himself. You just remember that every minute you're out there." He watched Harry walk to the door. "Good luck, bring Laura safely home."

~❖~

Harry was jerked out of contemplating the interview by a tap on his shoulder and a very insistent voice in his ear.

"I say! Could I trouble you? Can I get past, I'm afraid Sally needs a nappy change." The young mother, sitting next to him, was peering into his face anxiously. The little girl was whimpering. Harry drew in his legs to let them through, but his thoughts were still not fully in his present surroundings.

"What's your name?" The small boy near the porthole was peering at him.

"Jim. Jim Burgoyne." He replied quickly, remembering the identity Monty had given him. "What's yours?"

"Pete."

"Enjoying the flight, Pete?"

"No, I don't like flying, my ears popped ages ago and they're hurting me now. I wish the plane would land."

Harry slid over the middle seat and sat next to Pete. He could see the little boy was near to tears. Perhaps, the big American had been right after all.

"Why aren't you making the best of your window seat, Pete?" Harry asked. "You should be looking out of the porthole watching out for landmarks."

"I can't see anything."

"Of course you can," Harry leaned across. "Why yes, there's plenty to see. Stand up and look down, you won't see anything from where you're sitting."

When the mother and Sally returned, they found Harry and Pete both looking out of the porthole. Pete had cheered visibly, all complaints about his ears were forgotten.

"Mummy, Jim is showing me things. It's fun." Harry looked at her and she smiled gratefully again. She had her hands quite full enough coping with her young daughter.

Through the porthole, the coastline of northern Spain was clearly laid out before them, just like a mapmaker's dream. Every cove and inlet was etched incisively against the sea by a line of white, where sea met land and waves broke against the rocks.

"Where are we, Jim?" Pete asked.

"Fish out the map from the pocket on the back of that seat." Harry pointed to the string pocket and its contents. The small boy took everything out and eventually found the map. Harry peered out of the porthole, then pointed to a place on the map.

"That's about it, I should say. You follow the coastline as we fly. You're lucky it's such a cloudless day." Pete was so preoccupied with the route they were taking that he didn't bother Harry anymore.

Sometime later, the plane began its descent. The change in engine noise and cabin pressure affected Pete's ears again. He sat down looking pale. The same slim hostess who had come to them, at the beginning of the flight, brought two boiled sweets for him to suck. Almost immediately, he cheered up, but he didn't look out of the porthole for some time.

Harry, however, was eager to get a glimpse of the country he had known so well. He watched the houses appear with the tiny squares of cultivated land hugging them closely. There were small villages dotted around churches and marketplaces. It all looked exactly the same and the passage of time seemed to fade, the closer they got to Oporto.

Eventually the rusty orange rooftops of the city came in sight. From their height, it resembled some untidy patchwork quilt. Threading its way through the quilt of colour was what looked like a ribbon of shimmering grey silk. From high up, the sweep of the majestic Douro River seemed nothing more than a small stream. By rights, it should have been a golden river, if its name really was a true description.

Harry could feel his heart beating faster, as he peered down at the city. Somewhere down there were his enemies and somewhere, he prayed, there still lived the friend on whom he was pinning all his hopes.

The plane landed smoothly and taxied slowly along the runway. Some eager passengers began to undo their seat belts, until they were reprimanded by the head stewardess. Harry saw the buildings of Oporto airport; nothing had been added since he was last there. Somehow this reassured him.

There was a small coach waiting as they left the plane; it was to take them the short distance to the main airport building. Harry helped the mother to gather her things. His own luggage was on the trolley and being driven to the Arrivals section.

When they were safely inside, the young mother spoke to him: "I'm grateful to you, Jim, you've made the journey so much easier for me. Are you here on holiday?"

"Yes, and you?"

"No, my husband got a job here a couple of months ago. He came on ahead to get us a home. He works in the drinks business at home in England. The firm sent him out here to learn about Port wine. I suppose he couldn't have come anywhere better." She grinned at him.

The coach lurched to a halt next to the main building. Harry looked out of the window at Pedras Rubras Airport, it was almost exactly as he remembered it. Then he glanced at the other passengers, wondering which of them was Cattermole's angel. Or perhaps, the angel was already out there somewhere in the airport watching out for the arrival of this flight. That the angel was around, Harry did not doubt for one minute. It was who he was and where he was that bothered him. He knew quite well that Cattermole would not be able to keep out of his business for two whole weeks. At the very least, he would expect to know what was happening.

Harry helped Pete off the coach. Two straggling weary queues formed up to go through passport control. And although he did not need to comply with this formality, since Monty had arranged things, Harry did not want to appear different from the other passengers. The young mother paused to wave to him as she passed through ahead of him. The man at the desk hardly looking at her passport. Then the sallow faced uniformed man took Harry's passport. He thumbed his way through it, glancing at the stamps at the back and the visas.

"Okay." The man nodded and handed him back the passport, then indicated for the next person to step forward.

Harry was grateful for Monty's arrangements, as he watched the other passengers being quizzed. Once he had collected his luggage, he headed in the direction of the taxi rank. Out of the corner of his eye, he caught sight of a man rushing towards Pete. He smiled as he saw the little boy's face light up. Then his smile faded as he thought that he too could have been met by Laura if things had been different.

CHAPTER 6
THE FISHERMAN RETURNS

The queue at the taxi rank was gradually diminishing. Harry had not ordered the usual car service, wanting to be as inconspicuous as possible. Many couples seemed prepared to share taxis to the same hotel. Some enterprising drivers held up placards with the names of various hotels written on them. At last, it was his turn. A battered car was next in line at the rank. Harry eyed the driver for a second, then opened the door. He decided to try out his Portuguese straightaway, partly to get him used to speaking the language again, partly to let the driver understand that he knew a thing or two about Portugal and couldn't be cheated.

"Conduz-me a Sé."

The driver nodded and drove away at speed. It was only a journey of about fifteen minutes from the airport to Oporto and Harry had known every twist and turn like the back of his hand, at one time. Now his memory was jerked as the car travelled along the dusty road. He glanced out of the back window to see if they were being followed. But there was a stream of cars all jockeying for position and his angel could have been in any one of them.

The city streets were full of early evening shoppers. Cars and buses fought for space with arrogant, cheeky scooterists weaving their way in and out of any tiny gap they found. Each set of traffic lights was like the beginning of a Grand Prix with the leading scooter, car and bus determined to get away first. There was grim determination on the faces of some and sheer enjoyment on the faces of the young scooter riders. Harry smiled, nothing had changed at all, the same haste to go nowhere in particular, very fast indeed.

He caught sight of the Clerigos Tower in the distance, looming large and dominant over the city like some ancient stone guardian. Then he saw his own point of destination, the forlorn once resplendent Sé still standing proud and high above the old town and the riverbanks. The Sé glowed in the light of the dying sun. An untrained eye might pause for one moment as it swept across the building's façade. To anyone who didn't know the old cathedral, the golden light made it look magnificent. But a knowing eye could detect the creeping decay eating away the once splendid façade.

The taxi pulled to a sudden and under-signalled halt, causing the car behind to skid. The driver shook his fist and hurled abuse through his open window. Harry's own driver, totally unperturbed, didn't even glance at the havoc he had caused. Harry got out and paid the fare.

For a while, he stood on the pavement watching the traffic flow past. The air was hot and stagnant and hit him like the blast from a fan heater. He hadn't remembered it had been as hot as this before, in fact he thought there had always been a pleasant breeze in the city even in the summer. Either his memory was wrong, or this was an unusually hot heavy day for Oporto. He looked at his two bags and then at the steep stone steps, he would have to climb, leading to the side of the old cathedral. He decided to take it slowly.

The market stalls lining the steps were crowded with women eagerly buying fish and bread. Yet other stalls, sold rolls of linen and pieces of lace which were being bartered with much gesturing and shouting. Further up the steps, there was a stall selling cheap cotton dresses which brought a splash of colour.

Harry picked up his bags and began climbing slowly. It was pointless to hurry, since the steps were littered with small shoeless children playing or begging. Halfway up, he was halted by the sudden rush into his path of three scrawny, squawking chickens scurrying from beneath a wooden crate. Hot in pursuit came a skinny, mangy, black dog, its claws scratching and slipping on the stone, as he chased them across the steps and beneath yet another stall.

Harry continued his climb and at last, reach the top. He paused to get his bearings. As he did so, two small boys ran up to him, one of them held out a filthy hand for money. He realised he must look like the tourist he was supposed to have been for the purpose of the flight. He was irritated he had not had the presence of mind to change his clothes before coming to the old quarter and drawing attention to himself.

The small boys followed him. Wanting to be rid of them, Harry said:

"Vá-se embora." He spoke sharply and the boys looked surprised. "Vá-se embora." Harry repeated, "Clear off, you little devils!" He flicked his hand and the boys, thinking he was about to hit out, tumbled over each other in their haste to escape. Despite himself, Harry laughed and headed into the network of alleys.

After about ten minutes and having taken two wrong turnings, he eventually found himself outside a crumbling tenement block. On the front, there was a mosaic in blue tiles of Our Lady of Fatima surrounded by the remains of what had once been a beautiful blue ceramic frontage. The alley was deserted and silent, except for the faint sound of a radio coming from the far end.

Harry put down his cases and rubbed his chin thoughtfully. He pushed open the heavy wooden entrance door letting himself into the tiny courtyard beyond it. The apartment he wanted was directly to his right, as he crossed the courtyard. He knocked on the door and waited. No answer. He waited for a while and knocked again. This time he saw the small niche behind the central iron grille open just a fraction. He couldn't see who was there but before it closed again, he called out in a low whisper.

"It is I, O Pescador, I have returned."

He waited for the door to open, but nothing happened. He ran his foot along the worn stone edge of the doorstep, acutely aware of the danger of having used the old cover name. He also knew it was only the sound of that name that would get the door to open for him, if João and Angelita were still there. Minutes passed and nothing happened, no sound came to indicate anyone was behind the door. He knocked again and waited again.

Suddenly it dawned on him that he might, after all, have to see it through himself. The enormity of this fell on him like lead and, for a moment, he wondered whether he would cope. Perhaps after all João was gone, dead even. Perhaps the old network had also vanished. Standing there in the cool of the courtyard, he realised he should have considered that possibility before going to see Cattermole and conveying his plan to take on Leonid by himself. Maybe, he should have allowed DP1 to handle it for him.

"Damn them all to hell! I'll do it alone if I must." He muttered, as he went out of the courtyard and back through the doorway into the alley. He paused, then headed in the direction from which he had walked, with such hopes, only a short time before. As he closed the door, he heard a faint low whistle coming from an upper window. The sound made the hairs on his neck rise and a shudder of excitement went through him.

"Of course, what a fool!" He found himself talking aloud in reproach. Then he whistled three notes. To anyone listening carefully, they would have heard they were the next three notes following in sequence from the ones Harry had just heard. He repeated the original notes, followed again by the ones he had just whistled. He returned stealthily back through the door and into the courtyard. The apartment door was open, and unhesitatingly he went in.

Seconds later, he was engulfed in the darkness of the dimly lit passageway smelling of paraffin and garlic. The chill of the air made him shiver. Gradually, his eyes grew accustomed to the faint light and he saw, framed against the light coming from an open door, the solid stocky shape of someone he knew very well indeed. Harry stood still allowing the other man to scrutinise him carefully, to see if there was some detail that was out of place. Moments later, Harry saw the other man's shoulders relax and he heard the beginning of João's hoarse laugh.

"My God, Harry, O Pescador! Is it really you?" He seized him by the shoulders and hugged him so fiercely that for a moment Harry couldn't breathe or speak. At last, João released him and held him at arm's length.

"Why didn't you whistle, eh? Have you forgotten how careful we used to be? Anyone could come along and say he was 'O Pescador', but that plus the whistle was the sign, wasn't it?"

"Of course, João, I'll be truthful I had forgotten. Fortunately for me, you're still the old fox you always were. We'd never have survived if you hadn't been the cunning one."

All this time, in the shadows of the kitchen, Angelita had been standing anxiously waiting for a sign that everything was all right. When she saw her husband step forward and clasp Harry, she relaxed. Harry noticed her withdraw her hand from her apron pocket and flex her fingers as if they had been gripping something tightly only moments before. Then, looking over João's shoulders, he noted the look of anxiety still on her face.

"Angelita, it is really me, Harry Randall, I have returned."

She stepped forward and embraced him as João had done. As she did, he felt the hard form of a revolver in her pocket. Secretly, he was glad they were both so vigilant, after all this time.

João led him up the wooden stairs to a small back room. It was sparsely furnished only having a table, some wooden chairs, and a paraffin heater black with age.

"Your old room, Harry, no one else has used it since you were last here."

"So, I see, even the paintwork's the same colour, and I'll swear the heater hasn't moved an inch!" He laughed and went to sit on one of the chairs by the window. João followed and sat next to him.

"Do you want to stay here with us, as before?" He asked. "You are welcome and it is still safe here. Angelita is better than any watchdog."

"João, am I really welcome? After everything that happened at the end?" Harry didn't look directly at him as he spoke, instead he peered through the net curtains into the alley below. He didn't want to see João's eyes in case they registered a sense of betrayal.

"You old fool!" João spoke loudly and vehemently, so much so that Harry looked up with a startled expression. "Do you think I am such an ignorant man that I did not understand! Harry, you wrong me, Angelita and I, we understood everything. We knew why you left so suddenly and why you did not contact us again. If it was to save yourself and the other British agents, then it was as much done to save us. We knew, we understood." He reached out to touch Harry's shoulder: "you believe me?"

"But tell me truly, it hurt, didn't it? That I, who looked upon you as my friend and closest ally, just left?"

"Of course, it did. But you and I were not playing children's games, were we? We were dealing with life and death and the welfare of this country. For over a year after you left, we were suspicious of every stranger who entered the courtyard. Angelita has carried a gun ever since."

"So, I noticed!" Harry chuckled, "and she would have used it on me too, if you hadn't given me the okay." He paused, "so your cover was never blown?"

"Who knows, Harry? I'm sure Leonid's men knew where we live. I'm sure they knew our connections with you. But for some reason they have never, not once, threatened us."

"Then it must have been for a reason. I think that even four years ago, Leonid had planned he would get me back here. He left you alone so that when I came, I would be able to find you. Of course!" He thumped his fist onto the window ledge. "Christ, what a fool I've been! Yours was the last place I should have come to!"

"Why? What has happened? Something important, I can tell, you are risking so much after so long, what is it?"

Harry got up and walked slowly round the room. He felt riddled with guilt at having brought João and Angelita into danger. This time it was not for any idealistic cause, not for the future of Portugal, but purely a personal vendetta.

"João, I have to be honest with you. I'm not here representing DP1 this time. I still work for them; I still deal with the Iberian Peninsula. But that's not why I'm here. In fact, Sir George Cattermole was strongly opposed to my coming. I have no support this time from Sanctum. I'm on my own. So," he turned to look at João, "if you want to tell me to get out, then I will. Your government and your people certainly won't benefit from my presence this time, nor will mine."

"So why are you here? Why so many words, Harry? Tell me why." João was growing impatient to know the real reason for the return. He sensed action and part of him longed for it. But he wanted to know what sort of action and when it would be.

"I think – no – I'm sure that Leonid has kidnapped my daughter."

"What!" João exclaimed, "Laura? When? Where?"

"About three days ago. As to where, then you will never believe it. She was in Póvoa on holiday. And" he held up his hand, "don't tell me, I should never have let her come here. I told myself that, so has Sir George. But I couldn't stop her. Her husband and I don't get on and he seemed to see coming to Portugal as a personal battle between him and me. He knows nothing of my past, or about my present work with Sanctum. I was a fool to have reacted so badly when they first mentioned Portugal. But there it is! They came and with disastrous results. But I promise you, João, not even in my wildest dreams did I think anything like this would happen."

"How do you know she was kidnapped? Perhaps she went off with another man or…"

"No, I wish it was as simple as that. She went on her own to a local bullfight one of the very few held at Póvoa. She was never seen again, not a trace of her. Her husband didn't report her missing until the next day. Also, by then he'd had a phone call telling him Laura was being held and that he wasn't to do anything."

"Where is her husband now, still here?"

"No, he's back in London with the children. He was a liability out here; it was upsetting the children too. To be honest, he was only too pleased to get home. I gather the local police chap, someone called Lopes, opposed his return but our Consul squared it with him. Also, Sir George managed to pull some strings on my behalf; so there's been no reporting by the British or Portuguese press. If I'm right, and Leonid is involved, publicity wouldn't help."

"Why has he waited till now, Harry? He could have come at you in England. You would admit that such things do happen, even on your own doorstep. He didn't need to wait until your family set foot in Portugal. So why now?"

"It's a simple answer – Pedro Batista died very recently. The rest you can imagine. Of course, you're right, Leonid probably would have come to London. The irony is, Laura presented herself as the very bait he needed."

"I understand now!" João said, "Leonid never forgave you for breaking his cell. But, above all, he would never forgive you for what happened to Batista. You know, I think he would have preferred it if they had just shot him and that would have been an end. But Leonid hated us both for what the PIDE inflicted on Batista. So," he paused and nodded to himself, "now I understand."

"Those are the facts, my friend, you are free to tell me to leave. I wouldn't blame you, in fact …"

"Don't insult us, Harry! What do we care if all this is unofficial? Were we ever ones who did things by the book? Angelita and I will discuss things now."

Harry remained alone in the room. He peered through the curtains and into the alley. He had a clear view from there in both directions. There was little to see save for a couple of old women trundling heavy baskets from the market. He heard Angelita and João talking. Angelita returned carrying a tray with a bottle and three wine glasses. She dragged the table across the room and then she and João came and sat with him.

It was Angelita who spoke first: "he has told me everything. We have decided – you will stay here with us. It may be, as you say, that Leonid left us alone for just such an occasion. In my heart, I have always known we were not safe here. João did not tell you this, but in the winter, we shall leave the city. We have saved up and have enough money to buy a small guesthouse near Estoril." She laughed, "our

English, you see, is almost as good as your Portuguese. So English tourists will love to stay with us."

"What Angelita is trying to say, Harry, is that we were going to leave here anyway. Maybe, your visit means we will have to go earlier, if things go wrong but," he shrugged his shoulders, "it's not important."

"There may be danger …" Harry began.

"When has there not been danger?" Angelita interrupted, "now let us drink to our success in getting your Laura back." She poured out three large glasses of red wine.

They drank in silence. Harry letting the cool wine quench his thirst, he hadn't realised how dry his throat was. João poured him another glass. It was only then that the exertions of the last two days began to hit him, and he yawned. Angelita smiled and beckoned to João. They left him sitting by the window. She opened a cupboard in the corner and dragged out the frame of a camp bed. Harry half rose to help but was firmly told to sit still. The bed was made up and pushed to the wall opposite the window.

"Harry, lie down and sleep for a while. We will call you when supper is ready."

Without waiting for a reply they left him, closing the door behind them. Harry went over to the once familiar bed and within minutes was asleep.

When he woke, he smelt cooking coming from the kitchen. He swung his legs over the side of the bed and rubbed his face, then went downstairs. João saw him coming and pulled another chair to the kitchen table. The smell of garlic, spices and baked sardines made Harry feel hungry.

Angelita mixed an enormous bowl of salad and placed it in front of him. Then she pulled out of her old oven a dish of sardines. They were silvery and shining, the salt on their scales sparkling like jewels. He couldn't wait to start eating. They ate and drank without saying much, eating was always a serious business to Angelita. Harry looked up and saw she was smiling at him.

"What is it?" He asked.

"I smile with pleasure. Not since the day you left have I watched anyone eat my food with such appetite. You still like it, eh?"

"Angelita, this is the first real food I've had for years. I'm afraid the nearest we ever get to real food is frozen lamb and chicken. It all tastes the same to me. But this," he held up a grinning sardine head, "this is real food."

"Harry, what are you trying to do! She'll be impossible to live with if you pay her compliments all the time!" João laughed.

Suddenly, João stopped talking and held his fingers to his lips to indicate silence. There was a sharp rap at the door. João rose silently and left the room, Harry half rose as if to follow, but Angelita put her hand on his arm and shook her head.

The minutes passed; they strained their ears to catch something of the muffled conversation coming faintly from the hallway. At last, the kitchen door opened and João came in followed by a tall well-built young man.

"Hello, Harry." The young man spoke in perfect English. Harry didn't recognise him and looked puzzled.

"It's Mario! Surely you haven't forgotten him!" João said.

"When I last saw Mario, he was a scrawny youngster who we used as a courier. He was pale and undernourished. But now!" He looked again at the strong young man with the deep voice who stood in front of him.

"Well, I'd have known you, Harry, you have not changed at all."

João shuffled his feet rather impatiently: "Sit down, Mario, and let me tell Harry something of what we have been talking about." They gathered around the small kitchen table. "Harry, I should tell you Mario is a policeman now. He works to the north of here, in Póvoa, in fact. He works with Chief Lopes."

"Mario, I can hardly believe it! Have you been working on the case of the missing Englishwoman?"

"Why yes, I have. But how do you …" Mario was surprised and looked at João who turned away to see how Harry would react.

"So, you haven't told Mario about Laura?" Harry asked.

"It was not my place to do so. You tell him, as much or as little as you told us."

Harry hesitated for a while. Mario's job as a policeman was a two-edged weapon. True, it would mean that if Mario was willing, they would have access to valuable information. But if Mario was more loyal to his Chief Lopes, there would be a predicament. João watched him closely, he guessed what was going through his mind. He decided he would abandon his role of observer and give advice.

"Harry, Mario is like a son to me. You are my dearest old friend; I think that I must speak for you both so that you understand each other and the situation. First, Harry, let me tell you that Mario was completely loyal to the old network. He is a good policeman, do not think otherwise. But his loyalty to what we all stood for goes above all the rest. You understand what I'm saying?" Harry nodded. "Now, Mario, you must know that the missing woman is Harry's daughter." He raised his hand to stop Mario interrupting. "Also, Harry suspects and I agree, from what he has told me, that it is Leonid who has taken her." Again, he had to silence Mario who was now wide-eyed and sitting on the edge of his chair. "Harry does not have the blessing of Sanctum for what he is doing here. The most they have agreed is a two-week period during which they will keep out of his way. But I have also to tell you, Harry and you,

Mario, that he will not be acting alone. Angelita and I have talked we agree that we are here to help him."

Harry had not yet asked João whether he would help. He hadn't felt it right to put them in such a position. Yet now to hear what he said was almost too much for Harry's emotions. He looked at Angelita and saw her nod in answer to his unspoken question.

"João, what can I …"

"Say nothing, Harry. You will upset us if you say a word that might make me think you doubted that we would give you our help. But Mario must decide for himself."

Mario drank the wine Angelita had given him and considered the situation. He concluded it was not incompatible with his work as a policeman to assist Harry.

"I will help, I will give you as much information …"

"Mario, you must understand that what we want is that you help us, but that you do not divulge our information to Lopes. You see if the local police interfere, there is a chance Laura will be killed. What I am asking, is not easy for you. I am asking for your help to us, but nothing in return to Lopes."

"I understand, Harry. I came to that conclusion, before I offered to help. And before you ask, I can square my conscience easily. Lopes sadly is rather a fool; his enquiries never get anywhere. From what I recall of the old days when we worked as a team, we got things done. Leonid is an enemy, not only to you Harry, but to all of us. I see it as in no way going against the best interests of anyone, if I help in dealing with him."

Angelita gave a sigh of relief and João slapped Mario on the back and grinned at Harry.

"So, what has Lopes discovered about Laura's case? Anything at all?" Harry was eager to know if there were any leads that could help them in what seemed an impossible task, from where he now stood.

"So far there are no leads. That is not unusual for Chief Lopes. He was angry when your son-in-law left the country. He wanted to stop him, but the diplomatic service overruled him. Now he seems to have lost interest in the case because no reporters have been to see him. One thing that Lopes loves is publicity! Also, there is no one, in his opinion, whom the kidnappers can now contact in Portugal. He has a horror of any British police coming over here though. So, I suppose that is one way I could encourage him to be a bit more vigorous in trying to get a lead."

"Not too vigorous," João cautioned, "we don't want the police snooping around too much."

"Actually, I already made some of my own investigations in this case. If you like, Harry, I will do more. I have resources that you and João can't get your hands on. What do you say?"

"Mario, any help is useful. Time is short - only two weeks before Sanctum begin and then, well, you can guess the rest."

Mario got up, his face was flushed with excitement. Harry noted this with some degree of trepidation, he didn't like working with people who were too enthusiastic. Judgement often flew out of the window when enthusiasm bounded in through the door. At least that was his opinion. But Harry had not forgotten what it was to be young and eager for success. He and João had grown old and careful, and it was their careers and cunning that had kept them going. Now, their reflexes were no longer as fresh and responsive. Harry knew he had to trust Mario, there was no other way.

"I'll come again tomorrow. I can't be sure what time." Mario said.

Harry was totally exhausted by the events of the day. First, there had been the flight, then the tumult of emotion at being back in Oporto. Now the arrival and departure of Mario had roused feelings of hope and fear. Angelita saw the tiredness on his face, so after the three had sat and talked for a short time, she encouraged him to go to bed.

He lay down for some time before falling into a fitful sleep. He was woken in the early hours of the morning, by the sound of a dog barking in the alley beneath his window. He turned over and went back to sleep.

CHAPTER 7
A FARMHOUSE NEAR VIANA DO CASTELO NORTHERN PORTUGAL

Laura lay huddled on the floor of a narrow stone shed. The place reeked of rotten damp straw. The scuffling noise of rats' feet, as they ran across it, made her feel sick with fear. She had always had a horror of mice, spiders, and rats since she was a little girl. Now to be closed in with them in a dark, damp, narrow room was like the fulfilment of her worst nightmares. She tried to cheer herself with the thought that at least her hands and feet were now free from the tight leather thongs that had been used to bind her in the horse box.

She shivered and rubbed her bare shoulders with her hands; as she did, a rat came so close to her leg that its thin tail ran along her flesh. She started to scream, then quickly stifled the sound by putting her knuckle to her mouth. She wanted to scream, not just to let out her fear but to release her feelings of anger and horror. The memory of what had happened last time she screamed stopped her. She could still feel the swelling on her face from where a hard fist had pummelled her. She remembered how she had looked up for help from the woman who stood nearby; but the woman had only laughed and shouted encouragement to the fat man who hit her.

Laura tried to think of other things to keep her fear at bay. She held her wrist to her ear to hear the ticking of the watch, but it was silent. Either it been broken when she fell onto the floor of the horse box, or she had overwound it in her nervousness since being in the shed. She knew it was day, she could tell because of the light which streamed, like a laser, through the small chinks in the wooden door. But what day it was, she had no idea. All the usual needs such as desire for food and sleep had gone. Now all she wanted was to be left alone, not to be hurt anymore and to be allowed to breathe in fresh air.

Some hours later, she heard the bolt being drawn back and was blinded by a sudden dazzle of daylight. The door opened and the man, whom she come to know as Luis, stood in the doorway watching as she blinked and rubbed her eyes against the sudden glare.

"So, you're not liking the sunshine. I thought you English liked warmth." He chuckled to himself, delighting in her discomfort. "I have brought you some food." He threw it unceremoniously onto the straw beside her. "Eat it, go on. It is bread and fish."

He watched her pick up a piece of fish from the straw and eat it. He laughed again. "Different from the 3-course meal you could have been eating in your luxury hotel, eh? But," he paused, "perhaps if you had known what had gone on in the kitchens, you would have felt safer eating off the floor here!"

Laura tried to close her ears to Luis's taunts. She pretended there was no filth on the floor, and she was really on a picnic at home. Luis could see he was getting nowhere. He leaned against the wall and took the cork out of a bottle of red wine with his penknife. Then he swigged the wine slowly. Wiping his mouth on his sleeve, he handed the bottle to her. She shook her head but still he held it out. When she persisted in refusal, he became annoyed. He stepped further into the shed and forced the bottle between her lips. The wine stung as it dribbled into the cuts on her face and along the cracks on her dry lips. But as it trickled down her throat, it felt good. Luis slid down the wall until he too was sitting on the floor. He took the bottle back and drank some more, then handed it to her again. This time she did not refuse. Luis grinned.

"You learn fast, lady. You learn fast that you too can drink with an old peasant. Not so bad, is it?"

Although she wanted to say something in reply, Laura remained silent. She was afraid to say the wrong thing. If she agreed, it might annoy him; if she disagreed, it might anger him. She had indeed learned fast. She had learned that anything, but just the right response, produced a violent reaction from Luis. He had punched or kicked her into silence or into saying the right thing, nearly every time he had seen her. Now, he wanted to talk, or so it seemed, but she felt wary.

Luis drank, offering her a swig each time. She began to pretend to drink the wine. He became progressively more talkative and not interested in hearing her response.

"Do you know what life is really like, Senhora Bayliss? I do, I have seen it in all its ugliness. I know how people like you live in England and in America. I lived in America for five years – in Chicago. You know something, I liked it there. I might even have stayed there too but I had to come home to look after my family. When I had made enough money, I returned to set up in business. But I didn't have enough money. I tried to buy a small farm, but I lost it to a big landowner, after two years." He clenched his fist around the neck of the bottle and Laura thought he would hit her with it and flinched. But he wasn't even looking at her, his eyes focused on images from his memory.

"Do you know why I couldn't succeed? It was because of the Estado Novo and their godlike Presidente do Conselho, Antonio de Oliveira Salazar. That was why I failed!

No one who was a peasant like me could ever succeed under such a regime. And" he poked her with his finger, "and, Senhora Bayliss, it was your country, our oldest ally, that ruined things for me. It was your country and the Americans who helped to keep Salazar in power." He stopped speaking, gently stroking the neck of the bottle in his hands.

Laura waited for him to begin again. She knew he would because he was nodding to unspoken words going through his mind. However, she was startled when, at last, his voice came again with some vehemence.

"Why? Why did you do it? Let me tell you why. Because any regime here was better for you than a Communist one. We are part of your little defence network, aren't we? But you didn't care how we, the peasants, suffered." This time he kicked Laura but not with any great force. "I asked, did you?" She shook her head and Luis chuckled to himself. "Good, lady, you are learning."

Laura sat completely still, though her muscles ached, and she could no longer stretch her legs. For one thing she did feel grateful, that was as long as Luis sat there babbling on, the door remained open and fresh air came in. The sun's rays brought warmth to her cold arms and legs. Luis talked on and on, his English becoming less coherent the more he drank.

As the shed grew warmer, she watched him slowly begin to doze. At first, he fought sleep. As his chin fell onto his chest, he would wake and glance suspiciously around but within seconds his eyelids closed again. This little ritual happened several times, each time the waking became less dramatic, and the bouts of sleep grew longer. He began snoring, finally slumping into a lying position.

Laura held her breath and watched him closely. From the corner of his mouth, she saw dribble run towards his chin. He was obviously now deeply asleep. She drew her legs up and painfully twisted them to one side, kneeling on her swollen legs. Slowly, she stood up. In apprehension, she put her hand to her mouth in case he should wake. She leaned forward and carefully peeped out into the yard.

The yard appeared deserted, apart from a scrawny cat and some chickens pecking vigorously at the dirt. There was no sign of people. Laura thought for a while, trying to guess how many people there might be in the farmhouse. Recently, she had only encountered Luis. Perhaps the others had left. She decided this might well be her only chance of escape.

She looked at Luis's sleeping form and then at the deserted yard. She crept out into the full glare of the sun's rays. She waited for the inevitable shouts and blows to her head. There was nothing, nothing at all. She closed the shed door behind her and carefully drew the bolt into place.

The sun was directly overhead now, so there was virtually no shade to give any degree of cover. Her black and red dress stood out starkly against the grey walls of the outhouses. About ten yards away, and just beyond the enclosed yard, was a small cluster of olive trees. She knew she must make for them if she was to get away. She paused and listened for any sounds indicating the presence of someone else nearby.

The only noise came from Luis' snores in the shed; the hens clucking contentedly to each other and the occasional birdsong. There were no voices, no sound of cars or machinery, no dogs barking. She decided the risk was worth it. She ran as fast as her aching body would allow. She crossed the yard, slinking through the open gate and into the limited protection of the trees. Her heart beat so fast and so loudly that she felt certain anyone standing within feet would hear it. Again, she waited for the shouts and outcry to begin, there was nothing and no one.

She leaned against one of the olive trees and weighed up the situation. She was free! She was freer than she had been for what seemed an eternity. Yet, she was still only yards away from her former prison and might even be feet away from another captor. She was in a strange country and had no idea of the location, in relation to the hotel.

'Think positive' she repeated to herself. Ever since she had been a small child, her father's mantra was 'think positive'. He told her to turn any seeming disaster into something of a victory. Here, at last, was real disaster, so she decided to try to turn it to her advantage.

First, she must decide in which direction to run. It was obviously too dangerous to contact any local people since they might well be working with Luis and that awful Dos Santos. That meant she would have to get well away. The surrounding land was flat and barren. To the East, lay a range of what seemed to be small hills with higher ones beyond them. To the West, the land sloped gently to where she knew the coast must lie. Her instincts told her to head towards the coast since the coast meant the hotel.

After a short rest, she scrambled across the stony field, keeping close to the ground and out of sight. At the edge of the field, she found a small dusty track. Instead of using the track, she stayed in the field. She felt less conspicuous there. About a hundred yards further along, there was a small white farmhouse. She made out the figure of a woman hanging washing on a line. Laura longed to go and ask for help. Then looking back the way she had come, realised the place where she had been held was clearly visible. She decided against going to the farmhouse, reasoning the proximity meant the people there might know Luis and Dos Santos and might even be in sympathy with them.

The heat of the sun poured onto her head and shoulders which only a short time ago had been cold and numb. Now the intense heat and glare made her feel sick and exhausted. She hadn't realised how weak she'd become after being held in such cramped conditions without proper food. In such a weakened state, she knew she couldn't make much progress while the sun was so high. She decided to shelter somewhere until the sun was lower, even possibly until it was dark. Perhaps then she would make faster progress.

At the far end of the field, there was a dense copse of bushes and small trees. Laura raised the lower branches of the shrubs and crawled into the heart of one of the larger bushes. It was uncomfortable, the branches were sharp, but she was virtually invisible to anyone in the field or on the track. Despite the lack of comfort, she fell asleep.

In the shed, Luis vaguely heard the sound of the bolt being drawn on the door, but his stupor was such that he took little notice. It was a sharp kick to the ribs that finally brought him out of his dreams. Pain shot through his body like a hot knife, and he curled up to protect himself from more hurt. A heavy boot thudded into his back and head relentlessly, accompanied by swearing and shouting. Luis reached for his knife, but another's hand grabbed it before he could reach it. He held his arm over his face and peered up. Above him was the sweating red face of Dos Santos, his eyes bulging with fury.

"Where is she?" Dos Santos screamed.

Despite his stupor, Luis rapidly assessed the situation and guessed exactly what must have happened. He hadn't bargained on the woman having the spirit to break free. He thought she was too weak and fragile. But he could tell Dos Santos none of this. He knew that Dos Santos had killed in rage more than once. Normally, Luis would not have feared him, but without his knife, he felt defenceless. His brain worked fast to think of some way to pacify him and make his own actions look different.

He began to groan loudly and clutch at his stomach. "You don't understand, Esteban, she kicked me in the stomach after I tripped over her feet and hit my head. I must have passed out with the pain. I know nothing of what happened afterwards."

"You liar! You bloody liar!" Dos Santos screamed again, his face contorted with rage. He held the knife to Luis's throat. "You've been drinking again, you bloody old bastard, and you let her get away." He seized Luis by the neck and ran the knife's edge along his chin. "I tell you that you will die if we don't find her. And it won't be me who has the pleasure of killing you, it will be Leonid. He is due back in about three hours." He kicked Luis once more. "We'd better find her, or else you won't be around to make any more excuses." Pulling Luis to his feet, he pushed him towards the house.

Luis sat heavily on one of the kitchen chairs and watched Dos Santos fumbling in the large cupboard near the door. He shouted for Helga to come, as he did so. Helga came quickly, glanced at Luis, then asked Dos Santos what had happened. Luis could see her anger mounting, as she was told how snores were heard coming from the shed. Luis had been discovered sprawled drunk on the floor. Worst of all, Laura was gone.

At last, Dos Santos found what he was looking for: two smallish blue boxes. He opened one and pulled out a revolver which he threw to Luis.

"Take the Beretta." Dos Santos yelled, "Now go and find her. You head along the road towards the coast. Helga and I will go inland. Don't shoot her, just use the gun to frighten her. We need her alive, otherwise she is no good to Leonid. You understand?" Luis nodded. "Get going!"

"I want my knife back." Luis pleaded. "I work better with a knife than a gun." Dos Santos shook his head.

"No! You use the gun! I am keeping your precious knife."

"So, the little bird has flown, has she?" Helga burst out laughing. "Who would have thought it? She was not the sort to have any spirit, or so we thought."

"It's no joke, Helga, Leonid will be furious. I have to pick him up from Póvoa, in a matter of hours. I don't know what I shall say to him if we haven't got her back."

"This little vendetta of Leonid's is dangerous." Helga said. "It was not for this, that I was sent here – to kidnap a silly woman - to entice back a worn out, useless, old British agent. I was sent here, as Leonid was first sent here, to build up the cells and send information back to Malyshkin. I hope the woman dies if Luis gets his hands on her. Probably she will, regardless of what you said. Then, Esteban, we can do the work we are meant to do."

Dos Santos opened the second box and pulled out a small Colt revolver. He checked for ammunition and then put on the safety catch and slipped it into his belt. He handed a second one to Helga.

"Keep it, Esteban, I have my own. Those things you use are old, almost useless. The sights are no good and the trigger catches. Mine is always in perfect order. See," she drew a neat looking gun from her shoulder holster. "Where do we start looking?"

"We'll go together along the inland route; I expect she'll head for the hills. I must leave in an hour or so to meet Leonid. Let's hope we get her before then. But she can't have gone far."

They left the farmhouse and turned up the track towards the hills. Already, the sun was low on the horizon, inland the warmth of the afternoon was beginning to cool.

Laura was startled awake by the sound of a child crying. She carefully crawled out from beneath the bushes and looked across to where a woman had a child with her in the small farmhouse yard. There was the sound of shouting, and the woman smacked the child. Laura turned away and looked around to see if there was anyone else nearby. She noticed that the shadows from the trees were now long and straggly as they spread out across the dusty field. There was no one else to be seen. She got her bearings and headed, much faster now, in the direction of the coast.

After about half an hour, she reached a tarmac road. A donkey cart was travelling along quite fast towards where she stood. It was driven by a dark-haired peasant woman. On the cart, there was a huge pile of seaweed, some of it still dripping seawater as it went along the road. Laura hailed the woman who reined in the donkey.

"Please, help me!" She tried desperately to think of some Portuguese phrase that would indicate her predicament. "I need help, the police." Then she remembered a phrase from the handbook she had at the hotel, "Chame a policia. Va depressa!" The woman's expression changed at once from sympathetic curiosity to one of fear. She shook the donkey's reins and urged the animal into a fast trot.

Laura ran along beside her for some distance, trying to make her stop. But her efforts were brushed aside and soon the cart had trundled away into the distance.

She wasn't sure how long she had been walking along the road, but already the first signs of fatigue were beginning to overcome her. The sun had set over the sea and the inland hills were dark. There were no nearby lights and soon everything was black. The heat of the day lingered in the air and there was no breeze from the sea. She smelt the sage and rosemary bushes growing at the side of the road. The cicadas started throbbing rhythmically, as they began their night chorus.

She felt helpless having no idea where she was or how far the nearest town might be. Two more carts trotted past her, the urgent sound of the donkeys' hooves only increased her agitation, since she had now lost confidence to hail their drivers. At a sharp bend in the road, a car with its headlights full on, swerved to miss her and skidded. The glare blinded her, and she swayed almost into its path. The driver hooted angrily, speeding off into the night.

Gradually the long dark road grew steeper until she found herself labouring up a hill. She could just hear the faint sound of waves in the distance and pausing to listen, she felt a gentle breeze beginning to stir from the sea. Sitting on a large boulder lying beside the road, she rubbed her calf muscles which ached from unaccustomed exercise, after the long time when she had been tied up. She took in a deep breath and relaxed.

It was then that she heard another sound over and above that of the sea. She tensed and strained her ears to catch it again. For a while there was nothing, then again, she heard it. It was the sound of shoes crunching against gravel at the side of the road. It wasn't a regular pattern of sound, but it came every now and then as if someone was growing tired and occasionally dragging their feet.

Laura paused apprehensively and listened. This time she heard a faint dry cough followed by the sound of someone spitting. Then the sound of a man's voice cursing loudly. As soon as she heard the voice, Laura knew it was Luis. She wanted to scream to shout for help. But there was only Luis to hear and no one to help her.

She darted swiftly away from the boulder, forgetting the exhaustion she felt only moments before. Soon, she was running up the hill heedless of the noise her footsteps made. In her haste, she didn't see the branches of a stunted bush stretching out in front of her and she fell headlong onto the gravel. As she fell, she let out a cry. She stood up at once and listened. In the short silence that followed, she heard Luis exclaim then laugh and then call out to her. She didn't answer. She heard him break into a lumbering, unsteady run. She heard him coughing and panting with the effort of climbing the hill. Summoning all the strength and courage she had, she ran.

When she reached the top, she could see faintly that there was a long slow downward incline before her. She ran, arms and legs flaying wildly, as she tried to keep her balance. Somehow, she must get away from the old man. Surely, he could never hope to keep pace with her.

When she could run no more, she paused to catch her breath to discover where Luis was. There was no sign or sound to show he was anywhere nearby. But now she knew she was being pursued; she knew she would have to act at the very next opportunity that might present itself. If a cart came, she would stop it. If it was a car, she would wave it down. This was no time for caution.

Walking as fast as she could, she kept to the centre of the road so that the sound of gravel wouldn't give away her position. Time passed and no carts came by, no houses appeared. She felt quite alone in the midst of some vast friendless desert with Luis stalking her.

It was then that she saw the distant headlights of a car coming towards her. It was about a mile away and travelling slowly. Every now and then the lights disappeared as the car went down a dip in the road or around a bend that she couldn't see. She decided she must stop this car and try to make the driver understand she needed help. She ran towards it and momentarily it disappeared from sight. Then she heard its engine as it approached around the corner.

Stepping out into the middle of the road, she waved her arms frantically. For a moment, she thought the car wouldn't stop. The headlights blinded her, and she shielded her eyes. She heard the engine slow down; the brakes being applied. Finally, the car stopped. A door opened and a man called to her. She lowered her arm and stepped out of the line of the headlights, so that she could see who was approaching. He was a heavily built man wearing a beige coloured suit. He beckoned her to come to him.

"Por favor, por favor!" She said in Portuguese, then in English, "Please! Please, help me!" She gasped out the words, hoping he would understand.

"Ah! You are English?" The man spoke slowly without much trace of an accent. Laura's relief was too much for her; she felt the tears coming. She thought she would begin sobbing if she was not careful. Before that, she knew she must ask for help.

"Please, I'm being chased by a man. I must go to the nearest police station. I need help. Please, don't let him catch me." She began to shiver.

The man in beige said nothing, instead he put an arm around her shoulders and led her to the car. The driver had not got out. She climbed gratefully into the back, where she sank into the comfort and security of the seat. When the door was shut, the man went round to the other side and got in beside her. The driver spoke rapidly in Portuguese, then he started the engine and pulled slowly away.

As they drove up the hill that only a short time before she had been running down, the headlights picked out the shambling figure of Luis. The old man shaded his eyes from the headlights and the driver hooted. The man sitting next to her spoke to the driver and they both laughed.

"That's the man! That's him. Please don't let him get me." Laura said.

"Calm yourself, Senhora, you are safe with us now." The voice seemed reassuring.

"You will take me straight away to the nearest police station, won't you?" Laura was relieved to see the man nod and smile.

The car ran smoothly, and the driver switched on the radio. Laura closed her eyes. It was only the sudden movement of the car taking a sharp right turn that made her open them again. She sat up and peered out expecting to see a police sign. Instead, the car was speeding along a narrow road.

There was a small village with some people sitting outside in the market square drinking wine. The driver hooted and dogs scattered out of the way. Then as they left the village behind, she saw the entrance to a driveway, she felt certain it wasn't leading to a police station, so she looked at the man for reassurance. He smiled and turned away.

She saw they were heading towards what seemed to be a farmhouse. Though she had never been outside of the shed, until she had run away from it earlier, Laura knew that this was the main farmhouse where Luis and the others lived. Her heart began to pound.

The man next to her betrayed nothing by his manner; the driver was silent, but she knew. She reached for the door handle and forced it open. Instantly, the man next to her grasped her roughly, pulling her back across the seat.

"Be calm, lady. There is nothing to fear." He spoke in the same quiet tones, but this time she was not reassured.

The car came to a halt in the cobbled courtyard. The driver switched off the engine and headlights. The man in beige and the driver got out and conferred for a while. Then the man, whom she had at first thought her saviour, walked to the farm leaving her in the car. The driver, whose face she had still not seen, leaned over into the back and looked at her. As he did, the light above the door shone onto his face. Laura screamed; it was Dos Santos.

"Welcome back, Senhora Bayliss, why did you leave so hurriedly today? Luis was upset." Then he hit her with the back of his hand. His signet ring caught her nose and blood poured down her face. Roughly, he dragged her out of the car, pushing her in front of him to the farmhouse. "Your hero, the man who rescued you, he will be wanting to talk with you very soon. Maybe not tonight."

CHAPTER 8
CAPTIVE AGAIN

Dos Santos hauled Laura into the kitchen. Then he sat down and poured himself a glass of wine, laughing to himself. Laura stood unsteadily in the centre of the room. The nightmare had become reality again. A tall blonde woman came in. At first, Laura didn't recognise her, then remembered it was the woman from the hotel who had become so friendly with Tom. When Helga saw Laura, she gave her a look of sneering pleasure.

"You have come back in style. How nice." She went and sat next to Dos Santos. "Where is that old fool, Luis?"

"We passed him on the road. If we hadn't reached her when we did, he would have caught her." Dos Santos turned to Laura. "You are lucky we got to you first. Leonid wants you alive, for the moment. Luis wouldn't have had your welfare so much in mind."

From somewhere, a man's voice called Dos Santos and he left the kitchen. When the two women were alone, Laura looked pleadingly for some sympathy. The woman's pale blue eyes were cold, seeming to enjoy seeing her predicament.

"Stop the blood dripping onto the floor, you slut!" Helga said. "This is a kitchen; don't you see that?" She threw her a floor cloth. "Wipe it up. Get on your hands and knees and wipe the blood off the floor." Laura did as she was told.

Suddenly, the back door was flung open, and Luis rushed into the kitchen. His grey hair was soaked with sweat. He was breathless. He looked from Helga to Laura. Then in an unexpectedly swift movement, he seized a large bread knife in one hand and threw himself at Laura. In his rage and frustration, he struck out at her. The knife glanced off her arm and she cried out.

Helga jumped to her feet. Straddling herself across Luis, she twisted his arm sharply behind his back. Luis felt the ligaments in his shoulder tearing, as his arm bent beneath Helga's weight. Laura rolled out of harm's way and lay curled up in the corner.

"Let me go, Helga. I want to kill the stupid bitch." Luis pleaded.

As soon as he heard the commotion, Leonid sent Dos Santos into the kitchen. The sight that met his eyes amused him and he laughed. Luis lay on the floor gasping for air, beneath the crushing weight of Helga's body.

"Let him go, Helga. The old fool can't do much damage. Besides it's my duty to punish him for all that happened today. I'll deal with him later."

Helga got up then reached down to drag Laura to her feet. Then she saw Laura had vomited and turned away in disgust.

"Catherina, come here!" Helga shouted to a small Portuguese woman cowering nervously in the scullery. She had seen everything that had gone on but hoped not to become involved. Helga shouted again.

"Clean up this mess! Take off this pig's stinking dress and give her something else to wear. Then clean everything up."

While Catherina did her work, Helga left. Dirt of any sort nauseated her. Good Marxist that she was, there was a limit to her tolerance of the more sordid aspects of life.

Catherina returned and helped Laura take off her dress. She gave her a coarse black linen one to wear. Blood still oozed from the wounds to her arm and nose and Catherina wasn't sure what to do. She looked at Dos Santos.

Dos Santos opened a small cupboard and threw Catharina an old piece of linen. She looked at it then ripped it in half. She bound Laura's arm tightly, securing the rough bandage with a safety pin. When she was satisfied, she smiled at Laura, her eyes full of sympathy and understanding.

"There, Senhora, I think it will be all right." She helped Laura to a chair then began washing the floor.

Dos Santos had pushed Luis into the yard. He meted out what he considered to be just punishment for all the trouble the old man had caused. Even in her own state of shock and self-pity, Laura heard the sounds of Luis's punishment and felt sympathy for him. However, it only served to increase her fears, for if this was how they treated one of their own kind, she wondered what mercy she could expect.

The man in the beige suit came to the doorway and beckoned her to follow him into the next room. She found herself in a large room with a low ceiling. The walls were whitewashed and the floor tiled. Helga sat in one corner next to a large open fireplace.

"Come in, Mrs Bayliss, the former Miss Randall. Tell me, how is your father these days?" He spoke in a quiet voice; his accent was different from that of either Helga or Luis and Dos Santos. It took some moments for her to realise the strangeness of the question.

Laura looked suspiciously first at Helga then at the man in beige. She couldn't understand who they were, why they were treating her in this way. Now they talked about her father. She wondered if, after all, this was really a prolonged nightmare. But in the wildest and strangest nightmares, nothing like this had ever happened to her before. There was no sensible explanation for anything that had taken place. And now for her father to be mentioned, made her doubt whether she was really in touch with reality.

Dos Santos joined them in the room. Laura glanced at the bent figure of Luis passing the door and heard him groaning as he climbed the stairs.

"Well, my friends, at last we are all together. You so very nearly disappointed us, Mrs Bayliss. What would this gathering have been without you? You, the guest of honour, should not have tried to miss the occasion." Dos Santos laughed.

The man, who seemed to be in charge, went over to a large wooden cabinet and opened its doors. Inside was an array of bottles and glasses. He reached for a large green bottle and placed it on the table in front of Helga. Then he put four glasses next to it.

"Helga, fill a glass for each of us. We are to drink a toast. We have much to celebrate tonight. First, we must drink to the success that our new friend, Helga Kaufmann, is having." He turned towards Helga. "Yes, my dear, Malyshkin is delighted with your work and your reports."

Then the smile faded. "My only complaint, Helga, is that you should have kept me informed of the details in your reports. Malyshkin and I go back a long way together. Don't ever try to be too clever with me, my dear."

The smile returned, but Laura noticed that Helga was irritated. Then he turned to Laura. "The second thing we have to celebrate is the restoration of Mrs Bayliss to us. We would not be happy tonight, if she were not with us, would we, Esteban?" Dos Santos laughed.

Helga handed round the glasses, then went back to her chair. Leonid raised his glass first to Helga than to Laura. Everyone drank except Laura.

"Come, drink to your health, Mrs Bayliss. Tom would want you to do that."

Helga smirked at the puzzlement on Laura's face: "Also, I want to make a toast." Helga said, "I want to drink to the success of our leader, to Comrade Leonid Paustovsky!"

Dos Santos and Helga raised their glasses and drank. Leonid watched Laura and saw she still had a full glass. He put down his glass.

"So, you won't drink to yourself, to Helga or to me. That is not sociable, is it?" He walked over and raised the glass to her lips. She drank and the liquid scalded her throat making her splutter and choke. He laughed: "It isn't wine. Is that what you were expecting? Surely you wouldn't expect a civilised man to keep wine in a cabinet?"

He returned to the table and filled everyone's glasses again. Then he held up his hand for attention. "I give you all one final toast. I drink to one absent, shall I call him 'friend'? I drink to the speedy return of Colonel Harry Randall. The brave Harry Randall from DP1 and Sanctum."

Laura watched everyone drink, so she sipped carefully at the white liquid that had almost paralysed her throat. She watched Leonid throw back his head and pour the contents down in one gulp. He turned to look at her, then hurled his glass against the heavy stone fireplace. Helga and Dos Santos did the same.

"I see your father has not taught you any old Russian customs, Mrs Bayliss. Perhaps, I shall have the pleasure of educating you." Quite abruptly, Leonid Paustovsky left the room.

Helga and Dos Santos looked at each other, they said nothing. Each knew what the other was thinking. Helga had hoped Leonid's mood might have changed from the destructive path he had set for them all, in his desire for personal revenge. Dos Santos felt the same. Tonight, convinced them that he felt exactly the same and was not going to be deviated from his course.

Helga shouted for Catherina to clear the broken glass from the floor. Then she ordered Laura to follow her upstairs.

"It has been decided you are to stay here in the house now. We can't have you running off again. There are rooms upstairs and I shall look after you from now on. Leonid thinks you are too precious to be allowed to escape again; nor does he want Luis to kill you," She paused, "not just yet."

At the top of the stairs, the main corridor turned to the left. A much smaller passageway went to the right. At the end of the passageway was a small door. Behind the door, a narrow flight of small steps led to a long low room beneath the eaves of the roof.

Laura looked around the room. There were bare boards on the floor. In one part, there were some old rolled-up carpets; a torn straw mattress was next to them. A bucket and a bowl lay close by the mattress. There was a small window with heavy shutters pulled across. Helga crossed over to the window and pulled back the shutters, then she pointed to the heavy metal grille fixed to the window frame.

"There is no way for you to get out of here, even if the shutters are open. You are not the first person who has been here who had ideas of leaving." She switched on the light and a bare bulb gave an arc of harsh light.

"So how does it suit you?" Helga asked. "Not as comfortable as the room you had with Tom. But it will do. I shall come to see you tomorrow." She turned on her heels and left.

The door closed and Laura heard the key turning in the lock. The sense of relief she felt at being alone was greater than her fears for the future. She looked around for somewhere to sit. At the far end of the room, where the eaves narrowed so that it would be difficult to stand, there was a table with two chairs. She pulled out one of the chairs and sat down.

She could not understand what was happening. How did this man, they called Leonid, know her father? Why did Helga talk so familiarly about Tom? And hadn't she been called Greta, in the hotel? Waves of self-pity flooded over her, and she felt the same degree of forlornness and foreboding as on her first awful day at boarding school in Devon. Then the narrow, spartan dormitory had been filled with iron bedsteads and there was a smell of mildew in the air. Only then, there had been the promise of friendship from the little freckled redhead girl who had the bed next to her. Here was only the threat of the unknown.

CHAPTER 9
NEWS COMES TO OPORTO

Harry and João sat at a window table in the small café–bar near the corner of Rua 31 De Janeiro and the Praça De Liberdade. An hour earlier, Mario had phoned telling them to meet him there. Already, he was half an hour late and Harry became increasingly agitated. Nearly all the other customers were men sitting and talking or reading a newspaper. The slick moving waiters, edged their way round the sprawling arms and legs, carrying trays of Licor Brasão, wine or coffee high above their heads. João nudged Harry and nodded towards the door. Mario was looking round for them. João raised his arm to attract his attention.

"Any news, Mario?" Harry's voice was anxious.

Mario nodded and sat down on the chair next to Harry. He placed a folded map on the table, then ordered more coffees, before he began talking.

"Lopes has found your daughter's bag and sunhat. Anyone with ability should have found them long ago. They were in one of the storerooms beneath the bullring. She must have dropped them when she was taken. That's all Lopes has done!" Harry's face registered disappointment.

Mario put his hand on Harry's arm: "However, I have been doing my own digging, and I came up with some interesting facts. Firstly, do you remember old Luis, who worked at the Vasco Da Gama in Viana?" Harry and João nodded. "Well, he was seen at the bullfight by one of my informants. I looked up his files and it seems he was working as a temporary chauffeur for one of the Eastern European trade delegations. A short while ago, he was a driver to a Helga Kaufmann. I also discovered, Harry, she was the woman whom your son-in-law was with on the night of your daughter's disappearance. Only she wasn't using her own name – she was one Greta Peltz as far as the hotel was concerned."

"How did you find all this out so quickly, Mario?" João asked.

"I've kept up with several members of our old network and recently they've been sending me reports about the revival of communist cells here in the North. This Kaufmann woman seems to be recruiting new members. Luis has been quite active in the last few weeks too, so one of my friends was keeping an eye on him."

"You remember Luis, don't you, Harry?" João asked. "He worked with Dos Santos in the old days as a sort of agent provocateur. He infiltrated the workers' groups and incited them to strike. Later, he gave information about them to the PIDE. The leaders would then be arrested, then Luis would bring Leonid in to give a rousing talk to the rest and recruit them. Quite clever. What are a few ruined lives compared to the cause!" As João talked, memories flooded back to Harry.

"This Dos Santos has also been seen in Póvoa recently." Mario said.

"It's just as I hoped! You've done well, Mario." Harry was surprised at the young man's ability to get so much done, in such a short space of time.

"That's not all." Mario added. "This morning, I questioned several people who were at the bullfight your daughter attended. One of them is a forcado. You know who they are? They are the crazy ones who jump onto the backs of the bulls, once the cavalieros have finished with them."

He paused and drank his coffee. Then he sat thinking how he should explain the rest of his story. "One of the men I talked to knows Dos Santos. He had arranged to get a lift back to his village, as usual, after that very bullfight. However, when he went to the horse box, Dos Santos shouted at him and told him to clear off. This man was very angry, he had no other way of getting home." Mario paused to let what he'd said sink in. He noticed Harry was clenching and unclenching his hands.

"Instead of going away," Mario continued, "he hid near the horse box, intending to climb onto the roof when the others got in. He says he waited a long time; he saw a horse being put in. Sometime later, he saw Dos Santos and another man carrying out what looked like an unconscious woman. He saw them put her into the horse box and then another horse was led in. This horse kicked out and Dos Santos started shouting. The horses were obviously frightened. Then, Dos Santos came down the ramp, argued with the other man who wanted to go into the cab with him. He closed the ramp, leaving the other man inside with the two horses and the woman."

Mario paused and took out his notebook to check his story. "The man said he waited till Dos Santos started the engine, then he sprinted forward, climbed up the side of the box and sat on the roof." Mario laughed, "it's good he was a forcado, few other men could have held on across the roads around here!"

"Well, where did they go?" João asked excitedly, "did he tell you?"

"He said they took this route." Mario spread the map on the table and pointed at a small road leading directly north from Póvoa. "They went along here. Now, this man's village is just there." He indicated a small settlement a little way inland, away from the road that he was tracing with his finger. "He says, he waited till he they reached this point. It is quite a steep hill and the horse box had to slow down. When this happened, then my man jumped off and went the rest of the way on foot."

"Anything else?" Harry asked, hardly daring to hope for more.

"Not much more; the man said that the horse box went towards the North. Later, I checked the frontier post at Valença Do Minho and two other places. I even checked to the East as well. No horse box went across the frontier at the time when we might have expected it to."

"It isn't likely it would have done." João said. "They could have transferred to an ordinary car or van. Or what is more likely, they have a hideout in one of the outlying farms and villages. It'll be like looking for a needle in a haystack, if she's somewhere in the hills around Montalgre."

Harry sat listening to them as if he was an outsider. He felt as though he were suspended somewhere above the table, where they were sitting, as if he were an observer watching but not taking part.

"Harry, are you listening?" João asked and tapped Harry's shoulder, as he spoke. "I asked what you thought about our chances of finding Laura?"

"There's one important thing to remember," Harry said, "Laura's kidnapping wasn't for money. If it was, then we'd never find her. But she's being used as a lure. There's no point in holding a lure unless you intend to use it. Leonid will contact me somehow and give instructions; then we'll know where we stand. I need to make my presence here more widely known." Harry saw a worried look on João's face. "There's no other way, we haven't time for games. I won't endanger you and Angelita, so I've already booked into a small guesthouse on the Mercadores." He silenced João's protests. "No, I won't bring danger to your house."

"Harry, if Leonid is as well organised as he always used to be, I expect he already knows you have been with João." Mario looked from one to the other.

"Maybe, but let me do something for my conscience, João. If Leonid is going to contact me, I want him to do it in a neutral place, not on your doorstep."

"I must go," Mario said. "Lopes is doing some prowling this afternoon. I am to help him. But since his enquiries have got him nowhere yet, you needn't fear interference, Harry." Mario got up. "I'll be in touch with João when I have more news. If you need me, leave a message with Lopes' secretary for me to phone you. Use the name – Sebastien – no other information. Okay?" The three got up and shook hands.

Watching Mario disappear into the busy street outside, Harry noticed a man sitting alone at a table near them. He'd observed him earlier and thought his behaviour odd, at the time. Now he was sure there was something suspicious about him. He leaned towards João.

"I think we have an angel with us." He whispered. "Don't look round yet. He's sitting two tables away, to our immediate left. He's about thirty, wearing a checked shirt and jeans. Now, I'm going to get up and walk out of here. Wait and see what he does. If he follows me, as I think he will, then you come out too. If I'm wrong, give me fifteen minutes and meet me in front of the Clerigos Tower." João nodded.

Harry got up and walked slowly to the door. João picked up a newspaper and watched from behind it. The man was obviously undecided and peered from Harry's retreating figure then back to him. After a minute, he made up his mind, paid the waiter and hurried between the tables after Harry. João followed at a discreet distance. He could see the man ambling along behind Harry. He remembered the old routine they'd used in the past and wondered if

Harry would use it now. Harry went down a side road and the man quickened his pace. As he rounded the corner, João found Harry holding the man, by his collar, against the wall.

"Right then, just who the hell are you and who sent you?" Harry jerked the man's head.

"I don't know what you mean, I…"

"I haven't got time to waste on you to go through the niceties." Harry increased his grip. "I know you're an angel."

"All right – I don't know how you found out." The man sounded crestfallen and Harry laughed. "You're right though, I am from Sanctum."

"Sir George sent you to watch over me, I suppose."

"Yes."

Harry released him but maintained his threatening manner. He turned to João: "He doesn't know how we found out! Did you hear that?" He looked at him, "a child could have spotted you. You stuck out like a sore thumb; just how long have you been trailing me?"

"I was on your flight from Heathrow."

"Damn you! And damn Sanctum - this is my business, you understand? My business, not anyone else's, just mine! Sir George gave me two weeks, which is nowhere near enough time. But keep out of my way till then. I want a clear run to the end of the week after next. And if your ability as a tracker indicates your ability as an angel, I can do without your help, thank you very much. What's your name?"

"Logan, Peter Logan. Sorry you feel this way about it, Randall."

"Just you remember to keep your distance, Peter Logan. I won't be answerable for consequences if you don't!"

Logan was disturbed by Harry's response. Several people had told him Harry was a difficult person and could act up rough. But he never dreamed that, as a Sanctum angel, he would be treated in this way by another agent.

"It's all right, I'll keep out of your way." He pulled a card from his pocket and handed it to Harry. "Here's my phone number and address. You never know, I might be of help some time."

Harry was tempted to tear up the card, then he saw the look on João's face. The same look he'd always given him in the old days whenever he was too abrupt with one of their own men. João obviously saw Logan as one of them, not as a meddling outsider.

"All right then, clear off, Logan." Harry said, nodding for him to go.

When he had gone, João laughed: "you know my English is not so good that I understood all that went on between you. But you were not the polite Englishman, Harry! You know he was only offering help not trying to kill us."

"His help is more like the kiss of death" João looked puzzled. "Don't you see? If Leonid's men have been watching me or trying to pass a message to us, they'll have kept away if they spotted Logan. They won't want to get mixed up with the new Sanctum network here. From what I read in the files, the new boys have been tied up in knots by Leonid. He won't jeopardise everything he's worked for recently; Moscow would be livid. So, if Logan gets in the way, Leonid may have no option but to kill Laura. Even if he doesn't, this Helga Kaufmann might well force the issue."

João suspected Harry was right, Moscow wouldn't allow the new cells to be ruined by a personal vendetta. Malyshkin was ruthless in his pursuit of objectives and would override Leonid.

"You know, Harry, I don't understand what goes on in the head of men like Leonid. I never liked the man, but I admired his intelligence. I don't understand how he could have got mixed up with a shit like Batista. I mean that's all Batista was, wasn't it? No political convictions at all. It was all talk as far as he was concerned. Also, he enjoyed seeing men beaten and broken. Remember how Carlos told us Batista laughed when he saw him being tortured? How he beat up that young lad, Jorge? He was nothing more than a sadist. How Leonid became attached to him, I don't understand."

"You wouldn't, João. Not the right mentality to appreciate the likes of Leonid Paustovsky."

"When you handed Batista over to the PIDE though," João said. "I did feel sorry for him. I couldn't and still can't see how torture and brutality can ever be right. No matter whose side the torturers are on."

"I know your views and those of Angelita's." Harry muttered, "But, we're in a messy game you and me, not so far removed from outright war." He paused, "and in war, re-member, anything goes."

They ambled slowly through the streets. The sun's heat was overpowering and the smell of diesel fumes, from the cars, hung heavily in the air. To any casual observer, they looked like two middle-aged friends taking an afternoon saunter before returning to work in some small shop or office. Harry looked exactly like any other Portuguese man in the street, very different from the way he had appeared on arrival at the airport.

"Tell me, Harry, why are the big powers still interested in Portugal? I could understand it when there was a war on. But now!" He shrugged his shoulders and pulled a face, "now I don't see the point."

"Come on, I don't need to explain it all to you, João. War or no war, Americans want stable right-wing governments in power wherever they can support them. And war or no war: the Russians can't wait to promote revolt wherever they can. So, my old friend, both you and I know that Portugal will remain a focus of interest until one of them finally achieves what they're after. It may not be a hot war – but here the Cold War is still being played out."

They walked along in the direction of the Sé, Harry constantly glancing round. He was as nervous as a young puppy on its first walk. Every noise, every face, posed a source of interest to him. He suspected that not only Logan might have been trailing him these last few days, since he arrived in Oporto. Unlike João, he had kept remarkably in trim and his heightened sensitivity and alertness gave his step the tautness of that of a man many years his junior.

João had never been one for physical fitness, he almost appeared sloven. Yet this appearance belied his capabilities. When danger struck, it was João who reacted fastest and best. On more than one occasion, it was his quick actions that had saved the day. This afternoon, as they walked through the busy streets, it was his eyes and not Harry's that saw exactly what Harry had been searching for.

"Don't make it obvious, Harry, but in a moment, turn your eyes up to the raised walkway on our right. There is a young man in a white linen shirt and black trousers walking a few paces behind us up there. I know him, he is one of Dos Santos' men."

Harry curbed his instinct to look immediately and walked on several paces. Then he stooped as if to tie up a shoelace. The raised walkway loomed about six to eight feet above the pavement. He saw the young man quite clearly. João stopped and looked in the opposite direction.

"It's okay, I've seen him. Let's move off again." Harry straightened up. "That finalises it for me, I move out of your place today."

"What for? If you go, you leave us more vulnerable than if you were with us. If they can't find you, they will come looking for you at our place. No, Harry, the choice was made when you first came to see us. That was your instinct and that was right. You stay with us. It will be safer for us all." There was a firmness in his voice and Harry recognised the sense in what he said. But it didn't lift his feelings of guilt and he wanted Angelita's views on the situation.

They turned into the maze of alleys at the base of the Sé. The walkway was now at one with the original pavement and the young man hung back seemingly uncertain of what to do.

"Let's walk directly back to my place, Harry. Let him follow. We don't want him to think he's been seen. If we go somewhere else, or try to give him the slip, he'll become suspicious. Agreed?" Harry nodded.

Five minutes later, they were in the apartment and João peered through the net curtains down onto the alleyway. The man was nowhere to be seen.

"You see, he didn't come here. He is completely confident that we are here and unaware of him. He will report back now to Dos Santos. If we are wise, we can use him, Harry."

Angelita came into the room carrying a tray of coffee and some egg cakes, a Portuguese speciality, made from little candied egg yolks. She knew Harry loved them. She turned to leave but Harry called her back.

"Don't go, Angelita, I must talk to you both together. I want to move out to a place on the Mercadores. I think it would be safer for you both. I don't want Leonid's men coming here to contact me …"

"If you are thinking it will be safer for us, then you would be wrong." Angelita said firmly. "Leonid and Dos Santos have always known where we live. At any time, they could have come here. In fact, Harry, if anything, your return has given us more safety than we have had for several years. They now know we have, how shall I put it, still got friends in high places. They are basically cowards. They strike only those who will not be missed, the unimportant ones! Now once again, we are important. So, if you are truly thinking of us, you will not leave."

João sat back and grinned, he tilted his chair onto its back legs and laughed: "well said, my little angel! Your father knew just what to name you when you were a baby. You've just said what I've already told Harry. But you put it so much better." He looked at Harry. "So, you see, for our sake you must stay with us. We both agree on that."

Harry pushed his chair from the table went over to the bed. He knelt and took out, from under it, the leather suitcase that had gone with the diplomatic bags. He put it on the bed and beckoned for them both to come over.

"Well, what you think of it?" He asked them.

"It's an empty suitcase," Angelita said impatiently, she didn't like playing games.

"Take a good look." He urged, pushing it to João who examined it then shrugged his shoulders.

Angelita sat on the bed and folded her hands in her lap. She resigned herself to waiting until the two of them finished this irritating guessing game.

"It's not empty at all, João." Harry said with evident glee. "Even its weight doesn't give it away either. Leather usually weighs heavy, doesn't it? But look …"

He ran his hands along the inside of the case, pressed the lock a couple of times and lifted out the lining. A second layer could be seen and João and Angelita leaned forward to peer into the case. There were several small packages. Harry took them all out and laid them on the bed. He unwrapped the first, inside was a neat looking gun.

"The lining was made of some material so that metal wouldn't set off alarms at the airport. Otherwise, I could never have brought these things in. The guns are not quite what I'd asked for but then I'm a bit out of date. I tried one of them out and its excellent. Here," he handed it to João. "Get the feel of it. It's a Smith and Wesson Bodyguard Airweight Model 38. So, I've been told! I'm no expert on firearms – just how to use them! It's got a two-inch barrel. Overall, it can't be more than about seven inches. It's got fixed sights and only weighs about 14 ounces. Monty, back at HQ, said it's the best he's got in this weight."

"I wouldn't have thought it was powerful enough if we got into …" João began.

"This one's for Angelita." Harry handed it over. "I know she's got her own, I remember giving her that years ago. This one has many refinements. It's powerful enough for anything at close range and easily concealed in a pocket or," he reached back into the case and pulled out another package and unwrapped it, "or in this little shoulder holster." He gave it to Angelita.

Angelita's eyes lit up when she saw the holster. She strapped it on, with João's help, and slipped the gun in place. She stood for a while testing out the comfort and position, then shook her head.

"In the old days, this would have been perfect for me. But not now. See…" She lifted her hand to draw the gun. "My joints are too stiff for me to raise my arm quickly. I will go back to the old ways of keeping the gun in my pocket. And this is so small, no one will notice it. So, thank you for this."

"Here's the ammunition that goes with it. I'll feel happier knowing you've got it with you. We'll need to make sure you have some practice at handling it." He then took another package and gave it to João. "This is for you."

João remove the paper then whistled as he handled the gun. It was a beautiful piece of craftsmanship. He fondled it as if it were a piece of delicate jewellery.

"What is it? Another Smith & Wesson?"

"Yes, it's their 357 Combat Magnum Model 19. I chose the 4-inch barrel, it's a good deal heavier than Angelita's but I remembered you like to use a square butt. The ammo is .357 and we've got six rounds. I've got both shoulder and waist holster. Take your pick."

"I like it!" João said, "I like it very much, I'll use the shoulder holster, I never liked belt holsters. I always left the belt too loose. Remember it nearly cost me my life once? I couldn't draw the gun because the belt just moved up with it. My God, it gave me a fright!" He strapped on the holster, loaded the gun, and slipped it in place.

Harry pulled back his jacket and showed them both his own gun: "it's the same as yours, João. I tried it out on the test range and scored three bulls out of a possible five. Not bad for an old man!"

Angelita turned to leave but Harry put out his hand: "not yet, Angelita, still time for more presents." He winked. "I saved the best till last." He took a small square box and gave it to her and another to João. Then he took one for himself and opened it. Inside was a neat stainless-steel watch, slightly bulkier than usual with a heavy, black leather strap. Angelita examined the watch then put it in her pocket.

"Wear it, Angelita, not in your pocket!" Harry said, "and you too, João."

"I don't like wearing watches, Harry. I never have and this looks heavy." Angelita said.

"Wear it. You'll soon get used to it. It's important that we synchronise watches when necessary."

Reluctantly Angelita strapped it on and then asked· "Can I go to the kitchen now, sir?" She smiled, then left the two men together looking at the new watches.

"Press this button here," Harry said leaning forward to show João what he meant. "Then hold the watch up and speak a message for Angelita, directly into its face." João looked puzzled. "Go on, see what happens."

Angelita was in the kitchen waiting for the kettle to boil. Suddenly, she heard a small, thin, disembodied voice coming from somewhere. She recognised it as João. It sounded as if he was speaking over a phone. She looked around in bewilderment. Then she heard Harry calling out from his room.

"Angelita, can you hear João? If you can, press the winder on your watch, then press the small button on the opposite side and say something into the watch face."

She looked suspiciously at the watch and held it to her ear. There was silence, not even a ticking sound. She pressed the winder, as Harry had said, then the button as she been told. Feeling rather foolish, she spoke into the watch face. Then she heard Harry laugh.

"I hear you! I hear you, O Pescador, just like always, you surprise me!" She looked at the watch with astonishment.

"And I hope I will surprise you again!" Harry's tinny voice came over the speaker.

Angelita laughed, her large brown eyes sparkled with amusement and pleasure: "I'm coming back with more hot coffee." She spoke clearly into the watch. Then, with more freedom of movement than she had been able to muster for some time, she finished in the kitchen.

Some minutes later, the three were seated around the table again. Harry explained in more detail about the equipment he had given them. The watch had great assets, but it also had defects. The buttons and winder were small and, in the dark or if the fingers were cold, it might be difficult to press the right sequence. He gave them a brief outline of some of the important coded signals that could be used.

"This little gadget, according to Monty, will prove worth its weight in gold. We must face the possibility we may get separated for periods of time. It may not always be practical to talk to each other. If that happens, there are several things we can do. First – to attract attention without speaking – press the winder twice. That causes the numbers on the watch face to start flashing."

Harry glanced at Monty's notes: "Now if any of us is in trouble, we're to tap the watch face, just once. This will cause a small bleeping sound."

Angelita put her hands to her head and looked at João. He too did not look very happy.

"I know what you are thinking. With all these transmitter/receivers between us and Mario how will we know which one of us is in trouble?" Angelita nodded. "Well, I haven't worked that one out yet. These toys are only intended to be used by people working in pairs. But I'll think of something!" He handed out a piece of paper, to each of them, with the instructions typed on it. "Try to memorise this, as quickly as possible. Perhaps, we can all do a trial run some time with Mario. Luckily, I persuaded Monty to give me an extra set of everything."

CHAPTER 10
THE SEARCH FOR LAURA

An hour later, Harry was driving through the crowded summer resort of Póvoa de Varzim. João had hired a battered old Volkswagen Beetle for him. It was in as bad a state as most of the other cars on the road so didn't attract attention. At the far end of the promenade, there was a Circus Big Top, its loudspeakers blasting out a cacophony of music and shouting.

His heart skipped a beat when he caught sight of the hotel where Laura and the family had been staying. Goosepimples prickled in a shiver up his arms. He had seen enough pictures of the place, in the glossy brochures that Tom had waved in his face at Christmas. It towered like some white council flat tower block. As he looked at it, he thought he would have never have stayed in a place like that. But then he had never enjoyed foreign holidays anyway.

He drove to the side of the road near the small line of sand dunes that fringed the beach. Just beyond the dunes and closer to the sea were row upon row of beach tents and sun traps, carefully positioned by the hotel staff. Prior to setting them out, they had rid the area of the seaweed collectors with the help of the local police.

Now, each one was occupied by a holidaymaker laid out ready to be cooked by the overhead sun. Harry got out of the car, strolling along he surveyed the scene. He wondered why people paid vast sums of money to sit in this hell for a fortnight, pretending it was fun.

Further along the beach, he saw the hotel lifeguard prowling up and down. His eyes, however, were not scanning the waves for a swimmer in trouble. Instead, he was smiling at the rows of the many middle-aged and younger women who gazed admiringly at his tanned torso. And, no doubt, they saw plenty to admire. In contrast to their pale or reddened skinned partners, he displayed the physique of a Mr Universe. Harry reckoned he knew where this man's fortune lay, and he smiled to himself.

In stark contrast to the modern-day Lotus eaters spread in front of him, Harry saw what was going on a hundred yards further along the coast. Groups of ragged peasant children and women were still trekking up and down the steep slopes, dragging in seaweed from the water's edge and collecting it in mounds. At the mounds, others were raking it into flat strips to dry in the sun. Some of the children were little more than toddlers. The women looked like wizened old creatures, yet most of them couldn't have been more than thirty. Whatever the age or stage of physical well-being, they seldom paused in their work. Harry turned back to the sunworshippers and for a fleeting moment, he understood what motivated men like Leonid and Batista.

He crossed the road and looked through the tall wooden fence that surrounded the hotel grounds. As he peered through, a man in a white uniform came over and shouted abusively to him in Portuguese telling him to clear off. Harry did as he'd been told. His appearance obviously put him beyond the world of the wealthy tourist, in these parts. Realising there was little he could find out by hanging round the hotel and beach, he got back into the car and drove North.

Every now and then he stopped the car to check his position on the map. He was following the route, indicated by Mario, taken by the horsebox the night Laura disappeared. He came to the hill and the road junction that the forcado had described. Twenty minutes later, he passed one of the large traditionally built 'Quinta', or country house, that dotted that part of Portugal. The orange pantile roof sloped gently, and the sun reflected brightly off its white walls. Vines curled lazily around a pergola at the side of the courtyard. Harry stopped the car in the shade of a tall hedge and took out a bottle of water. Then, he ate some bread and spiced sausage that Angelita had packed for him.

He liked the look of this Quinta set into the low tree covered slopes around it. The atmosphere helped him to think more rationally about his own plans. After ten minutes or so he decided what he would do next.

He knew that Dos Santos originated from an area inland near Viana do Castelo. As he scoured the map, a couple of names stuck out to him. He started the car and headed for the first of those names. The village was little more than a single straggling street. He parked and walked over to a rather dilapidated looking inn. Some men were sitting outside, listening to a record of fado music. They looked up as he passed but showed little interest. Two or three men, dressed in working clothes, were inside sitting at the bar.

Harry went in and ordered a toasted sandwich and a glass of muscatel wine. While the sandwich was being prepared, he looked at the men sitting near him, he nodded to them. Despite nodding to him, they were not inclined to draw him into their conversation. He started talking to the man behind the bar. In the last few days all the Portuguese, he thought he'd forgotten, had come flooding back. He spoke with no hint of an English accent, according to João, and so the barman accepted him for what he appeared to be, a city worker who had stopped by for a drink.

They talked about football, tourists, about cars, about anything that Harry felt would attract the interest of the other men and induce them to join in. After a while he had succeeded, they were all chatting about the fate of Benfica and how many of its players were in the Portuguese national football side. Harry was grateful he had followed the fortunes of the club from England.

During a lull in conversation, he asked one of the men what it would be like to buy property in or near the village. He told him he had just returned home after several years working in Brazil. He wanted to settle in this area and buy a smallholding. This stirred a great debate amongst the others at the bar. One man said he was a fool to have left Brazil. Another said the land around the village wasn't worth having. The barman told him no property had changed hands there for many years. That was what Harry wanted to know. No new strangers had arrived recently. He glanced at his watch, it was nearly six o'clock and he aimed to call in to at least one other village before returning to Oporto. He bought his companions a glass of wine each, then left.

The next village he drove through was not one he considered worth scrutinising. But the one after that looked more promising. On the outskirts, there were two rather rundown quintas and some smaller farmhouses. They were all at some distance from the village centre. He went to the only inn and repeated the same performance. This time, the barman wasn't so friendly, and the locals were a morose bunch whose interest couldn't be roused by either football or the weather. He asked one man if there were any vacant properties in the village. The reply was less than encouraging, he said they didn't want any more outsiders there. He said he was sick of foreigners with their flashy cars driving through the village as if they owned it.

Harry was more than intrigued. The others began discussing the strangers who seemed to have taken over the 'o grosso' place. Harry wondered whether this 'fat one' might be Dos Santos. He felt, in his bones, that it was. He sensed it, as clearly as if he'd seen Dos Santos himself with Leonid. He thought he'd hit the jackpot and was hardly able to contain his excitement. But he controlled himself and listened as the others talked noisily of the disadvantages of having strangers in the village.

"At least this one is Portuguese, same as us! It would be better to have him here than those others." He pointed to Harry. "Remember that blonde woman and how she looked at us as though we were dirt!"

"O Grosso is Portuguese! What good has that done us. I say we've had enough strangers here." They turned their back on Harry and continued discussing their own concerns.

"I can see you are not like 'o grosso'." An old man had come over to Harry and was nodding sagely. "The others don't judge people as well as me."

Harry bought him a glass of aquadente and watched with admiration as he drank it in one swift movement. He had once drunk some of this local firewater and it had nearly blown his head off.

"Where does this 'o grosso' have his place? Is it near the village?"

"Just North of here. I remember when it was a thriving farm; when the vines were tended, and the wine from there was good. Now, the vineyards are overgrown, and the grapes are not collected." The old man shook his head sadly.

Harry left the bar and returned to the car, deciding to drive past the farm belonging to the 'o grosso'. He scanned the buildings from the road and saw that most of them were in a good state. Their whitewashed walls were gleaming, none of them looked neglected.

Then he noticed a small track leading off the road to the left. A gate hung loose from broken hinges at the entrance. He slowed the car, to look more closely, then speeded up until he reached an incline some distance away. From there, he could make out another building, previously hidden by trees. He brought the car to a halt, took out a pair of binoculars from the dashboard shelf. Then, he slid across the passenger seat and wound down the window so he could scan the scene. First the farm building and then the courtyard.

At first, nothing of interest caught his attention. Then, amidst the even colouring of pale green and faded beige, a sudden flash of colour attracted his attention. He focused the binoculars carefully on the brightly coloured material waving in the breeze. There was a line of washing and among the white sheets and pillowcases, he saw the black and red colour again. He shivered. He remembered the new sundress that Laura had bought just before leaving for the holiday. He leaned back in the seat and closed his eyes. He had found where Laura was being held.

The exhilaration he felt at the discovery was overwhelming. He drove fast to release his pent-up energy, paying scant attention to the villages that flashed passed the windscreen. But as he left Villa do Conde, he stopped to calm himself.

Arriving in Oporto, he parked the car in one of the side streets close to the Douro. He crossed the road and looked out across the wide majestic river. There were two or three sailing barges making their way upstream. Their characteristic dhow-like sails billowing full of the wind that came from the sea. He took in a long deep breath and let the cool air fill his lungs, before returning to the stagnant air of the old quarter.

After a short time in the alleys, Harry sensed he was being followed. He wondered if Dos Santos had somehow trailed him all the way back. Then he realised it was unlikely. So, who could be following him? He was annoyed, he had so much to discuss with João. This interlude only prolonged the suspense for him. He walked quickly down two left turnings, then ran up a flight of steep stone steps leading towards the wide terrace behind the cathedral. His rubber-soled shoes were soundless as he ran swiftly across the stone paving to one of the large ornate doorways facing onto the terrace.

Moments later, he heard rapid footsteps. The shoes were hard-soled and the sound they made echoed clearly. From the shadow of the doorway, Harry saw the man. To his intense annoyance, he recognised Logan. He waited till Logan had passed, then stepped out behind him.

"You bloody interfering bastard, Logan!" Logan was visibly startled. "I thought I'd made it more than clear I don't want you around."

"I've kept a discreet distance, I'm sure …"

"Discreet distance, is that what you call it? So discreet that I spotted you the minute I came into the old quarter. My God, man, with your pressed suit and your polished leather-soled shoes, you'd stand out in a parade of raw recruits. I've not been active in field operations for some years, but I spotted you even though I've been out of the way of surveillance. Your idea of discretion wouldn't fool a dead rat."

"You underestimate yourself …" Logan started.

"I never underestimate myself! Surely, Sir George must have told you that. You shouldn't underestimate me either. Forget you were sent here as an angel and go and view the tourist sights instead. Leave me to take care of my own business; I don't have time to nursemaid you as well."

"Don't worry about me, I can take care of myself. This may be my first solo assignment, but it makes it even more important that I do well. I can't afford to muck it up."

"Then don't!" Harry felt vaguely sorry for Logan. If it had been any job other than this one, he might have helped him along. Everyone needs to start somewhere. "Look," he sighed, "if all goes well, I'll put in a good word for you with the old man. If things go wrong – you're best out of it, anyway. Doesn't that sound like logic to you?" Logan nodded rather dispiritedly.

Harry held out his hand and shook hands with him. Something told him even now he hadn't seen the last of him. He walked across the terrace towards João's place. Logan remained standing on the open terrace. After he saw Harry disappear, he went down the steps and returned to the room he had rented nearby.

If either of the two of them had waited a few minutes before going their respective ways, they might have glimpsed a third man lurking in the shadows. Once they left, the man came out from the protective cover of the building and ran lightly and soundlessly along the narrow streets that led back to the Douro. He had information he needed to pass on.

CHAPTER II
HELGA'S SPITE

Laura heard the phone ringing before anyone answered it. She put her ear to the door and strained to listen. At first, Leonid, Dos Santos and Helga were speaking quietly. But gradually the conversation took on the tones of an argument. It was Leonid's voice that began to dominate and the other two were silenced. She heard the front door being shut loudly, then the sound of a car engine starting up and a car leaving.

Returning to the bed, she sat down again. A few moments later, she heard Helga walking along the corridor and then up the stairs. The key turned in the lock and she came in. Locking the door behind her, Helga stared across towards Laura. Her face was flushed with temper; her breathing was heavy as a result of climbing the stairs too quickly. She smoothed down the tightfitting cotton dress, where sweat had made it cling to her body, then she went over to the bed.

"If I had my way, you'd be dead by now! Esteban agrees. You're a hindrance to our proper work here." She kicked out at Laura's leg in temper. "The sooner Leonid's vendetta is over the better. Then I can put you out of your agony too, like a sick dog."

"What have I ever done to you? I'd never even seen you, till last week. Why do you hate me so much?"

Helga sat down, reached into her pocket, and took out a slim silver cigarette case. She took out a cigarette and began smoking: "you ask interesting questions. You personally, have done nothing to me. I neither like nor hate you – I don't feel anything for you as such. But what you represent, I can hate quite easily. How does it feel to be a symbolic victim, Mrs Bayliss? For Leonid, you are a tool to entice your father. For me, you are nothing."

For a time, nothing more was said, and they sat side by side both blonde and blue-grey eyed. But there the resemblance ended. Helga was the epitome of the ideal Aryan woman. She was tall, broad shouldered, firm strong muscles; her flaxen hair held back by a tortoiseshell clasp at the nape of her neck. Her posture was that of a confident narcissist who would not have looked out of place in one of Wagner's operas. In contrast, Laura seemed almost fragile, what were seen as her assets: slimness, delicate frame, wavy honey blonde hair, were a pale reflection of the other woman. The coarse black linen dress, she had been given, only served to emphasise her pallor and delicacy.

"You asked what wrong you had done to me?" Helga suddenly said. "I said that there was 'nothing', didn't I? Now I've been thinking, I wonder if you can guess what wrong I have done you?"

"Apart from aiding my kidnapping, I can't guess." Laura said. There was a long silence.

"Yes, you can. Try, Mrs Bayless, try." Helga waited for some minutes. She studied Laura, whilst taking an extra-long puff at her cigarette, so that the tip glowed white and orange. Then methodically, she held the stub firmly against Laura's bare arm. "Come on now, guess!"

The pain made Laura gasp and she wriggled to release her arm free from Helga's grasp. "Leave me alone, please, leave me alone."

"I told you to start guessing, Mrs Bayliss, and I dislike being disobeyed, as you have just felt. So go on, try some guesses." She rubbed the newly reddened skinned in the area where the glowing stub had been held.

"What is it you want from me?" Laura pleaded, "I don't understand."

"Then you are stupid." Helga sighed and released her arm. "I suggested a little game, I thought you English liked games. If you try to guess, I will tell you if you're right or wrong. Of course, if you are too stupid to get the correct answer, I shall have to help you. I will do a little miming for you, shall I? You have a game, I think, in England called charades." This amused her, she threw back her head and laughed.

Dos Santos was at the top of the stairs when he heard the laughter coming from Laura's room. He walked over to the door and tried the handle: "Helga are you in there? What's going on?"

"Everything is under control, Esteban, you can go away." Helga said firmly.

They heard him shuffling near the door. Then they heard the creak of the stairs as he went back to his own room. Helga tossed her head and turned back to Laura.

"Come on now, Mrs Bayliss, you don't want Esteban in here as well, do you? Now, he really can be unpleasant if he wants to be. And there's no Leonid here to keep him in check. So, let's begin the guessing game again, shall we? I'll ask you once more: what wrong have I done to you?"

"Why are you doing this, are you trying to frighten me?" Laura was totally bewildered by the whole situation.

"If this is frightening you, you have no idea what real fear is."

"I am being kept here as a prisoner and you seem to enjoy it. I guess that!" Laura said in desperation to end Helga's toying with her.

"You are part of the job, that's all. I neither enjoy nor do I dislike it. Just as it will be part of my job to kill you – eventually. Try again, what is the wrong I have done you?"

"Please, can we stop this? I'm feeling very tired."

"Tired! What have you done to be tired? Don't spoil my little pleasure, Mrs Bayliss, I thought we were playing a game."

"I don't know what wrong you have done me! I don't care what wrong you have done me! I just want to be left alone." Laura sobbed.

"Oh my, so Greta Garbo! The little lady is giving up, is she? Maybe, I should give her a clue." She used her words as if she were talking to a young child. She was deriving pleasure from the whole situation, that much was obvious to Laura. "Come now, you really are a very unimaginative woman, aren't you? Such a simple little mind, but then that's just what darling Tom said."

Hearing Tom's name, on Helga's lips, startled her. "I know you met him at the hotel in passing. But you talk of him as if he were a friend of yours. What has he got to do with all of this?"

"Ah! You're getting warmer now." Helga sat up and smiled almost maliciously. "Though, Laura, that is something Tom says you are incapable of being."

It was then, quite suddenly, that Laura knew what Helga was trying to get her to say. She knew exactly what the imagined 'wrong' was supposed to be. Instead of being hurt or even annoyed, she felt relief at the bitchiness of Helga's spite. This was something she could understand. It was the sort of pathetic bitchiness that she had heard from another woman, who'd been involved with Tom, long before Portugal.

What she had dreaded was some new form of subtle torture that this seemingly ruthless woman might have fabricated. Instead, it was something Laura could understand

and feel quite superior to. She sat quietly pondering over the advantage that the sudden realisation had given her. The ace, for the first time in this session, was in her hands and she didn't intend to give it away.

Helga eyed her suspiciously, hoping that she was beginning to understand the hints. There had been no outward sign that Laura understood anything. Nor did Helga realise the advantage, she thought she held, had just slipped away.

For the first time feeling in control of the situation, Laura endeavoured to look puzzled and crestfallen. She knew that, at all costs, she mustn't give away her strategy. She needed to appear to play along with Helga's game.

"So," Laura said, trying to sound hurt and intimidated, "what did Tom tell you about me?"

"It was a little bit more than just what Tom told me." Helga leaned back against the wall and drew her knees up to her chin with evident enjoyment. "Though he did tell me about your prim, unyielding, little body with…" She paused and gave Laura an appraising look. "How shall I say? It's lack of qualities. Poor Tom I felt so sorry for him. After all, he is such a vigorous man."

"I … I don't understand." Laura lied convincingly. Now she had something to use herself, her brain had grown alert. She felt challenged by this battleground of Helga's choosing.

"Well, Mrs Bayliss, you have seen what a real woman's body is like. My body is physically superb, so I have been told. I excel in all sports. I trained with elite Soviet troops and came near the top at my graduation. My brain is at its peak. I passed all the tests for entrance into the highest echelons of the Soviet system."

Laura was amazed at the endless boasting and posturing. But managed to look suitably awestruck and cowed.

"Tom was set as my target at the hotel. He was so easy! In a way I felt sorry for a vigorous man like him being shackled to a thing such as you! But the starvation of his physical needs made him such simple prey." She paused and preened herself.

Helga got up from the bed and walked around the room. Laura made sure she appeared suitably distressed.

"You see your husband, Tom, he really enjoyed my body. He said he had never had anything so good in his life. Believe me, I really satisfied him. When all this is over, I think I should go and find Tom again and make love with him once more. Send him into ecstasy, the way he was transported on the beach outside your hotel!" Like some spiteful child, she glanced at Laura out of the corner of her eye. "Did you think Tom believed in your ridiculous marriage vows: 'Till death us do part'?" She returned to the bed and leaning over, jabbed at Laura's head.

The smell of Helga's sweat was nauseating, and Laura turned away. She feigned a look of anguish. It was important for Helga to feel she had gained some sort of triumph. In that way, her own little surprise would be made more effective.

"Was that the wrong; the wrong you thought would upset me?" She asked.

"That's the ultimate wrong for a woman like you, so prim, so proper, so very English. So repressed, as Tom told me. So unresponsive in the bedroom!" Helga said with relish.

"Well then I'm afraid, you are mistaken." Laura said quietly. "That was no wrong at all. You have done nothing to me. I'm afraid it was you who was wronged." She paused for effect, "so dreadfully wronged. I feel sorry for you!" She looked away, shaking her head as if in sympathy.

"You silly little bitch!" Helga stood up. "Are you stupid, don't you understand? Your husband and I made love. I enjoyed his body, and he worshipped mine!"

"Oh, I understood all right! Your speech made it quite clear. But there is something that you don't know. Something that poor Tom didn't tell you, for obvious reasons. It's true I don't sleep with Tom. I haven't slept with him for a few years now. I wouldn't. I value my own health too much."

"What do you mean?" Helga caught hold of Laura's arm digging her nails into it. Then looking at the red marks from the cigarette burns, she rubbed them hard with her nails. Only this time, Laura did not cry out. She stared defiantly into Helga's face.

"Guess, Helga? You like guessing games, don't you?"

It was now Helga's turn to looked bewildered. Her sense of confident satisfaction had vanished. Nervously, she fingered the loose strands of hair at the nape of her neck. Laura, in contrast, was quiet and seemingly calm.

"I'll leave you to play your own silly game." Helga said, as she walked over to the door.

"I think you really ought to understand what I'm talking about," Laura paused, watching as Helga turned to look at her. "Didn't you recognise that Tom was quite ill?"

"Tom was not ill when I saw him."

"Perhaps, the sores had healed." Laura said nonchalantly. "They do come and go."

Despite herself, Helga had to know what Laura was talking about. She went over and shook her hard: "what are you talking about? I saw no sores."

"Maybe you didn't see them, sometimes they're quite faint. But then you probably had other things on your mind." Laura was amazed at the powers of imagination that the hours of pent-up frustration had suddenly given her. She went on, "I think I should tell you, though of course, I don't owe you anything." She paused and looked at her hands for effect. "But as one woman to another, I feel rather sorry for you. It's such a horrible disease, with such dreadful long-term effects! Penicillin doesn't seem to be of any real help these days either, in many cases."

"Bitch!" Helga shouted, "bitch, what are you talking about?"

"Syphilis, the pox. I don't know what you call it in Germany. Tom is riddled with it." She looked suitably disgusted.

Helga stepped back as if someone had slapped her. She walked away and involuntarily shivered. Dirt and disease nauseated her. She hated being in Portugal because of the dirt and poverty she had seen in some of the villages.

Laura watched her closely, then spoke again, determined to gain as much advantage as possible out of this situation. "He's been in the highly infectious stage, for a little while now. That's why I don't even sleep in the same bed anymore. I couldn't bear the thought of those sores near my body." She paused, "I do really feel very sorry for you."

Without a word, Helga left the room locking the door behind her. She went quickly to her room and retched uncontrollably into the bowl beside her bed. Then she went to the bathroom and locked the door. She stripped off her clothes and ran a hot bath.

While she was soaking, she went over Laura's words: 'I couldn't bear the thought of those sores near my body'. She examined herself assiduously and then lay back in the hot water. As yet, there would be no signs or symptoms she thought. She needed to act quickly to prevent the disease taking a hold. She wouldn't trust one of these Portuguese quacks. No, she would contact Dr Schneider in Leipzig. He was a superb clinician and knew her well. She would phone him and explain what had happened to a close colleague. He would send her the necessary drugs. Gradually, she grew calmer.

Meanwhile Laura, despite the blows and burns, was relishing the small victory that she had achieved. How she had managed not to give the game away, she would never know. She thought with gratitude of Miss Fox, her old drama teacher at school and the endless lessons with her. Now, no matter what lay ahead of her, she felt she would be able to cope.

When the euphoria had faded, she began to think about what Helga had told her about Tom. It hadn't come as a bolt out of the blue. There had been many several women in his life, since their marriage. Somehow though this seemed worse than all the others. He had been manipulated and she was suffering the consequences. All because as Judy, her best friend had said, 'He just can't keep it in his trousers!'

She wondered whether, in fact, he really did have some form of STD. It wouldn't have surprised her at all. In fact, she thought, it would have been some sort of poetic justice.

CHAPTER 12
THE FARMHOUSE – THE FOLLOWING MORNING

Early next morning, Luis brought Laura some bread and goat's milk. He sat on one of the rickety chairs and watched her eat and drink. It was some time before he spoke.

"Hey! What did you say to that German cow? She refused to bring you food this morning. She said from now on I'm to look after you. She said you disgust her!" He gave a hoarse laugh running his hand across the thick stubble on his chin. "What did you do?"

Laura shrugged her shoulders but didn't reply. Luis observed closely, genuinely curious to know what this fragile-looking creature could have done to upset Helga. He disliked Helga intensely, feeling no sense of comradeship with her at all. As for Laura, he had never bothered to think much about her, except when she had escaped from him. Then, he would have gladly run his knife through her without compunction. Now as he looked at her, he noticed she was not the quiet, delicate little mouse he had supposed her to be. Despite the scars and bruises she had sustained, since being kidnapped, she had lost the look of terror.

Luis was perplexed: "you are a strange one, you are not what you seem. You are not what I thought you were."

The peace of the morning was broken by the sound of car wheels crunching across the loose gravel of the courtyard. Luis looked up and crossed the room to peer through the slats of the shutters. He muttered something under his breath and left hurriedly. Laura went on chewing at the crusty bread and drinking the rather pungent milk.

Leonid's arrival back at the farmhouse caused a stir amongst everyone. The argument of the previous evening had created a tension between the three main players. That tension was now increased by the evident moodiness that Leonid showed. Luis kept to his tiny room, fearing lest the rancour might suddenly be directed against him again. In the old days, not one of these three could have disturbed him, but now he was old and felt less secure.

At 11 o'clock, Leonid summoned Helga and Dos Santos to the lounge. He told them what he'd been doing in Oporto: "Dos Santos, I don't know how you select your men, but they are useless. The man you sent to cover Randall lost him when he drove out of the city. First you lose Randall's daughter, then this!"

"So, you got no new information?" Helga asked.

"Fortunately, there are still some comrades from the days before you assumed responsibility for field officers, whom I can still trust." He glared at Dos Santos. "One of those men was able to tell me quite a bit more. He's been keeping an eye on João Da Gama's place. He found out that Sanctum sent someone to watch over Randall. He's direct from London and has been nosing around trying to find out what's going on."

"I told you," Helga spoke, "I told you this crazy idea of yours would ruin our plans. The last thing we want is Sanctum men investigating here. It will ruin our work…"

"Our work! My work!" Leonid interrupted. "What happens here in Portugal has been my concern for the last 15 years. Do I need to remind you of that? You know nothing.

Even Dos Santos owes his existence to me. I recruited him. You both would do well to remember I have a greater interest in what happens here than either of you."

"What about the new cells, Leonid? Is this revenge on Randall worth their destruction?" Dos Santos rarely argued with Leonid, but Helga's presence gave him a certain confidence. He thought the old guard was changing and he wanted to be in with the new. "A new Sanctum man is not good for us. London had begun to lose interest in what was going on here. They only kept a token couple of men in Lisbon who have barely visited Oporto in the last six months. Now they are again on our doorstep. I say shoot Randall now and his daughter. That's all the revenge you need, isn't it?"

"Don't tell me my business!" Leonid replied angrily. "One Sanctum man presents no danger at all. He is London based and only here to monitor Randall. He neither knows, nor cares, about my work here."

Helga listened to them arguing and it occurred to her that their quarrel might be turned to her advantage. Now, she was a mere underling, second fiddle to Leonid. To her, Portugal itself, seemed a backwater.

However, what if Leonid were to fall and bring down the wrath of Moscow? Then, she might be in line to take over the operations. To be in charge was a different matter altogether. If she had control, she might even be able to put up with this country. It could be her passport to somewhere like Paris or Rome. She decided it was to her advantage to stir things up a little between Dos Santos and Leonid. But for now, she would hold her peace. Her confidence had waned somewhat since the encounter with Laura.

Leonid sat by the window strumming his fingers along the sill. He was worried about the loss of contact with Randall the previous evening. He wanted the Randall affair over and done with. Although it had seemed a good idea at first, it was starting to sour. He had almost lost the taste for it. He took a packet of cheroots from his pocket and lit one. He inhaled the smoke deeply and breathed out slowly.

"Helga, bring the woman down here now. I want to talk to her."

"Luis will get her, I'll tell him." She shouted instructions to Luis.

Sitting in his room, Luis heard his name called out with a sense of apprehension. He opened the door and called down to Helga. She ordered him to bring Laura down to Leonid. Relieved it was nothing else, he walked down the corridor and climbed the narrow steps to her room.

Laura was sitting curled up on the bed. She eyed him suspiciously as he came in. He nodded to her to follow him. For a moment, she hesitated then asked why she was wanted. Luis shrugged his shoulders and pulled a face.

They entered the lounge together, Luis a pace or two behind. He purposely looked at Helga's reaction to Laura, as she came into the room. He saw the big blonde visibly flush and turn away. He was even more curious to know what had passed between them to so disconcert her. He began to have increasing regard for this pale little Englishwoman. First, she had outwitted him – that he would have agreed was no great achievement – but she had done it. And now she had done something to this Helga woman – that must have required quite something.

They stood near the doorway waiting to be told what to do. Leonid turned and smiled at Laura indicating for her to sit next to him. She crossed the room, aware of the hostility of both Helga and Dos Santos. Luis remained in the doorway, no one took any notice of him and for that he was grateful.

"Well, Mrs Bayliss, Miss Laura Randall that used to be." Leonid spoke in precise English. "We have need of you," he offered her a cheroot, but she shook her head and watched him light another for himself. "Nothing too exacting for you. I just want you to read a little speech that I have written for you."

He leaned over to a small, highly polished, walnut table which served as a writing desk. From it he took a sheet of paper which he glanced at for a while. Then he handed it to her. "Read it to yourself, Mrs Bayliss, it is not difficult. Read it a couple of times, so you are familiar with it, then I will record you."

Laura took the paper and read it. She had already guessed what the contents might be. She shook her head and looked defiantly at Leonid: "I'm not going to read that. I refuse to be used as bait for my father."

"I see," Leonid intoned softly, clicking the joints on each of his fingers so that they cracked sharply. His small grey eyes assessed her, then reassessed her. "What a loyal daughter you are." He shook his head, "sometimes, my dear, loyalty is misplaced when there's nothing you can do to save your father anyway. You see, he has already, how do you say? Taken the bait! He is here in Portugal trying to find you. All I want you to do is give him some pleasure before he dies. That pleasure would be to see you once again. But, with or without his having that pleasure, you both will surely die."

When she heard that her father was actually in Portugal, her heart beat faster. Perhaps, after all, he could save her and save himself. But the cold unruffled manner shown by Leonid rather dispelled that hope.

"If he has to die, I won't be a party to it, I won't read that message."

"I think you will read it, my dear. I don't think your willpower will be able to withstand the subtle persuasion that Esteban offers. So why make things unpleasant for yourself? Let's be civilised and mature, shall we? After all, what are these things," he tapped the paper she was still holding, "words nothing more."

Leonid got up; his impatience was beginning to surface. Laura's manner irritated him and though his movements and words were slow and precise, his mood had turned sharply.

"I won't do it." Laura persisted.

"Yes, you will." Leonid turned and pointed a warning finger at her. His eyes had narrowed, his thick brow was heavily furrowed with anger. "You will read it." He turned to Dos Santos. "Esteban, convince her! When she is ready, call me." He left the room, pushing Luis out of his way.

Laura saw Dos Santos take a knife from his pocket, as he heaved his bulk out of the chair. He smiled at Helga then licked his thumb and ran it across the blade to test its sharpness. He nodded approvingly and crossed over to where Laura was sitting.

Luis had moved into the room now Leonid had left. When he saw his knife in Dos Santos' blubbery hands, his fury returned. It was his knife! He had won it, years ago in a game of dice, and had carved his name onto its bone handle. It was one of his few treasured possessions. He wanted it back. His eyes followed it, like a dog watching a long-desired bone.

"Well now, I am to teach you a few lessons!" Dos Santos spoke with such a heavy accent that Laura found it difficult to understand. But she did understand the menace in his tones.

He stood behind her chair, then with one hand he pulled back her head, by her hair, so that her neck was arched and vulnerable.

"One small stroke with this knife across your thin neck …" He made a gurgling sound.

It was Helga who broke the ensuing silence: "Do what they want! It costs you nothing!"

Dos Santos giggled, as he held the knife, waving it slowly in front of her face in ever diminishing circles. Luis was mesmerised. He had killed. He had few kind instincts but watching Dos Santos made him feel angry. It was his knife being used in cold blood. Killing in hot blood, he understood. But not this…

"Do what they want!" Luis shouted to Laura. "It's no good!"

"Shut your mouth. Move back!" Helga shouted, seeing Luis step forward.

"Enough, Esteban!" Leonid, hearing the shouting, had returned. He assessed the situation and turned to Laura, "Are you ready now?" She nodded. Leonid waved Dos Santos away. "Luis fetch the recorder."

Luis crossed the room and went to the walnut table, where the recorder was lying on its side. As he stooped to pick it up, he lost his balance and stumbled dropping it heavily on the polished wooden floor. The noise made everyone jump. Instantly, Dos Santos rounded on him pointing the knife accusingly.

"You damned old fool, are you so senile you can do nothing right anymore?" He pushed Luis roughly to one side and picked up the recorder to examine it. Luis slumped against the wall feeling humiliated. Laura observed everything but understood nothing of what had been said. But she, even in her predicament, she felt sorry for the old man.

Dos Santos handed the recorder to Leonid for him to test it. It still worked. Leonid looked at Luis, then ordered him from the room. When he had gone, he shook his head at both Helga and Dos Santos.

"Luis is becoming a menace. He's too old to be of any real use anymore. When this is over, you will get rid of him, Esteban. And I don't mean retire him either. He knows too much to be allowed to run around on his own."

"Esteban and I know exactly what is needed, Leonid. I'm sure we will think of a suitable way to end his contract." Helga laughed.

Although Luis had left the room, his senses warned him he should hear what was being said behind his back. When he heard Leonid and Helga's response, his first impulse had been to burst into the room in anger. Instead, he walked out into the yard.

He walked to the far side, where it was shaded, and sat on the ground, his back to the stone shed where Laura had been imprisoned. He felt fury at what he'd heard. Was this where are all those fine sentiments of comradeship and brotherhood were to end? He knew he was getting old. He knew he was not as reliable physically as he had been.

He coughed and spat into the dust, watching as some ants ran to the spittle and exam it delicately. He leaned back and closed his eyes in the warmth of the sun. He had devoted years trying to establish justice in his country. He had desperately wanted to see the end of Salazar and Caetano. Now, for the first time, there was the possibility of having a real state of liberty in Portugal, free from dictators.

But where was the liberty that Leonid had talked about so passionately? Was it only liberty for those who were useful? Luis' head hurt. He had never thought too closely about the doctrines that Leonid and Batista preached. It certainly wasn't what was being said now, behind his back. He no longer understood anything anymore.

Two small white pebbles lay in the dust at his side. Luis picked them up, rolling them in the palm of his hand. The movement comforted him. He recalled how his mother and grandmother had run rosary beads through their fingers and said their prayers. He wondered if, after all, he had been wrong to reject the old religion. Perhaps, this was God's punishment on him.

He decided he would have revenge in his own way. They would learn just what a useless old man could do. How he would do it, he wasn't sure. Then he remembered Laura. Leonid had set great personal store on how he would use her. He also remembered how this woman had intrigued him. She was not the spoilt English baby that he had first thought. She had spirit. Yes! She would be his weapon against the others. It would be sweet justice to use her to get his own back. The pleasure and anticipation of revenge soothed him, and he began to doze in the sun.

"Luis!" Helga shouted from the farmhouse door. He woke with a start and looked in her direction and saw she was angry. Her face was flushed, she had her hands on her hips. "What the hell are you playing at? Come here! Didn't you hear me calling?"

Luis stumbled over, deliberately taking his time. He would no longer go out of his way to please them. He followed her back to the lounge. Laura was standing in one corner, her face swollen from crying or being hit, Luis could not tell. Leonid and Dos Santos were rewinding the cassette. Obviously pleased with the recording, Leonid turned and smiled at Laura.

"Quite a little actress, Mrs Bayliss. I congratulate you. Who knows, we may need your talent again."

"Get her back to her room." Helga snapped at Luis.

"Why not take her yourself? It's woman's work to look after another woman." Luis could have kicked himself for goading her. But he knew instinctively that she wouldn't go near Laura now, for some reason, if she could help it.

"Do as you're told!" Leonid ordered.

Luis and Laura climbed the stairs to the small room in the attic. It was hot and stuffy now the sun was directly over the roof. Luis lingered for a while. He wanted to talk to someone about how he felt. But even in his present state of mind, he realised the foolishness of doing this. How could he be certain she would not betray him to Leonid? She might want to get her own back on him for kidnapping her. Instead, he tried to appear gentler in his manner. Somehow, he needed to win her trust if he was to fulfil his plan. He gave her a weak smile.

"Don't worry, everything is going to be okay!" He spoke in his strange American–Portuguese accent.

Laura sat down heavily on the bed when she was alone. She felt emotionally and physically exhausted. She thought about the recorded message, she had been forced to make, and imagined the impact it would have on her father.

But did she, in fact, know how he would react? She thought she had known him better than anyone else on this earth. Yet, she had not even known what his job was. She lay back on the bed and wondered if her mother knew about it. She imagined that she didn't know either for if she had even suspected it, her mother would have never been so calm about his regular trips abroad. Her mother was not a calm individual, at the best of times.

Thinking about her parents, and then about her own children, made Laura anxious and restless. She got up and went over to the shuttered window. By peering, with one eye closed, she could just make out the farmyard through a small crack in the wood. The big black Mercedes was parked below the window and Luis was standing near it.

She turned away wondering what had caused the change in Luis. His whole manner, towards her, had changed. Since the first time she met him, she got the impression he took pleasure in seeing her distress. His sudden softening seemed out of character.

A scuffling noise coming from the wall made her start. A small blue backed lizard darted along the bare wall halting statue-like level with her eyes. The sudden movement made her heart pound and, although she knew they were harmless creatures, she shivered. She watched as it remained still and seemingly lifeless on the wall. Then with one swift scuttling movement, it was gone. It had found the minutest of cracks in the plasterwork near the ceiling. She peered at the crack then returned to the bed. If only she could slip away into some unseen crack and emerge through the other side of the nightmare that now engulfed her.

CHAPTER 13
A PACKAGE ARRIVES

Angelita heard the knock, as she sat in the kitchen preparing lunch. She went to the door and cautiously slid back the grille, all the time keeping her hand on the slim revolver in her pocket. There was no one outside who she could see through the bars.

"O que deseja? What do you want?" She listened carefully but there was no reply.

As she turned, her foot kicked something and sent it skidding along the polished stone floor into a corner. She stooped and picked up a small package, carrying it into the kitchen. She took it over to near the window to get a clearer view. It was light and oblong, slightly larger than a packet of cigarettes but much firmer and harder around the edges. On one side, there was some thin scrawly writing which she found difficult to read.

Getting her reading glasses from one of the kitchen shelves, she peered closely and was able to make out the name 'Randall'. She put the package on the table and looked at the big wooden clock that hung above it. Crossing over to the dresser, she found the watch that Harry had given her. She disliked wearing it, because it was rather bulky, but kept it nearby in case it was needed. Now was such a time.

Earlier that morning, João and Harry had told her they were not sure when they would be back. Something told Angelita that she should not wait for their return but call them now. She put the watch on the table and sat looking at it, trying to remember the instructions. After a few moments she realised it was impossible, so she searched until she found the paper instructions.

After two unsuccessful attempts, she, at last, spoke rapidly into the watch face. She waited, listening intently for a reply. Nothing happened, no voice, no bleep, no light. She repeated her actions, this time shouting much louder. Again, there was no response.

At that moment, Harry and João were walking along the busy Praça Da Libertade, on their way to meet Mario. The noise of the traffic completely drowned the faint tones of the tiny receiver.

Angelita became agitated with the lack of response. She wondered whether she had followed the right procedure. Had she pressed the wrong button? She closed her eyes and concentrated on recalling all she had been told. This time she decided she would use the bleep call method instead of speaking.

It was João who heard the faint bleep coming from his watch, as they were just about to cross a busy street. He put his hand on Harry's arm and pointed to his watch. They went to the side of the road and stood next to a wall.

"Angelita is trying to contact us." Harry held his watch to his ear and heard the continuous tones as well. They moved further down the road and took a left turn, until they found themselves in a quiet side street where there was a phone box. João called Angelita at once, she was relieved to hear his voice and told him she had found a small package and that it was for Harry. She said she thought it might be important.

Harry took the receiver and asked who delivered it. She told him she had seen no one but that it was about the size of a small packet of cigarettes; it was hard, and she didn't think it was cigarettes. The fact it hadn't exploded when it hit the floor meant it wasn't a bomb. She laughed nervously as the thought suddenly struck her it might have been some kind of incendiary device.

"Leave it well alone, Angelita! I don't want you to touch it anymore." Harry told her, "We can't be certain what it is. I'm coming back now."

"I understand." Angelita said and nodded to herself with satisfaction. Obviously, she had done the right thing.

"Do you think she's in any danger?" João asked anxiously.

"No, not so long as she does what she's been told. You and I know Angelita is no fool. You go on to meet Mario, I'll go straight back to your place." He saw the worried look on João's face. "Don't worry, I'll take care of everything. You come back as soon as you can."

Logan had watched them talking, then he saw them split up. He was now in a quandary; which way should he go? Should he follow João or Harry? Then he remembered that his real function was that of an angel, so he turned back and followed Harry. His hesitation was of sufficient duration for someone else to get between him and Harry. That this had happened only became apparent to Logan, after several minutes. He congratulated himself on his judgement and perceptive ability. He saw Harry being followed by a tall, slim young man who shadowed his every change in pace and direction. Logan followed them both until they reached João's home.

Logan saw the other man pause at the head of the alley, then quickly go in the direction of the Rua Dos Mercadores. Following him at some distance, Logan mused that if he discovered something important, Harry would be well pleased. Surely, he thought, it was time to do something more than just watch.

Angelita let Harry in and led him to the kitchen. He saw the package and even before picking it up, guessed what it was. When he felt it, he knew for certain. He didn't need to remove the paper, he turned and headed for the stairs and looked back at Angelita.

"Don't worry, I know what it is. Come upstairs, we'll find out what friend Leonid has to say."

The anxiety of the morning had brought on pain from her arthritis and Angelita ached as she climbed each step. By the time she reached Harry's room, he had already plugged a small cassette recorder into a wall point and was inserting the cassette. She sat on a chair in the corner and waited. For a second or two there was a faint hissing sound, followed by the crackling noise made by a microphone being roughly handled. It was only then that Laura's voice came faltering across the room. Angelita saw Harry tense as he heard the voice:

"Daddy, I've been told to record this for you … I am all right. I'm not hurt at all … I'm…" Another voice interrupted her, and the recording stopped for a second before beginning again. *"I'm with some people who say they want to meet you. They say that if you want to see me alive again, you must meet them. If you do as they say, nothing will happen to me. They say they will release me unharmed. They want you to meet them on Monday at the northern end of the King Luis bridge. They want you there at 3 o'clock in the afternoon."* There was another pause, then crackling, then the muffled sound of voices. Harry and Angelita looked at each other.

Harry was about to rewind the tape when another voice suddenly began. This time it was a man's tones. It was deep and the accent was unmistakable to Harry's ear.

"Hello, Harry! Such a nice daughter you have. She is all right. She's not been harmed in any way. But you must do what she has told you. Not much for a girl to ask her father to do, is it? Just walk across a bridge, not so difficult, is it?" There was a pause. *"You can leave a message for me at the Automovel Clube on Rua de Gonçalo Cristóvão. Address it to 'Pedro Batista'. It will find me. Does that name bring back old memories? It seems a lifetime ago, doesn't it? I think about the old days, all the time. You will reply, of course, Harry and soon. You won't need time to work out your priorities."*

Harry heard the microphone click. Then there was silence apart from the faint hissing noise of the empty tape. He clenched his fists and swore under his breath then he looked at Angelita.

"I doubt if you understood much of that. I always find it difficult to follow a foreign language on the radio or tape when I'm not completely fluent in it. That was my daughter's voice you heard first. Then it was Leonid. But I expect you guessed that. He wants me to meet him on the King Luis bridge on Monday afternoon. Then he will release Laura."

"And you believe him?"

"No, I don't believe him. I think he wants me to see Laura suffer in the way he feels Batista suffered. It wouldn't be satisfaction enough for him just to kill me. He always wanted tit-for-tat in everything and what better way than torturing Laura."

"It was a bad day you and João handed Batista over to the PIDE." Angelita said.

"Maybe, but it had to be done. He had crucial information. I didn't condone their methods but unfortunately they were allies in a dirty war."

"But some of the methods…"

"Not now, Angelita, the PIDE didn't have the monopoly on torture and cruelty. Batista was no saint. And as for Dos Santos, well you know his methods. If I had my time again, there are many things I would not have done, but that's in the past." He paced around for a while. "It's Thursday, isn't it?" Angelita nodded. "There's little time." After a few moments thought, he took out a notepad from his jacket and began writing.

Angelita left him alone and went back to the kitchen. She made a pot of coffee and then returned with it. He was still writing, so she sat in silence. After some minutes he looked up.

"I've got to make Leonid think I agree to their terms. Likely as not they intend to kill Laura anyway. But if Leonid thinks he can get me as well there is just a chance they will leave her alone, until I'm in the web too."

Angelita made no comment, she knew better than to offer advice of her own. So, she poured out a cup of strong coffee for him, then rose to leave.

"No, don't go, I need your help. I have to play for time?" She nodded. "I can't just say I'll meet them at the bridge. I need to keep the dialogue going. Agreed?" She nodded again. "Then how does this sound?" He started reading from his notepad.

'How can I be sure that Laura is still alive? She could have recorded the tape some days ago. I want proof she is still alive, before I agree to anything. The only way for me to have such proof is for her to answer some questions. Only Laura will know the answers.

One: who is Rosie?

Two: how many children has Mrs Magoo?

Three: where does Peterkin go in a storm?

When I get the answers, I'll tell you whether I agree to your terms.'"

He looked over at Angelita. "What do you think?"

Angelita said nothing for a while. Then a broad grin spread across her face: "you are still - O Pescador, the Fisherman. You prepare your bait well and you watch the waters with care. The idea is good, send the message. What have you got to lose, Harry?"

Harry gave a long sigh, leaned back to stretch, then patted her on the shoulder. He carefully tore the paper out of the pad, folded it, then slipped it into an envelope.

"Right then, I'm off to the Automovel Clube. I'll be back by about one o'clock. João will have returned long before then. Tell him what happened, will you?"

The streets were crowded and the hot air almost stagnant. Harry found it oppressive walking along the busy streets heading towards the Clube. Once there he paused for a moment in the foyer, then crossed quickly to the reception desk. He handed over the letter to a uniformed man who was scrutinising everyone as they came in.

Moments later, he left the building and looked up and down the street, wondering which one of Leonid's men was watching him. It was then that it struck him as odd he hadn't seen Logan all that day. He dismissed it from his mind.

Harry felt he should phone home to Beth. He wanted to know how she was coping and how the children were. He guessed she would start to cross question him about Laura; he wasn't sure how he was going to respond. He'd think of something as they talked. Glancing at his watch, he headed for the main Post Office.

Inside, it was cool and a welcome relief to be out of the heat. He waited until he saw an empty phone booth. To get through to London was like asking to be connected to the other side of the moon. Harry's temper began to fray long before he heard Beth's voice.

She sounded cautious when she answered. There were none of the old enthusiastic tones that he associated with her answering the phone.

"Beth, it's me, Harry."

"Harry! Where are you? What's been going on? Is Laura with you?"

"Hey! Steady now, I can't answer everything at once. I'm fine and so is Laura."

"Let me speak to her please, Harry."

"Not just now, Beth, I thought you'd like to know things are coming along fine, that's all. How are the children?"

"Harry, where is she? Are you sure she's all right I…"?

"Trust me, Beth. Don't ask too many questions. I asked how the children were?"

"They've been very good but they're fretting now. They both keep asking where their mummy is. I don't know what to say to them." She gave a stifled sob. "I'm so sorry,

I know it's difficult for you too. Tom is here next to the phone; would you like to speak to him?"

"Not yet, Beth. Look you go ahead and cry if you want to. I phoned to talk to you and to find out if you were coping. I can't get on with things if I think you're fretting."

"I'm trying, I really am. Just come home soon and bring Laura back to us."

"I'll have a quick word with Tom now."

"Harry!" There was a tremendous cracking sound as Tom dropped the receiver, then fumbled with it. "Where the hell have you been? I've not known what to think or do. The least you could have done was to…"

"Don't you tell me what I should or should not do, Tom! The least you should have done, was to look after Laura in the first place. Understand?"

"Where is she? Is she with you?"

"All you need to know, is that I've got things under control. I can't talk any more now, Tom."

"So, what do I tell the children? Just that their grandfather has got things under control. Bloody lot of comfort that will be."

"Use your sense, Tom, if you've got any. Tell them that mummy and grandad send their love. What else can you tell them? I've got nothing more to add. I'll be in touch as soon as I have more news. Till then, you'll just have to sit tight."

Harry replaced the receiver when Tom began saying something else. He didn't want to hear more of his whining. And he could not face saying any more to Beth. As he left the booth, he looked around once more for Logan. Either the man had developed a new technique of shadowing, or he had given up being an angel.

CHAPTER 14
THE ANGEL AT JOÃO'S APARTMENT

When Harry arrived back at the apartment, João was waiting: "I've listened to the tape and Angelita told me what you've done. We don't have much time, do we?"

"You don't need to remind me." Harry said. "But we have the advantage that we are pretty sure we know where she's being held. We need to go back there tonight to get some idea of the layout of the farmhouse. We might find out how many of them are there and whether it's feasible to get Laura out before Monday."

Angelita called them for lunch. The three sat huddled around the small wooden table, for a long time no one said anything. Harry and João were each engrossed in their own thoughts.

"I think Mario should come to the farmhouse with us, when we go." João said"

"Won't he be on duty?" Harry asked.

"No, he's been dropped from the case. That's why he wanted to see us. Lopes ordered it yesterday, but Mario only found out this morning."

"Why? Why should Lopes do that?" Harry was disturbed by the news.

"Mario thinks Lopes didn't like the amount of time he was putting into the investigation. Apparently, he dislikes competition and thinks that if he solves the case of a missing British tourist, he will be promoted to one of the Lisbon offices. He doesn't want another officer to get any credit!"

Just as they had finished the meal, there was a faint knock at the front door. Angelita went to find out who was there. They heard her call for them to come at once, her voice sounded anxious. She was peering through the metal grille, as she beckoned to them.

"There is someone out there, I can hear them breathing heavily as if they were in pain. No one answered when I called out. I can't see anyone through the grille, but they are still there."

"Who's there? What do you want?" João called. There was no response.

After a while, with his gun at the ready and with Harry covering him, João opened the door. As he did so, a man's body fell inwards pushing the door wide open. Harry stepped forward and helped to bring the man inside. Angelita closed the door behind them.

"It's Logan! Harry, he's badly hurt." João said, as he laid him down on the floor.

Angelita hovered around, then recovering herself ran to get a cushion for Logan's head. She fetched a bowl of water and an old sheet. Logan's face was pale and his eyes were closed, his breath came in short gasps. Gently, Angelita rolled him onto his side and, as she did, they saw blood oozing fast through the back of his jacket. She slit open the jacket and examined the wound. It was a narrow slit and close to his heart. When she looked up again, at Harry and João, she shook her head.

"He's been knifed, it doesn't look too good for him." She spoke quietly.

Harry bent down and knelt beside Logan: "Who did this?"

Logan's eyes opened and he reached out for Harry's hand: "I'm so sorry I didn't mean to mess things up. I followed you this morning, I don't think you noticed me. I was trying really hard." He gave a muffled laugh, "when you both split, I decided to follow you. I thought I'd be clever. So, I waited until you were almost out of sight. But there was someone else following you. Only he hadn't waited as long as I did, he set off after you straightaway." Harry looked at João and Angelita to see what they were thinking. Angelita's face was full of concern for Logan.

"He shouldn't talk, Harry. He's very bad."

"He must talk, Angelita, we must know what's happening and who did this to him." João spoke roughly and moved her out of the way.

"I trailed both of you until we were at the end of the alley leading here." Logan said weakly, "the other chap set off fast towards the river. Difficult to keep up with him." He stopped and Angelita brought water for him and looked accusingly at both João and Harry.

"He went to a café bar and made a phone call. Later, a large Mercedes arrived and a fat man got out, he joined the man in the café. I wanted to hear them, so I went into the café." He shook his head "my Portuguese isn't good enough – I didn't understand much. But I heard your name, Harry."

Harry and João were alarmed. If Logan had disturbed Dos Santos' plans, then the exchange fixed for Monday could be jeopardised.

"Enough," Angelita said. But Logan shook his head.

"I must tell what happened. Then – I can rest." He closed his eyes and took in a deep breath which he let out slowly. "You were right, Harry, not much good at being incognito. The fat one kept looking at me … he spoke to the man I'd followed. I panicked – got up to leave – just outside I was grabbed and bundled into a back room at the café. They … tried to make me talk."

"What did you tell them?" João asked?"

"Nothing. The fat one didn't want to be involved - he left very angry. While they were both out of the room, I got out of a window and ran. The young one caught me and stabbed me. He thought I was dead. I lay in the yard then somehow, I got here to warn you. So sorry, Harry."

"Call an ambulance," Harry said, "he can rest on my bed till they come." Harry looked at Logan and shook his head. "You shouldn't have been in this business, Logan, you've not got the survival instinct."

João put his arm under Logan trying to sit him up, to help his breathing. As he did, Logan gave a sharp intake of breath and his head fell forwards. Harry put his ear to his chest and then felt for his pulse.

"He's dead! My God, he's dead!" Harry was shocked. He sat on the floor next to him for some minutes. Then he looked at João and Angelita. "We can't leave his body here. Sanctum will need to know. They'll want to inform the family." He leaned back and thought about the situation. "We'll have to drop the body off near a hospital, where it'll be found. They'll attempt to identify him and do the necessary. They'll contact the British Consul."

"I hope you're both satisfied." Angelita said, "we should have called an ambulance …"

"He was a dead man before we found him! No ambulance could have saved him. Anyway, he had a job to do and tried to do it. Don't take that last dignity away from him." João was cross with her. "We'll get the old carpet from the cellar; we can use it to wrap his body. I'll call Mario, he was going to meet us tonight, anyway. We can put Logan in his car."

Harry helped drag the carpet up the cellar steps and they rolled Logan's body firmly inside. Harry and João would wait till nightfall before putting it into the boot of the car. Angelita washed the already congealing blood from the marble floor and soon there was no evidence that Logan had ever been there.

The three sat in silence in the kitchen, each one deep in their own thoughts. It was Harry who broke the silence.

"I should never have come here. Logan told me that he was sorry, but I am the one who should be sorry. I should have let Sanctum deal with it, after all."

"What are you saying! Don't give us such bullshit! You came here because you're the only one who can do this job." João took Harry's arm and shook it forcefully. "Didn't the mess this Logan got into prove that. These new boys can't cope, they haven't had to run the risks that we've had to take all our lives."

"I didn't mean all that I said, Harry," Angelita spoke sadly. "It was just seeing that young man lying there. It brought back so many painful memories. And what João said is right, you had to come back. We don't choose our fate, do we? You've only done what you were forced to do, and we joined you, because we wanted to."

João looked at the clock and grunted: "if we are to meet Mario, I should phone him." He got up: "I'll go to the phone near the cathedral, after what Logan said, I won't risk using our phone in case it's tapped."

"Good idea." Harry said, "tell him to take his car to the road leading to this alley. It'll be a shorter distance to carry Logan's body. I suppose, in all fairness, Mario should be asked if he wants to get involved in this. He is in the police, after all."

Half an hour later, João returned obviously well pleased with the way things had gone. "We meet in twenty minutes at the entrance to the alley. He will park at the bottom of the steps. So, we won't have far to carry Logan."

"Will you be all right, here on your own?" Harry asked Angelita.

"What are you thinking, Harry?" She smiled. "This is the first time you've ever asked such a thing! Do I look so old and frail now?"

"No, but I …"

"No buts are needed, I hope! I have my new gun; I have my watch; I have my own good senses. You and João are not needed."

The effort of lifting the carpet containing Logan's body onto their shoulders was greater than they expected. Logan was not a lightweight and they staggered for a while, uncertain of the load. The alley was quiet, most people were indoors having their evening meal. Only some ragged children were playing at the far end. A scrawny old dog sniffed his way along the cobblestones. João shooed him away and saw that he'd been licking at some red stains on the ground behind them. He realised with a shudder that it must have been Logan's blood trail.

Angelita watched them from the upstairs window. She turned and went back into the kitchen making sure all the doors were locked. Then she settled down to wait, her watch nearby in case she needed them, or they needed her. Soon she dozed into a fitful sleep, exhausted by the traumas of the last few hours.

Mario saw them approaching, nervously he looked about but there were few people nearby and nobody seemed to notice anything out of the usual about Harry and João. Just two men carrying a heavy carpet to another apartment.

Mario opened the car boot and the three of them struggled to get the bulky load inside. Despite their efforts, it was difficult to get the carpet bent sufficiently to put it inside the boot and close the lid. It was then that João had an idea.

"Tie down the boot lid with the cord we put around the ends of the carpet. It's tough enough to hold it down for the short distance that we need to take it."

"I'll never make a good crook," Mario muttered as they secured the boot lid: "perhaps that's why I'm such a lousy policeman."

"You'll learn!" João slapped him on the back. "You have to learn or else you'll get the chop like this poor bugger."

"What exactly happened?" Mario asked. João explained, leaving out no detail.

Harry drove, since he knew precisely where they should leave Logan's body. Quite close to one of the smaller hospitals near the Douro, there was an area of public gardens for people to sit and relax in the heat of the day. The streets around there were now quiet. Harry stopped the car close to the gardens just where the streetlights were not too bright.

Mario and João got out, opened the boot, and carried the carpet with its heavy contents to the edge of the grass. With one swift movement, Logan's body rolled out unceremoniously. João straightened out the limbs so that it appeared Logan had been attacked near that spot. Mario folded the carpet flat and put it back in the boot. Harry said a prayer, under his breath, wishing Logan had been better trained.

Once they were back inside the car, he drove them away towards the north, hoping Logan's body would be found quickly and taken to the hospital. At least then it would be treated with dignity.

Harry took the more direct route along the Estrada da Circunvalação and headed towards Matosinhos, the crowded dockland area. He thought that by going along this route, they would give the slip to any of Dos Santos' men, if they had been watching. His twists and turns through the old quarter would have been almost impossible to follow.

Sometime later, on the open road, Harry speeded up. They passed the village of Vila do Conde and skirted round Póvoa de Varzim. The sun was setting over the sea and the intense red and orange glow blinded Harry every time there was a sharp bend in the road.

As they approached the river Cavado, Harry slowed down drawing into the side of the road. There was a long stretch of sand between them and the sea. The area was covered with pine trees gently swaying in the breeze. The river itself shimmered in the golden light. It flowed lazily but surely between low banks to the sea, just beyond where they were parked.

"This will be a good place to dump the carpet. It'll be carried right out to sea if it doesn't sink immediately. What do you think?" Harry looked at Mario and João.

"No point in carrying it around any longer." Mario said. "Difficult to explain a blood sodden carpet in the boot of the car if anyone stops us! It would make Lopes' year to get such news!" He laughed.

Harry started up the engine and drove slowly along not wanting to miss the track leading to the river. He turned off the road and onto the rough track. They stopped next to a large pine tree and got out. Mario carried the carpet to the water's edge. He and Harry swung it back then threw it forwards into the river. It didn't sink at once being pulled by the current into the mainstream. They watched as it disappeared into the shapeless mass of dark water.

"I suppose we should have said something over Logan, back at your place, João. I don't know if he was a believer or not. I don't even know whether he had a family. I just hope the hospital will notify the British Consul when they work out, he's British. I'll have to let Sir George know what happened if I get out of this. If I don't, then one of you two will need to. Only fair in case he had a family. They need to be told he died in 'the line of duty'."

CHAPTER 15
NIGHT STALKING AT THE FARMHOUSE

Harry drove back to the main road and a couple of miles further along turned inland. He knew exactly where he was heading. The village street, he was looking for, was crowded with people taking an evening stroll. Outside the small inn where he had first heard about 'O Grosso', there were several people sitting around tables listening to a young man playing a Portuguese guitar. He continued straight through the village passing the track leading to the farmhouse. He brought the car to a halt, about a quarter of a mile further along.

"Was that the farm we just passed?" João asked.

"Yes, there's a small track leading to it down there." He pointed just to the right of the car. "But there are other ways of getting near to the main building. I had a good look round the other night. Maybe, it would be wiser if we split up when we get there, agreed?"

"I suppose so, but we should keep in contact." Mario said.

"We could use the watches. We'll be easily within transmitting range and we needn't speak, just flash the lights if we are in trouble." João added.

"Right then, Mario, if you take the back of the farm; João, you check the outhouses." Harry said. "I'll go round the front. I brought along these small night binoculars – a pair each. It means we can get a good look, without having to approach too closely. Remember, as much as anything, we need to find out how many of them there are in the farm. Also, if possible, where Laura is being held."

They got out of the car and Harry showed them a gap in the hedge. This gave them a side view of the farm and had the advantage of not being visible from any of the farm windows. They each took in the general aspect of the place and the outhouses.

"Let's meet back here in about half an hour." Harry glanced at his watch. "If either of you find anything interesting or want to spend longer and don't want to use the radio, then the one who gets back here first should just wait."

"But, at all costs," Mario said, "we must avoid attracting attention of any sort."

Anyone observing the three would have seen them split up and merge with the background. Each was an expert at his job and the untrained eye would not have noticed them converge, from different directions, upon the farm.

Mario sidled around the main building keeping as close as possible to the shadows cast by two enormous eucalyptus trees on the eastern flank. The moon was full, and the trees' shadows were long and dark. The back of the building was relatively simple, two doors leading from what he assumed was the kitchen and scullery. One of them was ajar, he could hear a woman's voice, singing in Portuguese, as she worked near the window.

Mario focussed his binoculars on one of the downstairs windows and saw the slight figure of a young woman washing up. He ran the binoculars over the other ground floor windows, but the rooms were all in darkness. The rooms on the upper floor were also in darkness. He swung the binoculars up to the pantile roof. There was a small skylight set into the far end and a window under the eaves. A pale light came through the skylight and from certain points through the eaves window.

He zoomed in on the window and saw that it was shuttered. Something caused him to start, and he let the binoculars drop from his neck, as he looked around. Seconds later, he saw Dos Santos enter the kitchen and peer out of the window, then go outside into the courtyard. Quickly and silently, Mario crouched down low and watched him.

João was in the process of exploring the outhouses when he too was disturbed by Dos Santos' loud voice. He stepped back into the shadow, offered by the shed, and waited to see what Dos Santos would do. The fat man stood for a while puffing at a cigar. Then he shouted something to the girl and went back into the kitchen slamming the door behind him. João returned to his reconnaissance. He had already explored one of the outhouses and discovered it contained broken farm equipment and an old bicycle. The second one was full of mouldering hay.

The third and final outhouse still needed to be explored. Carefully opening the door, João found a padlock lying on the ground. The outhouse was quite small, hardly bigger than a shed, with no windows or shelves. There was a layer of straw on the floor and as he stepped inside, his foot hit something. He stooped and picked up an empty bottle of wine. He closed the door, convinced he had discovered where Laura had been held prisoner.

Harry approached the front of the farm with caution. He noted the Mercedes parked near the front entrance, remembering what Logan had said about a Mercedes. He scanned the building with his binoculars and saw nothing that gave any real clue as to Laura's whereabouts. All the windows were open to let in some semblance of air. In the still air, he heard voices. But it was impossible to distinguish anything being said.

Suddenly, lights came on in two downstairs windows. Harry focused on them immediately. He saw the figure of a man cross the room and go to the window. The hairs on the back of his neck rose, as he recognised Leonid. He drew closer to the building and saw the familiar outline more clearly. Leonid was smoking a cigar and talking to someone else in the room, but who it was Harry couldn't see.

Mario had almost finished his examination of the back of the farm, when he caught sight of a small door right at the far corner of the building. It was not as large as the other doors. He surmised that it must be a cubby-hole of some sort or even an entrance to a cellar. Just as he was going to find out more, he heard a bleep from his watch. He put it close to his ear. João, crouching further back in the grounds, also heard a bleep. He too stopped and listened.

"It's Leonid! He's here" Harry's voice whispered excitedly.

"So is Dos Santos." Mario added.

"I've not seen anyone." João commented.

Luis, standing only a few feet away from João, heard the first bleep of the receiver and then João's comment. He froze, first with alarm and shock, then he listened carefully to what was going on. All evening, he had felt vaguely uneasy as he patrolled the grounds. His instincts told him there was someone around, though he hadn't seen anyone. Now he knew his instincts had been right.

In the old days, he would have gone straight into action. His knife would have slit João's throat before he knew what was happening. Now, his precious knife was gone. He had also lost confidence in his own speed and skill. Also, he was no longer concerned about what happened to Leonid and the others.

His curiosity, however, drew him closer to where he'd heard the voice. He leaned against one of the outhouse walls and saw João. He recognised him immediately as the one whom they had called 'The Helper'. In the old days, he was the right-hand man of 'O Pescador'. It was then that the enormity of what he'd discovered hit him.

If 'The Helper' was there, then so was Harry Randall. Luis's heart beat faster with excitement. His training should have made him alert Leonid and the others immediately. His new-found resentment urged him to be still and do nothing.

Luis followed at a safe distance, as João made his way back to the rendezvous. His mind was racing with possibilities. He saw the tall slim figure of Mario and then the heavier form of Harry Randall. He followed them for some way until he was sure there was no one else. Luis's mind was not used to making decisions of any great magnitude. He was certainly not renowned for his speed of thought. But that night as he watched the three figures retreating, something spoke loud and clear in his head. It was almost with a sense of shock that he heard his own voice calling out.

"O Pescador'". He called out from behind the cover of a tree. He watched the three men tense and turn. "I have been watching you. I want to talk." He paused, as he saw Mario reach inside his jacket. "If you shoot, all the others will be out, and the woman will be dead."

"Who are you? What you want?" Harry rasped as loudly as he dared. He restrained Mario's arm.

"There will be time for knowing my name when we talk. Now, all you need to know is that I have the key to your daughter's life in my hands. I cannot talk now. But I will meet you on the road that runs by the sea at the bottom of the first hill. I will be there in about one hour from now."

"How do we know we can trust you?" Mario asked.

"You don't! No more than I know I can trust you. But O Pescador has much to lose if he does not trust me." Luis knew that for once, he held power in his hand.

"In one hour then." Harry said.

Luis hid himself and watched as they disappeared out of sight. Then when he was sure he could not be seen, he hurried back to the farm. When he had regained his breath, he went through into the kitchen. He poured himself a large glass of wine and sat drinking it for a while. He considered the enormity of what had taken place. He now knew exactly what he intended to do.

He walked into the lounge, a thing he would seldom have done before, unless he was sent for. Helga and Dos Santos were sitting and talking. He'd noted that his presence irritated Helga and hoped she would react to her annoyance tonight. He began coughing and spat into his handkerchief noisily. He knew she hated this habit. He had judged correctly.

"Luis, you should be on duty patrolling the grounds. What are you doing here?" Helga looked at him with disgust.

"Nothing happening. I walked round several times; only the rats are running tonight!" He coughed and spat again. "Besides, comrades, I don't see why I should have to do all the dirty work. I thought we were all supposed to be equal with our duties. So, I come in, now one of you can go out."

"Get back to your duty. Surely, you aren't comparing yourself with us?" Helga snorted.

True it was what he knew she would say and just what fitted with his plans best. But hearing the words still grated on him. One day soon, they would know who he was! He slammed the door behind him. Then he waited just outside to find out whether they would make a remark about him. He heard Helga laugh at something Dos Santos said.

"Esteban, that's how he needs to be treated. He is like any old dog. Be firm and he'll obey. The trouble with you, is you'd kick him to death while there is still some use in him. The time for the kicking will be when he is no longer of use." Helga's voice was loud. Everything she said carried clearly.

Dos Santos's reply was muffled. Luis turned away, no more doubts in his mind. He would develop a plan that would amaze them all! He went upstairs, fetching a torch, notebook, and pencil from his room. Leaving his room, he cautiously checked to see nobody was about. He stealthily climbed up to the next landing, near Laura's room.

Listening outside her prison, for a few moments, he nodded to himself. Then, he walked quietly further along until reaching a tiny door. Most people would not have seen the door since it was coated in the same whitewash as the walls. Looking over his shoulder, he opened the door then closed it quickly behind him, switching on his torch to avoid tripping. He made his way down a narrow staircase enclosed within the thick old walls. At the bottom, he switched off the torch and fumbled with the lock. He opened a small door leading directly out of the back of the house.

Luis grinned, none of the others knew about the staircase. He had often used it in the past when he wanted to get out of the farm quickly without being seen. Certainly, snooping had done him no harm in the past and promised to be of great value now.

Once in the yard, Luis hurried to the outhouse containing the bicycle. He lifted it out and carried it some distance along the path. The wheels were squeaky, and he didn't want to risk anyone in the farm hearing it. When he felt he was at a safe distance, he shone the torch onto his watch. He had half an hour until the meeting. He mounted the bike and rode up the farm track, then out onto the road. Once through the village, he rode fast. When the salt in the air hit his lungs, it gave him a feeling of exhilaration.

He reached the shoreline and laid his bike down. He sat on the shingle and shone his torch onto the notepad. He wanted to get his plan straight before the meeting. The idea was still so new in his mind that the audacity of it amazed him. He knew he wanted to spite Leonid and the others – that was important. But there was more. He wanted some tangible proof of his success. Money would be such proof.

Luis knew that O Pescador would do anything to get his daughter back and that included providing him with a large sum of money. He curled his toes in anticipation and excitement. Years of work in the movement had taught him caution. Now, he was no longer taking orders, he urged caution on himself. The newfound realisation of power made him excited. He, Luis, the one whom Helga had called 'an old dog' would manipulate the lot of them.

He jotted down his scheme on paper. Then he read it over twice nodding to himself with satisfaction. All the omens were in his favour; it was the right time of year; he was in the right part of Portugal. He hugged his knees with excitement, then switched off the torch. He got back onto the bicycle and pedalled fast to the meeting point.

Harry, João and Mario waited in the car. The road was deserted, only one car had passed in the last half an hour. Harry saw the outline of Luis riding along, he had no lights on the bike, but the moonlight silhouetted him against the pale shingle.

"Here he comes!" He said.

"I will stay back a little," Mario spoke quietly. "He'll feel safer and more likely to talk freely that way. Also, if João also stays back with me, we can cover you more easily, in case it is a trap."

Luis couldn't stop himself chuckling, as he stopped pedalling and lay the bike down. He recalled the way he had pursued Laura such a short time ago. If he had caught up with her then, she would be dead by now. She would have been a useless body instead of the key to his success.

"That's close enough!" Harry called out.

"Okay, okay! Suits me fine." Luis held his arms high in the air. "You see, I have no gun, no weapon. Also, I am alone. I come to talk." His English was halting but understandable.

"You can speak in Portuguese; it'll be quicker for us all and less likely to result in misunderstandings."

"I am right, aren't I, you are O Pescador, The Fisherman? Harry Randall?"

"Yes."

"You have João Da Gama with you. The one they call The Helper?"

"Yes."

"There is another with you. A man who I think is a policeman, I do not know his name. No matter. I am Luis. You know me?"

Irritated by all the talk, João called out: "we know you! What do you want?"

"Good!" Luis said with satisfaction. "Now, perhaps, we can all come closer. I have nothing to lose, you have a great deal to lose, if you try to play tricks on me."

"All right then, no tricks." Harry moved closer beckoning for João and Mario to join in.

Luis sat on a large boulder lying at the side of the road. Harry and the others remained standing.

"I have something you want." Luis said cryptically. "I can give you this something very soon."

"Stop playing games, Luis." Harry said.

"I know where your daughter is."

"So do we." Harry replied, "if that is all you came to tell us, then you waste your time."

"You may know where she is." Luis grunted. "But I spoke to her an hour ago. I shall see her in an hour's time. You cannot."

"What are you offering?" João asked impatiently.

"I can give you your daughter, O Pescador."

"And why should you do that?"

"Because it pleases me. That is why. Let's say, it pleases Luis to bring your daughter to you."

"What's the other reason?" Harry was genuinely puzzled.

"I want some American dollars. Yes. Many American dollars. I want $50,000 or 50 grand as they used to say in Chicago." He had suddenly switched to English and chuckled at the exaggerated American accent he had used.

"$50,000 – where do you think I can get hold of that sort of money. I don't have it." Harry was quite genuine in what he said. To acquire such a large amount of currency was not within his remit.

Luis rose and shook his head before replying: "then sadly you won't have your daughter." He shook his head again. "Such a pity! A nice woman but she will be a dead nice woman very soon." He turned and walked slowly towards his bike.

"Wait!" Mario called after him. "Let's not be too hasty, Luis."

"Why should I not be hasty?" He turned to face them. "I say you agree, or you do not agree. It is simple."

"I might be able to get the money. When do you want it?" Harry asked.

"Might is not good enough. You must say you will get it by Sunday."

"We will have the money." Mario spoke firmly and decisively. "Where do you want it?"

"You know that Sunday is the great feast of Our Lady of The Assumption, Nossa Senhora da Assunçao. It is the great festival day for all the fisherman of Póvoa de Varzim. Well, I will bring your daughter to the festival. A very good place for your triumph, yes?" He chuckled again to himself. "I will bring her to the little church of the fishermen, and you will bring the $50,000, O Fisherman! Yes?"

Harry did not reply for some time. His head reeled at the notion of the money and the bizarre proposition that Luis was putting forward. He remembered the great festivals of Our Lady that were held all over Portugal and the vast crowds that they drew.

Obviously for Luis such a crowded scene would be ideal. But for him, João and Mario it could be a trap. How could they be certain this wasn't Leonid's own plan? An event of symbolic importance for 'The Fisherman' and his daughter to be killed at the festival near the fishermen's church of Póvoa. Leonid would relish the symbolism and the shock waves it would send to Sanctum. It was João who asked the question that had been going through his own mind.

"And what part does Leonid play in all of this?" asked.

"Leonid! He is nothing to me now!" Luis, spat onto the road, he seemed genuinely angry when he spoke his name.

"And the Kaufman woman and Dos Santos ..." João got no further.

"Shit! Shit! That's what they are. Leonid and the rest do not know my value. I, Luis, know more about real Marxism than they will ever know. Yet, they treat me like dirt, like an old dog. They are nothing!"

Harry looked at the others in surprise. He was now beginning to understand why Luis was doing this, but it still surprised him. Leonid, in the past, had been so careful to nurture the members of his cell.

"So, O Pescador, is it agreed then? I will bring her to the entrance of the church when the big procession arrives back. You will give me the money and I will give her to you, just after the priest has gone inside the door."

"It is agreed, Luis." Harry said simply.

"Remember, I have your daughter's life in my hands. If I am double crossed, she will die. You understand?"

"I understand that, Luis. You have made your points very well. You have made a very clever plan." Harry said.

"That is good." Luis was pleased, as much as anything, with the recognition of his plan and his ability to draw up such a plan. "Now the three of you are to leave here first."

Luis stepped behind the boulder and watched them as they walked back to the car. Mario got into the driver's seat. He saw Harry was trembling with both rage and alarm and in no fit state to drive. Then, when they were all inside, he drove away without saying a word. João peered out of the back window and saw Luis step into the road and then run to fetch his bicycle.

"My God! It was bad enough having to deal with Leonid on Monday. But now this!" João said.

"Can we rely on Luis being able to do what he says?" Mario asked. "Leonid is no fool and this Luis is an ignorant old peasant. Surely, he can't outwit Leonid and the others. In any case, can we believe he really intends to?"

"Oh yes, I believe him." Harry said, "what he said rang true. He feels he's been badly treated. In English, we have a saying: 'Hell hath no fury like a woman scorned'. But that can equally well apply to an old, scorned comrade. I believe he is genuine in his hatred for all of them. What worries me is his ability to carry out the plan."

"I think he'll carry it off all right." João said confidently. "He was never a great one for ideology, that Luis. But in the field, he was excellent. He wrecked more than one of our plans. I think he'll carry it off okay. Anyway, what other options do we have, other than to believe him? We can't storm the farm, that's obvious from what we saw tonight. So, in my opinion, we must pray for Luis's success."

"Then - there's this little matter of $50,000. Sanctum won't be involved. And..." Harry was stopped in his ruminations by Mario waving his arm.

"Don't worry about the money. No problem. I'll get hold of it, if necessary." Mario looked over his shoulder for a moment. "You want to know where I can get hold of that sort of money?" He laughed, "I'll tell you. I was investigating a big counterfeit racket in Oporto. We uncovered the whole works, the press, the notes, the lot. There were almost $200,000 in ready-made notes, plus British pounds, and Escudos. We've got everything under lock and key in security. I can ask for $50,000 of this forged money and say I need it for a drug investigation case. I need it to catch a dealer. If I sign for it, there'll be no fuss."

"Could Luis spot they're forgeries?" João asked.

"What that old fool! Not even experts could tell the difference, not until the notes were analysed and then examined under a microscope. So, Harry, the money is the least of our worries."

"There's no option then. If it was anything other than Laura's life at stake, I'd be tempted to storm the farm. But it's too risky." Harry leaned back against the seat, suddenly feeling completely exhausted.

CHAPTER 16
LUIS EXAMINES HIS PLAN

Once Luis was satisfied that they had driven away, he got his bike and pedalled quickly back to the side road. He skirted past the village and returned directly to the farmyard. He carried the bike the last few paces and put it back in the outhouse. As he turned away from the door, he was confronted by Dos Santos who had been observing him from the shadows.

"Hey, you! What have you been up to, Luis?" He prodded Luis roughly in his side.

"What do you think? I've been patrolling the grounds."

"Like hell you have! I watched you skulk your way back here carrying that clapped out old bike. You've not been on any patrol, you old bastard. You've been to the village, haven't you? You've been drinking, instead of doing what you were told to do." He pushed Luis hard and sent him sprawling onto the cobblestones. "You're finished, old man. Once this job is over, you'll not be needed any more."

Luis staggered to his feet but said nothing. His impulse was to kick out at Dos Santos. But now there was too much at stake to risk getting hurt. He walked slowly ahead and into the kitchen.

"What does it feel like to be finished, old man? Perhaps you should try getting into Helga's or Leonid's good books. Who knows, they might still have some use for you. You'd be lost without having orders to carry out, wouldn't you?"

Luis opened the kitchen door and saw Helga standing in one corner. She looked past him towards Dos Santos who nodded to her.

"So, not been doing what you were told. You were sent out there to act as an early warning." She said in accusing tones.

"I've been out there for hours. There's nothing going on." Luis replied.

"How would you know that? You were nowhere to be found in the last hour." She pushed him against the table.

"He's not worth bothering with, Helga. I looked around the grounds and he's right, nothing is happening." Dos Santos was irritated by the extra work that Leonid's vendetta was causing him personally. Then prodding Luis in the back, he said: "Go up and check on the woman. Take her bread and water and tell her that's all she'll get until she answers Leonid's questions. You tell her that!"

Luis belched loudly as he passed close to Helga. He made no attempt to cover his mouth and let her feel the full effect of his garlic-laden breath. It amused him to see the look of disgust on her face. He picked up Laura's tray and slowly climbed the stairs.

The minute she heard the lock being turned, Laura got to her feet and backed against the wall. When she saw it was Luis, she returned to the bed. It was strange, she thought, how her ideas had changed. Only days earlier, Luis's presence filled her with foreboding, now he seemed a lesser evil.

"They want you to answer some questions. They say only bread and water till you do. I think they will do more than that, unless you do what they want. I think you should do what they ask. Don't give them hassle, eh?" He peered at her, then left the room.

He went to his own room and locked the door. He had a great deal to think about and to plan. He needed to arrange things fast. There were several things he needed: a car, gun, an escape route for him and Laura. He lay on his bed and closed his eyes. He knew he could get the car and the gun. His old friend, Ferreira, would obtain those for him, no trouble. The route for him and Laura, however, was another matter.

He rolled onto his side and the questions slipped from his mind. He had some hours yet to work that problem out. Instead, he revelled in the situation and all he had so far accomplished. He smiled as he anticipated the impact his actions would have on Dos Santos, Helga, and Leonid. He wished he could be around to see their faces when they found out that he, Luis, had outwitted them all. Then he fell asleep, basking in his own sense of self-satisfaction. It was the first time he had felt that way for a long time.

~❖~

João called Angelita from a phone booth at the side of the road, once they were within distance of the city. The relief in her voice was unmistakable, even though she joked. When they eventually arrived back at the apartment, she hovered around like an anxious little bird. She brought wine then cake, then coffee, in quick succession. Agitation always made her feel she had to do something.

Her activity reminded Harry of Beth who would find work to do in the house, whenever she was anxious. However, Beth had never had to cope with the problems that Angelita had dealt with in her life. In fact, if Beth had suffered one iota of them, Harry surmised she would not have survived. He watched Angelita's activity with both amusement and admiration. But for João it only served as an irritation.

"Sit down, Angelita! For Christ's sake stop bobbing about." He put out his arm to restrain her from fetching yet another plate of food for them. "Sit down and help us to think about the problem we have in hand."

Angelita sat between Harry and João, her hands folded in her lap. She had plenty of ideas but was disinclined to air them. Instead, her big brown eyes went from one to another, scrutinising each one in turn. In Mario's face, she saw the excitement of youth; the eagerness of a young man to engage in a fight. He had no anxiety or fear, only the expectation of facing a challenge. She looked at João. He was tired and anxious but in him she also recognised the desire to face a challenge. She realised how much he had missed being involved in Harry's business. She felt grateful for João being given this new lease of life.

Finally, she looked at Harry as he sat hunched over his coffee. Everything about him showed anxiety and exhaustion. She knew he had not been sleeping for the last couple of nights. She saw no eagerness for the fray in his face and she understood why. She also saw Harry's face had lines of sheer determination etched deeply around his mouth. Something that Mario had not yet developed and João did not have. He must be a difficult man to live with, she thought. He was stubborn, self-willed, and uncompromising. Thank goodness, her man did not have such traits! She squeezed João's arm, and he looked at her in surprise. She nodded to herself and thought they were a well-matched trio who would complement each other's strengths and weaknesses in the coming days.

"I'll arrange for the dollars, Harry. Also, I'll get some more men to help us." Mario said.

"No need for more men, Mario. The money, yes. That will be more than welcome. In fact, it's essential. But don't ask for more men, I don't want that." Harry seemed quite adamant.

"Surely, we can't handle this completely on our own?" Mario protested.

"Not 'we', Mario, it's just me. I'm not going to risk anyone else in this affair. Now Luis has made contact, there's no need for you or João or Angelita to be involved."

"Too late, Harry, we are involved!" João said. "You can't keep us out of this. The more we know, the safer we'll be. But I agree, Mario, we need to keep it just to ourselves. Too many outsiders could cause trouble."

Mario listened to them, he decided argument was pointless. However, in his own mind, he was sure he would have to involve at least one other person. There was no reason to make Harry and João anxious about this. He left soon after they'd agreed to meet again the following day.

When he had gone, Harry looked closely at João: "you agree, don't you about not wanting any of Mario's po-lice pals to help us out." João nodded. "With Laura's life at stake it's too risky. This Logan business, when it gets back to Leonid, will make him even more jumpy. And if Dos Santos keeps it from him, we are catering for unknown circumstances. Let's face it, despite what you say, Luis is not the most gifted of men. I just hope he knows what he's doing."

"What else could be done? Could we wait somewhere near the farm and then just jump Luis as he comes out with your daughter?"

João answered his own question: "Of course not! Firstly, we don't know how Luis plans to get her away. Secondly, we don't know whether anyone else is involved with him. It's too risky. We have to take it on good faith and wait by the church for the right moment."

"We are going to Póvoa tomorrow to meet Mario; we did decide that didn't we?" Harry found himself yawning. "My God! What a mess!"

~❖~

Leonid had received Harry's note earlier in the evening. He had taken it straight away to his room. He wanted to be alone when he read it. The reasoning behind the reply was impeccable, so typical of Harry Randall, Leonid thought. He had always admired the logic of Harry's mind. Harry Randall was never one to be flustered, the typical Englishman, who would not allow emotion to impinge upon a strictly business commitment.

He read the questions, Harry had posed, several times and smiled to himself. As Harry had written, only Laura could provide the answers. He wondered how easy it would be to persuade her to give him those answers. The previous recording had posed enough problems. Undoubtedly, she would resist again this time.

Now the time for the fulfilment of his vengeance for Pedro was so close, Leonid was surprised to discover he felt no real satisfaction or pleasure. Whatever he did to Harry Randall, or his daughter, would never bring Pedro Batista back or give him the vitality that he had lost when Batista died. He lit a cigarette and drew on it slowly, allowing the smoke to fill his mouth before blowing it out in one long withdrawing sigh. Without finishing the cigarette, he threw it angrily away and ground it into the floorboards with his heel. He picked up the letter and a pad of note paper and left the room.

He walked down the corridor and climbed the short flight of steps leading to Laura's room. He could hear Helga talking loudly to Catherina in the kitchen. He knew Dos Santos was checking the Mercedes in the courtyard. Luis, he guessed, was on patrol in the grounds. No one would interfere with what he had decided to do. He went into the long low room. It was the first time he had been in there since Laura had been locked up in the house. He saw her tense as she saw him, wondering what he wanted from her. He represented the unexpected. He crossed the room slowly and pulled over one of the wooden chairs and sat near the bed.

"There is no need to be afraid, Mrs Bayliss, I have just come to get some answers from you. Nothing difficult, is it?" He spoke softly. When he was calm, he spoke languages other than his native Russian quite well. But whenever he grew angry, his accent would disintegrate. Now he felt quite confident of success, so he spoke English very well.

"Your father, ever a cautious man, wants to be reassured you are still alive. Now, Mrs Bayliss, you wouldn't want to upset him in any way, would you? So, of course, you will answer his questions and put his mind at rest." He smiled.

Laura didn't know what to make of this situation. The questions had been read to her earlier by Dos Santos, but no one had tried to persuade her to answer. Leonid clicked his finger joints and smiled again, only his eyes didn't smile, they stared straight through her. Their grey colour seemed expressionless in the light provided by the bare light bulb.

"You will answer the questions now. I'll read them again for you, then give me the right answers. First: who is Rosie? Second: how many children has Mrs Magoo? Third: where does Peterkin go in a storm?"

He looked at her. For a while, Laura said nothing. The names Rosie, Mrs Magoo and Peterkin seemed so incongruous coming from Leonid. Images of her childhood flooded her memory. Little had she ever thought then that one day she would be stuck in a garret in Portugal being cross questioned by a Russian agent. She shook her head in disbelief, perhaps after all, she had gone mad, or this was a nightmare.

"Answer, will you Mrs Bayliss? You know very well you can be made to answer, so why not they make things easy for yourself?"

"All right then," Laura said. "Rosie is the name of my aunt, my father's sister. She looked after me when my parents were abroad."

"Wait a moment." He held out his hand to stop her while he wrote down the answer. "All right, what about this Mrs Magoo?"

"Mrs Magoo was the name of my aunt's goat, nanny goat, in fact. She had ten little kids."

"What do you mean 'nanny goat and kids? I don't understand." Leonid looked puzzled.

"Really?" You surprise me, I thought Russians were so clever." She smiled sweetly, "A nanny goat is a female goat and kids are what baby goats are called."

"Who is Peterkin and where would he go in a storm?"

"He was my dog. He used to hide under the cushions, whenever there was a storm."

Leonid wrote down the final answer, then carefully put the notebook on the table. He went over and hit her hard twice across her face with the back of his hand. The force of the blows sent her reeling against the wall.

"And that, Mrs Bayliss, was for trying to be too clever. And this is for Pedro Batista." He hit her hard again so that she almost lost consciousness. She felt a rib crack and a searing pain shot through her side. There was no emotion on his face just a look of total hatred.

Laura wiped the blood away on the back of her arm. She had bitten her tongue and began choking on the blood as it trickled to the back of her throat. She reached out for the tin mug on the table next to the bed. The water eased her choking.

"What a frail little creature you are, Mrs Bayliss! Are you sure that Harry Randall is your father? You must be a disappointment to him! He would have wanted a son: a resolute man like himself. Instead, he has you – a frail insipid woman." Leonid looked again at the paper on which he had written her answers.

"Who was Pedro Batista?" Her voice was quiet but steady. If she was to suffer, she wanted to know why.

Leonid peered at her without replying. Then he sat down heavily on one of the chairs and held his head in his hands. It was the first time he had registered any outward show of emotion, in company, since Pedro Batista's death. From his appearance, Laura could not tell if he was feeling anger or grief.

"Pedro Batista." Leonid repeated the name twice before looking at her. "Pedro Batista was what you would call my lover. He was the most important person in the world to me. Your father sent him to his execution. But it wasn't a quick execution, as yours and his will be. Pedro's was a slow lingering death that lasted for years. Years of suffering!"

"What did my father do, how was he involved?" In the desire to understand, she almost forgot her own pain.

"Your father was head of the British espionage services for the Iberian Peninsula. He organised anti-Soviet agents here in Portugal and Spain. He liaised with the Blue Army of Fatima! They see themselves as the saviours of Portugal and Spain. Your father had orders to work with them! You didn't know this?" He looked genuinely surprised.

"No." She shook her head. "I thought he worked for the British Government Trade Department."

"I suppose it is typical," Leonid said. "British agents have a remarkable record of being anonymous at home but totally infamous abroad." He shook his head.

Each of them sat in silence. Laura was still trembling from the blows to her head and chest. Looking at her frail form, everything suddenly seemed rather pointless to Leonid. He almost felt a twinge of guilt at having involved her in his plan for revenge and satisfaction.

How would Pedro Batista benefit? Her agony would never bring him back. Even Harry Randall's death would only add to the crazy game of kill and counter kill between both sides in the so-called Cold War. He wondered who would gain satisfaction from his own death and when that would come. No doubt when it did, the Blue Army of Fatima would claim the credit.

Laura no longer felt afraid of Leonid. He was, after all, human and fallible like everyone else. She remembered her old schoolteacher telling her once before going into an oral exam: *'if you can only picture people without their clothes on, dear, no one seems quite so frightening.'* Laura smiled to herself; it was true. Without our clothes and our mystery, we are all vulnerable.

Leonid got up and waved his piece of paper at her: "Your answers will speed up the resolution of this little game for all of us."

Laura watched him leave the room with relief. She went over to the enamel bowl in the corner of the room and washed her face trying to soothe the swelling on her cheek. The water in the bowl turned pink from the crusted blood. She went to the window and breathed in the fresh air. The intake of breath caused the pain in her side to make her gasp. But she had survived so far and survive, she vowed, she would.

Leonid returned to his room and rewrote the answers on a new sheet of paper. He reminded Harry that time was passing fast and that he needed a reply by return. Then he heard the bulky weight of Dos Santos on the creaky boards outside his room, so he called to him.

"Esteban, come here." He waited for Dos Santos to appear, then held out the letter. "I want this taken to Oporto now. Give it to that courier of yours. Tell him it must be delivered tonight."

"Perhaps Luis can take it, he ..."

"No!" Leonid thundered, "I told you to take it! I expect you to do what you're told. Luis is not to be relied on, haven't you told me that? He is finished, no good for anything, and must be dealt with soon." He pointed a finger menacingly at Dos Santos. "And you, you will go the same way too, unless you learn to obey orders the first time they are given."

"I just thought that…"

"Don't think! You are not so good at that. Just do what you're told." He handed him the letter. "Tonight, Dos Santos. Understand?"

Dos Santos cursed Leonid under his breath, as he clambered down the stairs. The sweat ran down his armpits in cold trickles until it settled somewhere above his belt leaving a ring of damp on his blue shirt. He was irritated at the thought of having to go out again. He had promised himself a relaxing evening, drinking wine and then sleeping. Instead, he now faced the prospect of two hours in the car.

Helga came out of the lounge and looked at him questioningly. She had heard Leonid's voice raised in anger. Dos Santos shook his head.

"He's going mad, Helga. He is totally consumed by his little private war; he never thinks about our real work here."

"I think," she paused for a moment. "I think it's time Moscow knew about this. Come, I'll walk with you to the car, we can talk more easily outside."

The courtyard was deserted but, from her little window, Laura could see them, walking together towards the Mercedes. She saw they were deep in conversation, but she heard nothing.

"Tonight, when you are at Eduardo's place, take the opportunity to call Malyshkin on the radio." Helga said. "We don't want ourselves involved in this business. Too much could go wrong, then we'd be implicated too."

Dos Santos hesitated. He had worked with Leonid for years; he knew he was not a man to cross. The thought of going behind his back to Moscow alarmed him considerably. Anyway, he didn't care that much for Helga either, if it came to it. She was arrogant and officious, and he knew she rather despised him too. So, when he responded, he was cautious in his reply.

"Perhaps, we ought to give him time to finish his plans, Helga. After all, it will be over by Monday evening. Not long to wait." He suggested.

"Are you mad, Esteban? What do you think Malyshkin will say if something goes wrong, and the new cells are jeopardised? We will all be blamed. And you know what happens when Moscow blames someone!" She paused, "No, the time has come for Moscow to know one of their top men is putting at hazard the future of the new network. I'll give you my code number, it will get you direct access to Malyshkin."

Dos Santos was troubled, the idea of radioing Moscow with news like this did not appeal to him. Also, there was the possibility of Leonid's plan working and then only he, Dos Santos, would be regarded as a traitor.

"Wouldn't it be better, Helga, if you radio Moscow yourself? After all, you know Comrade Malyshkin personally. You would know what to say and …"

"How can I, Esteban? I am tied here to this wretched farmhouse to look after that precious cargo. Besides, neither you nor I dare use the radio here, now Leonid is so on edge."

"But you never go near the woman anymore. Luis does everything. You have time to go to Oporto yourself."

"Maybe, but Leonid insists I stay here until Monday. No, Esteban, it is you who must do this."

CHAPTER 17
DOS SANTOS GOES ON A MISSION

Dos Santos found himself driving in the direction of the port of Leixões with two major worries on his mind. Firstly, whether he would find Eduardo at his flat. And if he didn't, he would have to deliver the letter himself. Secondly, he was now in the invidious position of having to inform on the top Soviet agent in Portugal.

He drove the big car slowly along the twisting road wishing to postpone the moment of truth when he would speak to Malyshkin. The very name caused him severe anxiety. Although he had worked for the party for years, he had never once been out of Portugal. It occurred to him that he had been taught everything he knew about Communism and the Soviet System by Leonid and Batista. Moscow was just a name to him.

The Lubyanka, amongst other things the training ground for important agents, had never seriously crossed Dos Santos' mind. Yet now he was driving to a small flat where he would have to speak to someone in the Lubyanka itself. He wished Helga had taken the responsibility After all, she was Moscow trained she knew Malyshkin. She understood the intricacies that existed between spymaster and agent.

He shook his head as he peered through the windscreen at the glare of oncoming traffic. However, he thought,

Helga was possibly the future in Portugal. If she thought this was the thing to do, then so be it.

The lights of Leixões came in sight, he had reached his destination. The port was even more crowded than usual. The sardine fishing fleet had just docked, the ships' holds laden with a fine catch. Seagulls were swooping and shrieking, even though it was dark. The dockside lights were sufficient to allow them to catch the entrails of gutted fish thrown overboard.

The local traders crowded alongside the wharfs, their cars blocking the way. Dos Santos cursed under his breath as he slowly forced the car through the narrow streets. He leaned forward and peered anxiously down one small street. The sweat from his back made his shirt cling to him. Peeling himself away from the seat, he looked for Eduardo's flat. It was with relief that he saw the lights were on.

He squeezed into a small space further down the street from the flat. Then, he wheezed his way up the steep stone steps to Eduardo's place, from where music was blasting. He knocked and waited and knocked again. A small dark girl in a skin-tight red dress opened the door, stared at him then smiled, putting a hand on his shoulder.

"You must be one of Eduardo's friends." The girl said, "come in, we are having a party."

The flat was cramped and though there were only about twelve people, it seemed like eleven too many to Dos Santos. He looked at everyone suspiciously, searching for Eduardo. At last, he caught sight of him, standing in the corner, his arms around a woman. Dos Santos felt a tug at his shirt, he turned irritably towards the dark girl who still had hold of him.

"You want a drink?" She guided him to a low table laid out with an array of bottles and tins. He shook himself free and pushed her away.

"Come on, sweetie, we're all here to have fun." She said.

"Get away from me, I've got business to do!" The girl shrugged her shoulders and headed off to a group sitting and laughing near the record player.

Dos Santos pushed his way towards Eduardo who was still engrossed in the woman. Eduardo looked up in surprise when he heard Dos Santos' voice. He could not recall having invited him to the party. Why ever would he, he laughed at the thought. Giving the woman a pinch on the bottom, he followed Dos Santos into the small kitchen.

"We have private business, get out!" Dos Santos said to a young woman standing beside the sink preparing food. She hesitated, looked at Eduardo, who nodded to her, then she left.

"Why the hell are you giving a party? We pay for this flat, remember? You use it, but you have no right to bring others here." Dos Santos' voice was angry.

"I happen to live in it. I do all the chores you give me, and I do them well. What else do you want from me? I have a right to a life, you know."

"As long as we pay you, you have no rights to anything." Dos Santos pushed Eduardo against the edge of the ceramic sink, then leaned his full bulk against him. "Understand?"

"Okay, I understand. No need to bring on the heavy stuff, Dos Santos."

The witticism was lost on Dos Santos who took out the letter from his pocket, waving it in front of Eduardo: "see this? It's important, very important! It must be delivered tonight to Da Gama's place. Right? Also, I must use the radio now."

"The letter, I can deliver. But as for the radio, it will be difficult with so many people here."

"Get rid of them. I don't want any left here when you go. And you're going in a few minutes."

"I can't just tell them all to clear out, there will be a riot. Then you will never achieve anything." Eduardo protested.

"Get rid of them now."

"I suppose," Eduardo said, eyeing Dos Santos closely, "I suppose, if there was somewhere better for them, then I could coax them out."

"What do you mean, somewhere better?"

"Somewhere such as the casino in Póvoa de Varzim. They'd enjoy that."

"Tell them you'll meet them there. I don't give a damn where you take them. Just get them out." Dos Santos was beginning to get frazzled.

"Then, I'll need more money, if I'm to take them there." Eduardo said.

Dos Santos took out his handkerchief and mopped his sweating head. He was hot, thirsty, and tired. When he heard Eduardo's last demand, he realised he was being played for a fool. In other circumstances, he would have taught him a lesson, but he felt too exhausted to deal with him. Besides, he wanted the flat empty and he wanted that done quickly.

"Look you little bastard, I don't give a damn how you get rid of these people. Get this through your head, I'm not paying you one extra Escudo to go to the casino or wherever. Drive them all into the dockside for all I care – just get them out while..." He paused, "while you're still in one piece yourself."

Eduardo realised he wasn't going to get anywhere with his tactics. He took the letter, put it in his pocket, and went into the lounge. It took him almost twenty minutes to persuade, cajole or forcibly shove everyone out of the flat. Some went away in search of another more promising party; others shouted abuse at him then headed for one of the noisy café–bars on the waterfront.

At last, he was left with just the woman and two friends. He got them into his battered blue van. He started up the engine noisily and revved it up. Looking in his rear mirror, he caught sight of the black Mercedes parked across the narrow street. Laughing and shouting out of his van window, Eduardo accelerated and drove close enough to the sleek Mercedes to cut a deep scratch along the entire side with his own twisted fender. He looked up at the flat: "that'll cost you, you shit!"

Dos Santos didn't hear, or if he heard he paid no attention to what was going on in the street. He sat in the bedroom facing the radio. He rubbed his hands together. Never one for quick action or decision–making, he found the situation agonising and disturbing. He had always accepted Leonid's orders, now he was about to betray him. Yet, he didn't want to do so on Helga's say-so alone. He sat thinking for some considerable time.

If things went wrong on Monday, he could easily be made the fall guy. He got up and went into the kitchen to pour himself a drink and sat there debating what he should do. It occurred to him that if Leonid was out of the way, then he would be well placed to inherit the leadership of the Portuguese section. True, Helga was more senior to him, after all she'd been to the Lubyanka for training, but he was Portuguese and that must surely count for something. He drained his glass and returned to the radio. He now knew what he was going to do.

Back in the cramped bedroom, he began fumbling with the small dials on the radio. He hadn't worked this particular set before and found it difficult to tune in to the correct wavelength. At last, he got the right signal, gave out Helga's code number and name, then waited for a response. The go-ahead took some time; the operator in the Lubyanka was doubtful about Dos Santos' authenticity. It took several queries and responses before Dos Santos was able to dictate the message for Malyshkin. At last, he was told to wait by the radio for further instructions.

In Moscow, the radio operator carefully checked the message he had taken down. Then, he took it along one of the narrow grey corridors criss-crossing the Lubyanka building. Eventually arriving outside Comrade Malyshkin's office, he hesitated for a moment, then knocked. Malyshkin had a reputation for not suffering fools gladly and the pale eager young man didn't want to be considered a fool.

When he heard the instruction 'enter', he opened the door carefully. Malyshkin was sitting behind a large wooden desk several neatly arranged piles of paper in front of him. He was studying one in particular, as the young man crossed the thickly carpeted floor and stood to attention in front of the desk, waiting to be noticed.

Malyshkin was a thickset man with a tremendous breadth of shoulders emphasised even more by the uniform he wore. He looked like a prize wrestler brooding over an opponent. After a grunt and a smile, Malyshkin put down the papers, pushed his chair back from the desk, and looked closely at the young man.

"Well, what do you want?" he snapped.

"I apologise for disturbing you, Comrade Malyshkin, but I have a message from Portugal. A man is using Helga Kaufmann's code name and number. He says she told him to radio you urgently."

"What's the message?" Malyshkin leaned forward and took the flimsy paper from his hand, reading it for a few minutes. "This line, is it still open?"

"Yes, Comrade Malyshkin, I told him to wait for your response."

"Good, that was clear thinking." Malyshkin looked at him. "What's your name?"

"Bogdanov, Boris Bogdanov."

"Well, Bogdanov, we'll have to see your work is kept under scrutiny. We need more young men with common sense." He got up and straightened his jacket. "It's a commodity lacking around here these days."

Meanwhile, Dos Santos waited by the radio nervously, wishing he'd never been involved in the situation. The sudden sound of Malyshkin's voice startled him, and he banged his elbow against the radio in his anxiety.

"Hello, comrade leader – this is Dos Santos. I am using Helga Kaufmann's code, at her request. Over."

"What is this personal vendetta I have read about in the message? Over."

"Comrade Leader, Leonid Paustovsky, has a score to settle with a man called Harry Randall. Over."

"What!" Malyshkin's face registered shock and even though Dos Santos couldn't see him, he heard it in the tone of his voice. "Randall, Col Harry Randall? Over."

"Yes, sir, he arrived from England a few days ago. Comrade Leader Paustovsky had been planning this for some time, I think. Over."

"Does he plan to kill him, do you think? Over."

"Yes, comrade. Over."

"Any other British Sanctum agents involved? Are our new cells in any danger? Over."

"As far as we know, no other British agents are involved. But it is because, Comrade Helga Kaufmann is concerned about the new cells, that we thought you should know. Over." He decided to emphasise the 'we', in case Kaufmann was right, after all.

There was a long pause while Malyshkin took stock of the situation. For a man of his high ambitions, the last couple of years had been singularly unimpressive. He foresaw a situation where he might be stuck forever as a mere spymaster in the bowels of the Lubyanka. The idea did not appeal. A success now, one that he could present to the tough chief of the KGB, Yuri Andropov, would be of great advantage. At the same time, he could not afford another fiasco like the Khokhlov incident only a few years earlier. This was still deeply embedded in the minds of all KGB agents. Another failed assassination would be a disaster. He leaned close to the radio and spoke again.

"Listen to me, Dos Santos, I want you and Comrade Kaufmann to watch the situation closely. This Randall caused considerable trouble for me and for our agents right across the Iberian Peninsula. Not for nothing was he called O Pescador, The Fisherman! If anything, now he is London-based, he is more active against our cause than before. If Comrade Paustovsky succeeds in dealing with him, then I shall have no cause to complain about any of you."

There was a long pause and Dos Santos thought he had lost the connection. But then he heard a bang reverberate down the radio signal.

"However, things may go wrong and Paustovsky's actions could bring disaster to the new cells. If that happens, and only if, then you and Comrade Kaufmann must act swiftly to prevent such a disaster spreading. Even if that means dealing directly with Paustovsky. You understand? Over."

"When you say 'deal with ', do you…"

"Kill him." Came the reply, without the usual rules of the airways being observed. "Do that as a last resort. Keep the situation under control and inform me as and when it changes. Over."

Interference flooded in as the line from the Lubyanka closed. Dos Santos wriggled uneasily, unsure whether to feel relief or disappointment now the ordeal was over. With trembling hands, he pushed the set back into the cupboard and locked the door. He took out his handkerchief and mopped his head and neck. Then he wiped his chest free from the clammy sweat that seemed to have oozed from every pore, at a greater rate than usual.

He returned to the kitchen and opened a bottle of wine he found in the fridge. Without bothering to get a glass, he swigged from the bottle, enjoying the cold liquid as it ran down his parched throat. He went to the bedroom and lay on the bed taking swigs from the bottle, until it was empty.

His own task completed, Eduardo went with his friends to a nightclub. He was still angry at the treatment he had received from Dos Santos. He didn't return to his flat until the early hours of the morning. When he discovered the blubbery form of the fat man lying on his bed, he had a tremendous urge to kick it. Instead, he kicked the foot of the bed. Dos Santos woke with surprising speed, his hand reaching immediately for the revolver he had placed beneath the pillow. Eduardo was glad he had only kicked the bed.

"It's been delivered." Eduardo said.

Dos Santos swung his legs over the side of the bed and surveyed Eduardo: "if it hadn't, then you would not be standing so calmly before me now. When you're told to do something, it is taken for granted you will do it."

"So, what do you want done now?" Eduardo watched Dos Santos heave himself to his feet.

"Same as before. Collect the reply and bring it to us at the farm."

CHAPTER 18
DECEPTION

João woke early, he'd had a restless night but didn't want to disturb Angelita. He went downstairs and made coffee. Since Harry's return, João had woken each morning with a sense of excitement.

He drank the coffee and then padded out barefoot into the hallway. It was then he caught sight of the envelope. He snapped his fingers and bent down to pick it up. He knew, without opening it, exactly what it was. The large, scrawled handwriting was the same as that on the outside of the cassette. He and Harry had waited up the previous night expecting this reply but by the early hours it had still not arrived. Now it was here.

João glanced at the clock and saw it was still only five. He decided not to wake either Angelita or Harry. They were fortunate to be able to sleep. The time was rapidly approaching when they would be as restless as he already was. He took the letter back to the kitchen and held it up to the window, trying to make out the writing. Once satisfied he could not decipher the message, he poured himself another coffee and settled down to wait for the others to come down.

Angelita was next downstairs. João nodded towards the letter and pulled a face. They talked for a time and decided Harry should read the letter alone. It would be easier for him.

Angelita put a fresh pot of coffee on a tray, together with some rolls and butter, then João took it upstairs. He knocked on Harry's door leaving the tray outside.

Harry woke feeling refreshed from a good night's sleep. He went to the door and picked up the tray. He knew at once why he had not been called down as usual. He tore open the envelope and read the note with mixed feelings – relief that Laura was alive – anger that they were both puppets in Leonid's game. The letter informed him the deadline was still set for Monday, there would be no more prevarication, Leonid had written.

Harry sipped at his coffee, pondering all the time what his next move would be. Leonid had to be lulled into a sense of security now that Luis was on the scene.

But at this moment in time there was another matter that had to be dealt with. Sir George would be getting suspicious at the long silence from Logan. Harry knew that he liked regular reports from his 'angels' and quite possibly Logan's routine was already broken. Harry dreaded the prospect of Sanctum sending in a team of their Lisbon men to find out what was going on.

He crossed over to the box in the corner of his room. It contained the few personal possessions that Logan had on him when he was killed. Harry and João had removed them and put them away in case they might come in useful. There was a small red notebook with names and addresses in London, a packet of cigarettes and a lighter. There was no gun which surprised Harry; until he remembered that Dos Santos had held Logan for questioning. Lastly, Harry looked at a small Yale type key with a brown label attached to it.

He took out a crumpled piece of paper from his own jacket pocket, it was Logan's address. He felt certain the key belonged to Logan's room. He paused momentarily, then made two rapid decisions.

Firstly, he implemented the most immediate decision by writing a reply to Leonid's letter. There was little to say, and it took a matter of minutes. He put on his cream linen jacket and went downstairs. João and Angelita were still sitting anticipating his arrival in the kitchen. They looked up as he came in.

"João, I'm going to take this to the Automovel Clube. It'll keep Leonid happy for a time at least. Then I'm going down to find Logan's room. I'm sure this key will fit the lock."

"Why bother, Harry? We've got so much else to do urgently." João protested.

"If Logan doesn't call in to Sanctum in London, then Sir George is bound to get restive. Knowing him, he'll take the opportunity to send in some of his new boys to give them experience. We can't afford to let that happen."

"So? I still don't understand …"

"The codebook and transmitter are probably somewhere in Logan's room. He didn't know anyone else here in Oporto to be able to use their gear."

"I'll come with you then." João half rose from his chair.

"No, I can manage this, it would be better if you took my car, leave yours here. Then go to Póvoa to meet Mario. I'll join you just after 2 o'clock outside the Grand Hotel. Wait for me in the park outside the hotel. I'll get a train there, it'll be quicker than driving." He paused to gauge the response from João. "Agreed?"

"If you say so, Harry, but for god's sake be careful."

"Leonid won't do anything until he gets my reply – then he'll wait for Monday."

"That may be true, but Dos Santos and this Kaufmann woman might not be so particular. We've still got to think of the possibility of Luis making a mess of everything. So don't take anything for granted."

~❖~

After Harry had delivered the reply, he caught a bus heading in the direction of Logan's address. The bus was full of women with shopping bags talking loudly and incessantly. He envied their absorption into each other's news and gossip. When the overcrowded bus finally arrived at the stop he wanted, he struggled to squeeze by two women who monopolised the exit. After polite requests and failed, he elbowed them out of his way. As he clambered onto the pavement, there was a chorus of abuse hurled in his direction through the open windows. It amused him and he waved.

Walking away from the main thoroughfare, he headed down a narrow dark side street. A young woman was scrubbing the ceramic tiles at the front of her house and singing a fado song to herself. He stopped and listened for a while, then asked the way to the Pensão Fernando. She brushed loose hair from her eyes, with the back of her arm, and smiled at him. She was tall and slim with golden tanned skin, so different from the women who had been on the bus whose skin was of a faded muddy brown complexion. Harry smiled back and repeated the question. She pointed along the road, telling him to turn left. She said that he would find it two houses further along on the left.

As she was directing him, an older woman obviously her mother, came out of the front door. She looked at Harry, then at the girl. Without waiting for any explanation, she gave the young woman a hard blow to the back of her head which sent her stumbling against the bucket of water. Harry stepped forward to intervene, then thought better of it. Instead, he hurried off in the direction she had told him to go. At all costs, he could not get involved and draw attention to himself.

The Pensão Fernando was one of the more undistinguished looking boarding houses that littered the back streets of Oporto. Harry wondered what had made Logan chose it. The outside was dilapidated and there was a strong smell of drains. As he entered, another smell hit him. It was a mixture of mustiness and diesel fuel. An old woman dressed in black sat in the corner of the entrance hall. She was reading a newspaper and toying with a huge bunch of keys that hung from a cord attached to her belt. She looked up at him questioningly.

"I've come to collect Mr Logan's things for him." Harry said simply.

"Logan?" She wrinkled up her nose and pulled a face. "Who is this Logan?"

"The Englishman in room nine."

"Ah yes! He didn't come back here last night." She coughed and her chest wheezed loudly.

"He's had to return home to London unexpectedly, so he asked me to collect his things for him." Harry said with total conviction.

"I can't let you into his room." She shook her head, as she said this.

"You don't need to; I've got his key." He dangled it in front of her. "He gave it to me yesterday. It's all right, you won't be blamed for anything."

"But I don't know who you are – you ..." She protested.

Harry pulled out several 100 Escudo notes from his wallet. He counted them out in front of her: "he gave me these to pay for the room till the end of next week. Since it's Friday, I'd say you were doing very well out of it."

The old woman grinned, showing a mouthful of decayed yellowing teeth, she reached out for the money and stuffed it inside her blouse. Then she coughed again and spat into a handkerchief before returning to her newspaper.

Harry went up the narrow staircase to the second floor. Room nine was at the far end of the corridor. The door was painted a dismal green and the number nine was painted on it in uneven strokes of black paint. Harry unlocked the door, closed it behind him and then locked it.

It was a small room with a wash basin in one corner, a heavy old-fashioned wardrobe in another and a matching chest of drawers and dressing table along another wall. The bed was large and draped with a spotless Portuguese linen bed cover. Harry sat on the bed and took stock of the room. Then he went over to the window and drew the thin cotton curtain, so that anyone in the house opposite could not observe him.

He opened the wardrobe. It was pathetically bare and for a moment Harry felt a surge of pity for the dead Logan and anger at the futility and brutality of his death. He took out a couple of pairs of trousers, a navy jacket, and some shirts. All of them were marked 'Logan' with name tape, so typical of a certain type of Englishman. Harry shook his head and mused. It was no wonder British espionage was in its present mess. He felt a surge of anger that Sir George and Sanctum didn't train their 'angels' better.

At the bottom of the wardrobe there was a pair of black shoes. He felt inside the shoes, inside the pockets and turn-ups of the trousers and the jacket. All he found was some small change, a couple of bus tickets and a comb. Next, he tried the chest of drawers, but again they only contained the expected neatly folded pants, pyjamas, and socks.

He stripped the bed and turned over the mattress. Nothing to be found. He took out the dressing-table drawers but still couldn't find what he was seeking. He looked under the bed pulling out a suitcase from beneath it. Inside, there was a handbook on Portugal with pencilled in comments, presumably Logan's own; there was a small shaving set.

Harry tried the lining of the suitcase, wondering if it was Monty who'd kitted it out. There didn't appear to be any hidden compartment but just to be sure, Harry stripped back the lining on the edge of the suitcase. It was bone fide, just what it seemed to be, a simple suitcase.

Harry surveyed the chaos he'd created; it had been a very tidy room. He looked at his watch and saw time was passing. He would need to hurry if he was to get to Póvoa at the arranged time. He began picking up the clothes and stuffing them inside the suitcase, feeling frustrated and angry. Finally, he picked up the shaver. He was about to toss it into the case when he realised it was a good deal heavier than he expected.

He sat down on the bed again and examined the shaver itself. Then he looked more closely at the case. Running his thumbnail along the metal strip that ran right around the base, he saw the bottom fall out effortlessly. The base of the case was hollow, inside was a tiny transmitter and a wafer-thin codebook. Either because it seemed so well hidden or because he was careless about such things, Logan had committed the unforgivable sin of leaving codebook and transmitter together; something that all agents were specifically ordered never to do. Harry shook his head with disbelief at his luck.

He scanned the little book and then smiled. One thing, he thought, could be said for Sanctum, that was they were nothing if not conservative in their methods. He was able to decipher the code Logan was using with ease.

He picked up the case and began tapping in a coded message. Since it was only a transmitter, he had no means of knowing whether the message had been received, so he repeated it once more as he had always done on operations. Then he closed the case and slipped the transmitter and codebook into his pocket.

A quarter of an hour later, Harry put the suitcase, containing Logan's clothes and spare shoes, on the pavement outside the apartment block. His action was deliberate and conspicuous. He was aware of the group of street urchins watching him. He turned and walked away from the case, for several paces, then looked up and down the street as if he were expecting someone. Out of the corner of his eye, he saw one of the boys creep stealthily towards the case, then make a sudden grab for it. The lad scampered off up a side street followed by the others whooping and yelling and running full pelt across the cobbles. Harry turned grinning to himself, as he watched the last of them disappear with their newly acquired treasure. They had served his purpose well.

At 2:30 precisely, Harry strolled along Póvoa's promenade opposite the inappropriately named Grand Hotel. He crossed over to the small park area that straddled the road and waited. Minutes later, João and Mario were with him.

"Nothing went wrong, João. I think I've taken care of Sanctum's anxieties for a while at least." João visibly relaxed.

"We've been looking round the area that Luis suggested for the handover period. It's a clever idea of his." Mario said. "We need to go back there with you, to show you exactly what the layout is like."

The little seaside town was crowded with holidaymakers. Music blared out from the strategically placed loudspeakers attached to the lamp posts. People sitting on the low seawall chatted happily above the racket being blasted out above their heads.

Everything seemed overpowering to Harry's ears and eyes. It took them some time to get to the quieter part of town. They reached the old fish market which lay between the centre of town and the sea. There were several stalls still with fish on them, even though the heat of the day had taken away their freshness. In the early morning, crushed ice cubes had been placed over them, but they had long since melted.

Some peasant women were bartering over the remains of the fish; their arms moving through the air in wild gesticulation. A few fishermen sat on the edge of the beach or on upturned rowboats mending nets and chatting. It was all so different from the scene, only a few hundred yards further back along the promenade, where tourists swigged their cocktails and children ate ice cream.

João picked up a dismal looking crab and asked the cost. He threw it back after the stall keeper gave, what he considered to be an extortionate price. There were more stalls selling shoes and belts. Another had on display garish ornaments including varying sizes of plaster figurines of the Portuguese cockerel. Yet another sold religious images, rosaries, candles, and statuettes of the Virgin Mary. There was a special section reserved for Our Lady of Fatima in her blue robes.

"They are already getting ready for the fiesta procession on Sunday." Mario said nodding over toward some of the houses behind the stalls. Harry turned and saw women and girls hanging up bunting; whilst others, who had houses with balconies, were busy decorating them with banners and streamers.

At last, they arrived at the small fishermen's church which would be the centre of attention on Sunday. It was a plain building, on the outside, with no spectacular stone carvings or a large ornate tower. The windows were unremarkable and the low terrace around it was almost drab. The terrace was enclosed, on three sides, by a low wall. The fourth side faced towards the fishermen's cottages and a small square.

"This is where the procession begins and ends." Mario pointed to the church door and a short flight of shallow steps leading down to the square. "They process around the town and return sometime later."

"There will be a crush of people on the day, many of them in a state of ecstacy." João said. "And over there," he pointed to the road along which they had walked. "There will be coaches, cars, stalls, and a great deal of pushing and shouting. An ideal place for Luis to merge back into the crowd and disappear."

João looked at the church, the streets and then back at the church: "Clever old sod! I'd never have given him credit to plan anything like this. Leonid would be amazed. That is, if he's not behind it. I'm not sure whether I could have chosen a better place and time!"

They sat down on the wall to consider their own strategy. Harry turned to look along the road, then across to the rows of small houses.

"Harry," Mario spoke quietly, "I've made arrangements to get the money. I'll bring it over to you and João tomorrow. We can pack it away then in a suitable bundle." He paused and chewed on his lip: "I just hope I can retrieve at least some of it when this is over. Lopes is becoming increasingly suspicious of me."

"I'm more than grateful for all you've done, Mario. Don't worry, if anything goes wrong, I'll do all I can to get London to put things straight with your senior officers. I'll leave a note for Sir George with João in case something happens to me." He held up his hand to stop either Mario or João interrupting him. "So, you'll be covered whatever the outcome. After all, this Lopes doesn't seem the best man for the job, a word to the right people will soon fix him."

"We need to discuss where we're going to position ourselves." João said impatiently. "All we know is that Luis said he'll bring Laura to the church when the procession returns. The only way into the church is that large wooden door." He pointed to it.

Harry got up and stood at the door, then he looked around: "Obviously, I'll have to stand somewhere about there," he pointed to an area almost adjacent to the door.

"Otherwise, Luis won't come forward. João, I'd like you nearby so you can get Laura to safety if things begin to go wrong. Mario, you say there'll be a very large crowd."

Mario joined them and looked around. "Yes, there will be hordes of people, both locals and holidaymakers."

"We can't afford to get separated. So, Mario, I think you'd better be positioned somewhere over there." Harry pointed to an area just beyond the square, in a direct line to the route the procession would take.

"What about getting away with your daughter if things get rough. We need some sort of escape route." Mario said.

"The streets will be too crowded for us to use a car, which would have been the obvious first choice." João said. "Using a boat might be possible. So, Mario, what do you think? Is a boat an option?"

"No good. We can't get one of the right type in the time we have available. Also, you'd be a sitting duck trying to get across to the beach. It would be asking for trouble."

They sat thinking for some time. Harry could imagine all sorts of things going wrong and was reluctant to put forward any ideas. For once, he felt stymied. He knew it was because Laura was at the centre of the operation. Anybody else and he would have had plans galore.

"I have a police informer," it was Mario who broke the silence. "He lives in a small cottage, just down that street." He pointed to it. "He gives me tipoffs about smuggling activity. I could ask him to give me the key to his place and make himself scarce for the day. It could provide us with a bolthole. What do you think?"

"Ideal!" Harry said with enthusiasm. "Do you think he'd agree to it?"

"For money, Fonseca will do anything." Mario, who had been sitting on the wall, swung his legs over and got up. "I'll go and see if he's there now. You two wait here, I shouldn't be long."

João and Harry watched Mario disappear into the dark narrow alley. They went inside the little church to get out of the heat. Although from the outside it looked drab and small, Harry was taken aback when he entered the building. It was full of larger-than-life wooden and moulded plaster statues of the Nossa Senhora, Angels and Jesus. Each was decked out with vividly coloured silks and velvets. Some appeared to be rising out of enormous clouds made from cotton wool and netting. Others were held in place by ironwork. All of them were standing on large wooden biers waiting to be lifted high on the shoulders of strong young men and carried around the town in glory.

Harry stared at each of them in turn. One particular statue of the Virgin seemed familiar to him. He drew closer trying to recall where he had seen the image before.

"That's Our Lady of Fatima." João said, noticing Harry's attention to the statue.

"Of course! How could I have forgotten! It's seeing her amidst all these others that confused me." He turned to João. "How is the Blue Army of Fatima, these days? Still striking fear into the Red Army?"

"Who knows." João said. "I think since Salazar went it's not been quite so active. But the Vatican is as cagey as the Kremlin about its activities. I sometimes wonder whether there is much to choose between the Soviet Red Army and this secretive Blue Army of Fatima. I know that's heresy to say so – but you and I know more than most about it."

"The Soviets were quite paranoid about the Blue Army." Harry said. "Several eminent philosophers were encouraged, by Moscow, to discredit the supposed revelations of Fatima. It's alleged that Andropov tried to get men infiltrating the ranks of the Blue Army by joining the Portuguese priesthood. Personally, I doubt that. I think he worked according to Tolstoy's adage that '*he who has learned to think, will find it hard to believe.*'"

"All I know, is that Salazar found the revelations of Fatima very useful. Very useful indeed! There was a saying, that he used three things to keep control of Portugal. They were: Fado, Football and Fatima!" João gave a wry laugh.

"Of course," Harry said, "they conveniently overlooked the Polícia Internacional e de Defesa do Estado – the dreaded PIDE. I suppose it would have spoilt the alliteration."

João pondered for a moment: "To the old guard like you and me and Leonid, despite the fact Caetano changed the PIDE name to DGS - the Direcção-Geral de Segurança - the new General Security Directorate is still run by the same type of men."

"Most of the PIDE's leaders must have retired or be very near to it now. One has to hope they didn't pass on their methods." Harry grimaced.

The sun dazzled their eyes, as they stepped out from the cool dark shade inside the church. They returned to where they had been sitting and waited. Mario walked over looking pleased with himself, some half an hour later.

"It's all fixed. Fonseca is going to give me his key tonight. I'll bring it over tomorrow. I'll get two extra ones cut, so we can each have one. Come with me and I'll show you exactly where the house is. Don't forget, that on Sunday it will take at least twice, or even three times as long, to get through here. But the crowd will provide some form of cover."

Mario led them across the tiny square and along the alley. The houses were typical fishermen's cottages. The informer's place was tucked away at the end of the street. Already, it had a festive appearance, women were polishing ceramic tiles and admiring their handiwork. Small girls were being fitted out for their costumes and some were parading up and down showing off to each other in brilliantly coloured frills and headdresses.

Harry and João noted the exact position of the house and then the three of them walked back towards the main streets of Póvoa. They went to a café bar and ordered a bottle of wine. They sat at a table on the pavement, watching the passers-by; each of them was feeling tense and apprehensive.

"Harry," Mario spoke hesitantly, "I have a man who works with me in the police here. I trust him completely. Do you think it might be helpful if I asked him to keep an eye on Luis for me? Luis wouldn't know him; he is new to this part of Portugal. He could carry a walkie-talkie and let us know when Luis is bringing your daughter to the church. It could be useful."

"No", Harry shook his head. "In theory it's a good idea. But don't forget Luis is going to be as edgy as hell. He'll be on the lookout for Leonid's people as well as for us. He'll be on high alert, and anything could push him into taking a false step. That could be disastrous for Laura. I can't risk it, Mario."

"He's right, Mario, Luis is not used to playing a double-blind game. He'll be jumpy as hell." João could see both their points of view but agreed more with Harry. "If anything, we need to bolster Luis's confidence."

CHAPTER 19
COUNTDOWN

Leonid watched Eduardo drive his battered old van to the front of the farmhouse and went out to meet him. They got on well. Eduardo had something about him that reminded Leonid of Batista. For his part, Eduardo liked the way Leonid treated him, with a degree of respect and encouragement.

"Well, is there a reply?" Leonid asked, leaning against the side of the van, trying not to show his eagerness to have the answer.

Eduardo slammed shut the van door and nodded. He held out the envelope. Leonid slit it open with his finger and read what Harry had to say. He smiled approvingly and, feeling satisfied with the response, put his arm around Eduardo's shoulders.

"Very good, Eduardo. We can take things easy for a while. Come and have a drink with me. Dos Santos is asleep, and Helga is instructing some new agent we've recruited."

They entered the farmhouse and went into the lounge where Leonid poured out two glasses of vodka. He handed one to Eduardo.

"Here's to success!" He said, downing it in one. Eduardo was more circumspect and drank slowly. "It's time we talked about what I have in mind for Monday." Leonid poured himself another glass. "I'd like to use your place as a rendezvous in the morning. We'll be bringing Randall's daughter with us. Then you and I and Helga will travel in your van, I think, into Oporto. Dos Santos can follow us in the Mercedes. When we get within sight of the bridge, we will park. I want you to take the woman by the arm and lead her, with me, towards Randall. Then I will tell him to come with us."

"Do you think he will?" Eduardo asked doubtfully.

"He adores his daughter and would do anything for her. He'll come all right."

"Then what?"

"You turn the woman round and take her back to the van. Helga will go with you. I will take Randall to the Mercedes and Dos Santos will drive us back here. You should drive just ahead of us, so that Randall can see the van." He stopped talking for a while, deep in thought. "I have a few things I want to do before Harry Randall is dealt with finally. But it should all go quite smoothly." He nodded in satisfaction.

"What about João and the other one, the policeman? They will be there, for sure."

"Harry Randall will signal them to stay out of it. He won't want his daughter's safety compromised."

"Ah! So that's what Dos Santos was telling Moscow, last night."

The words shot through Leonid like a bolt. He stopped his thoughts about the Monday triumph and stared hard at Eduardo: "Did Dos Santos radio Moscow last night?" Eduardo nodded not noticing the change in Leonid's attitude.

Crossing the room, Leonid went over to the window. He needed a moment to absorb the information and its implications. He had not been in his sort of work without developing a sense of paranoia. In recent weeks, he had felt there was a subtle change in Dos Santos' relationship with Helga.

He knew that she was scathing about his plans for Randall. He also knew she was exerting an increasingly powerful influence over Dos Santos. Now, with this unexpected news from Eduardo, he suspected there was plotting behind his back.

Leonid clicked his finger joints one after the other methodically, while he took stock of the situation. He was furious that anyone should dare to contact Moscow without asking his permission first.

He knew Helga had her own code to contact Malyshkin in a crisis, in the same way that Batista had always had his own code. But that code was only to be used if he, Leonid, were incapacitated in some way. Since Batista's death, he knew he had become somewhat distant from the field workers. Helga could well be exploiting that as well. He was well aware of her ambitions. It was time to remedy the situation, he turned back to Eduardo.

"Come, my friend, another drink." Eduardo smiled and handed him his glass. "You know," Leonid said, as he returned a full glass, "you know, Eduardo, I should like you and I to work together more closely. To be frank with you, I am not happy with the way things are being managed here in the North. As yet, I can't put my finger on why things are not progressing as they should. However, I have my suspicions. From now on, I'd like to think of you as my new eyes and ears. Do you understand?"

Eduardo listened intently. This could mean an opportunity for him. He might get his own back on the fat slob who constantly ordered him about and treated him like dirt. He nodded and grinned.

"That means, I want you to keep me informed about everything that's going on. Even about them." He indicated with his head the upstairs room where Dos Santos was sleeping and the back room from where Helga's voice could be heard."

Eduardo had been waiting for more action. This was what he thought the movement was about, a more dynamic approach. Of course, he knew about Leonid's relationship with Batista, and he guessed what else might be involved. But if that was a way to the top, then what the hell! So, he nodded again and smiled.

"Come over here again on Sunday, Eduardo. You can stay for lunch with the new agents. It will be useful for you to meet them. Afterwards, we can have a final briefing session on our plans for the Monday dénouement."

Leonid walked back to the van with him and waved as he drove away. It was the noise of the van's engine that woke Dos Santos from sleep. He dressed and came downstairs. When he entered the lounge, he saw Leonid reading the note.

Controlling his emotions, Leonid turned and waved the note at him. The expression on his face betrayed nothing of his inner turmoil. Dos Santos was relieved to note that Leonid seemed to be calm.

"See, it's arrived! We don't need to worry for the next couple of days, do we?" He paused and looked intently at him. "Nothing's been worrying you, has it, Esteban?" Leonid decided to give him the opportunity to explain his actions of the previous evening.

"Of course not," Dos Santos wiped away the sweat already running down his brow. "With you to guide us, I worry about nothing." He gave a weak smile, remembering the radio talk with Malyshkin and dreading the possibility of it being discovered.

For one fleeting moment, he wondered whether he should confess all to Leonid and about Helga's involvement. However, his mind was made up for him by Helga's sudden entry into the room.

~❖~

Luis sat alone in his tiny bedroom. He too had heard Eduardo's van leaving the courtyard. He had not been asleep like Dos Santos; his mind had been feverishly checking all the plans he had made. His main problem was to solve the issue of getting Laura away from the farm, without being seen. The next problem was to ensure they had a sufficient head start to make a clean getaway. He knew that Sunday mornings at the farm were usually busy. Leonid and Helga gave regular instruction sessions for new recruits and local agents. Often, Dos Santos helped out too.

Luis began crossing himself for luck, hoping that the same routine would hold good for this particular Sunday. Then he remembered the saying that Leonid had, time after time, tried to imprint on him: *'For a true Marxist, superstitious ritual is an indication of an uncivilised mind.'* But Luis decided, long ago, that if that was the case, he would have to live with the fact that he possessed an *'uncivilised mind'*.

He considered his plans with a growing sense of excitement. If it all went his way, then… But he dared not think too far ahead. He came to a decision that during the afternoon, he would walk to the village and catch a bus to Viana do Castelo. He thought he could borrow an old car from his friend, Marcello. He'd already planned where he would hide the car so that no one from the farm would find it. But again, the same problem raised its head and bothered him; how to get Laura to the car without being seen.

Luis went downstairs and passed the entrance to the lounge from where he heard voices. Helga and Dos Santos looked up but ignored him. There was not even a nod of recognition or civility. Even now, at this late stage, Luis thought that if they treated him as an equal, with some degree of respect like in the old days, he would give up his mad dash scheme. He would work with them for the good of the movement and the country. Then he would not have to risk all on a gamble with the Bayliss woman.

He caught sight of Dos Santos paring fingernails whilst sitting at the table. Luis noted with fury that Dos Santos was using his treasured knife! The knife he had always kept with him until it was taken from him. It reminded him, if he needed reminding, of all the slights he had suffered at Dos Santos' hands. No one had thought of his feelings then, as he lay bruised and bloodied on the ground. So, why should he now have any qualms or guilt? He walked out of the farmhouse and took the track towards the village.

Laura was standing near the tiny window that provided the limited supply of light into that hothouse of an attic room. Through the bars, she caught sight of Luis leaving. She saw him pause for a moment and look up at her window, then shuffle off out of sight. He was still limping from the beating Dos Santos had inflicted on him.

She no longer knew what time, nor even what day, it was. Like most prisoners kept on their own, for any degree of time, she had become almost totally self-absorbed. Anxiety for her children and her father had become secondary to anxiety for herself. Now everything she saw or heard had significance only in so far as it related to her. She watched Luis disappear, wondering whether his departure had anything to do with her. If, of course, she had known exactly what was going through his mind, her anxiety would have greatly increased.

She went back to the little bed and pondered what her father might do to get her out of this mess. She wondered whether Tom were with him and if the children had been sent home.

There was one thing about which she had made up her mind, during the long, lonely hours. On her return home, if she returned home, she would divorce Tom. She felt he was partly to blame for the situation she was in. He had become as infatuated with the German woman in the hotel as he had been with countless other women before her. The women flattered his ego.

Yes! She would divorce Tom and start life afresh. She would take the children with her to Devon and send them to a local school. None of this private school nonsense that Tom had insisted on. If Tom had his way, then both the children would be packed off to boarding school. The thought of life with just him made her feel sick. Yes! If she got out of this, she would begin to live the life she wanted.

Her daydreaming was interrupted by the sound of Helga's voice coming from downstairs. She sat up and tensed as she heard the clicking sound of Helga's heels coming up the stairs. The footsteps, however, did not approach her door. Instead, they disappeared somewhere down the corridor. Laura relaxed breathing a sigh of relief. Reality came flooding back: plans for her future were futile in the present situation.

Rumblings in her stomach told her that it was well past the time for the evening meal. However, Luis was not yet back from wherever he had gone and no one else bothered to bring her food.

In fact, Luis had for some time been struggling to camouflage the car he had successfully acquired from Marcello. Earlier, he had driven a quarter of a mile along the road leading to the farm. There he spotted the ideal place where the vehicle could be hidden.

There was a small track, just off the road, finishing in a dead end near some old vines. It seemed ideal. Luis reversed the car, with some difficulty, into the area so that he would be able to drive out again at speed. He got some sacking from the boot and placed it over the windows and headlights. He didn't want the sun to reflect off them and reveal its presence. He stood back and surveyed his handiwork and nodded feeling pleased, then he set off on foot back to the farm.

Helga caught sight of Luis ambling up the drive. She went to the door and yelled at him like some port fishwife. He pretended he hadn't heard.

"Where the hell have you been? We aren't running a holiday camp for your benefit, you old fool!" She grabbed his shoulder as he came into the kitchen. "That slut upstairs needs feeding, that's your job." She shook him vigorously.

Catherina was surprised at Luis's response, instead of snarling back, which was his usual reaction, he merely removed Helga's hand from his arm. Then he went over to the tray. Helga glowered at them both and left the kitchen slamming the door behind her.

"That bitch! I hate her!" Catherina said. "She threw a plate at me when she found you weren't back! I'm glad you arrived when you did, Luis. She has a temper that one, not at all like Leonid. Some comrade, she is!"

"Never mind, Catherina, life is hard for all of us." He picked up the tray and took it upstairs.

Laura was relieved to see it was Luis bringing the tray. She dreaded another visit from any of the others. He put the tray on the floor in front of her, then leaned forward and whispered quietly in her ear.

"If you are good, I think I can help you." He put his finger to his lips. "You must be quiet, no one must hear us. I am going to help you, do you understand? You have to trust me."

"Why should I trust you, it was you who kidnapped me." She replied quietly.

"You must, Mrs Bayliss, there's nothing else you can do. Either you take a chance on what I have to offer, or you take your death walk with Leonid on Monday" He put his grizzled old head on one side and peered at her. "You see, there is no real choice, is there? You must trust me." Again, he put his finger to his lips, grinned then left her.

As soon as the door closed behind him, Laura jumped up from the bed in a state of acute agitation. Her heart was pounding with excitement and apprehension at the same time. She walked around the room several times, before calming down. The uncertainty of everything alarmed her but at the same time, the old man's whisper had given her a possibility of hope. Any hope, however faint and however tinged with uncertainty, was better than total despair.

CHAPTER 20
POLICE HEADQUARTERS - PÓVOA DE VARZIM

Mario was aware Lopes was keeping a close eye on him. It had already caused him to delay collecting the dollars. For the third time that morning, he went back to the main office and typed additions to a particular report that Lopes insisted on having.

Lopes, for his part, was increasingly suspicious of Mario's behaviour, since he had been taken off the kidnap case. He never liked the young police officer considering him to be arrogant. Now, he wondered why Mario was collecting such a large number of dollar bills. He suspected it was somehow connected with the Englishwoman and he would not tolerate that.

So far, he had made no progress in finding the kidnapped Englishwoman, no progress at all. He blamed everyone around him for this fact. First, the stupid husband had been totally uncooperative and left the country without his knowledge or permission. Finally, there had been the ridiculous directive that he received from Oporto that the Press should be told absolutely nothing

In a fit of paranoia, he decided there was a plan afoot to thwart the upward trend in his career. Lopes took everything personally. He saw any lack of progress in the case not as an example of his own inferiority, but as malice and interference from those who envied his position in society.

Sitting at his large mahogany desk, he ordered his secretary to get him coffee and, when it came, drank it slowly and reflectively. He would investigate what this young policeman was up to.

Mario saw the coffee being taken into Lopes' office. It was then he decided to collect the dollars. He went quickly to the security section and was handed a brown paper package. He returned to his desk slipping the package into his briefcase. Half an hour later, when he was about to go off duty, he received a message to report to Lopes' office.

Mario cursed under his breath knowing he would be late for the meeting with Harry and João. Before going to Lopes, he went to the washroom, combed his hair, and straightened his jacket feeling it would give him a psychological boost over the pretentious little man who always looked uncomfortable in his uniform. However, it was with a degree of unease that he knocked on the door.

"Sir, you wanted to see me?"

"What are you up to? That's what I want to know." Lopes snapped.

"I'm sorry, sir, I don't understand." He was genuinely taken aback by the abruptness of Lopes' manner.

"The $50,000 that's what I'm talking about. A great deal of money. I asked myself, what sort of case would require that amount of money? I conclude it can only be a kidnap case. I'm right, aren't I?"

"No, sir, you are mistaken. You could conclude the money was to be used in a kidnap case. But in this instance, I'm investigating a drug smuggling case. The money is bait for a drug dealer. Drugs are big business, sir, in fact $50,000 is a small sum in comparison with other entrapments, as you well know."

"I don't need you to teach me my business!" Lopes was still acutely agitated. "Why this weekend?"

"I'm sorry, sir?"

"Why this weekend?"

"As you know, sir, it's the Feast of the Assumption and Póvoa will be packed with foreign visitors. My informant told me the money is needed this weekend, some Brazilians are…"

"Are you telling me the money has nothing to do with my case?" Lopes leaned forward endeavouring to intimidate Mario.

"Of course, sir, you took me off that case. I would never presume …"

"Don't tell me what I did! I took you off that case because you were arrogant and insubordinate and hindering our efforts. I said as much in a report I've sent to headquarters in Oporto. If I were to find out that you were using those dollars for any other purpose than what you have stipulated, I'll have you on a charge. Is that understood?"

"Understood, sir. May I go now?" Mario was increasingly irritated by Lopes' manner.

Lopes leaned back in his chair and dismissed Mario with a cursory wave of his hand. Mario felt like slamming the door, instead he swore to himself all the way down the corridor to his own desk.

To relieve the tension that had built up, Mario drove fast along the main road leading to Oporto. The road was relatively free of traffic, and he opened all the windows to let air rush through the car. By the time he reached the cathedral, he felt calmer. He arrived at João and Angelita's apartment and knocked on the door.

"Come, Mario," Angelita said as she ushered him in. "Join us in our meal. I saved food for you because I expected you earlier. I got a plate of spicy sausages, tomatoes and peppers and some freshly baked rolls."

They all sat around the small kitchen table. After a few moments, Mario told them about his interview with Lopes. Then he handed Harry the package of money.

"Are you sure Lopes is not up to anything more than just being suspicious?" Harry asked.

"No, I don't think it's more than that."

"He's not put a tail on you?" João asked.

"No, I checked for that, don't worry, that's not to say he won't. But I doubt it somehow. However, there is a chance that I'll be asked to report for duty somewhere that Lopes chooses tomorrow. We have to face that possibility, particularly since he is acting up so strangely. The excuse he'll use is that tomorrow will be a heavy day for the police." He paused again, "we ought to prepare and have alternative plans just in case it happens." He reached into his pocket and pulled out two keys. "Here, these are the spare keys for Fonseca's house where you will take Laura. One for each of you."

"Damn! It'll be a nuisance if you're assigned to some other part of town. We really need you near the church." Harry said.

"It will be like the old days, eh?" Angelita said, "you and João against the world." She laughed.

"They won't need to be on their own, Angelita, not this time. Even if I'm on duty, I'll be sure that I'm near the church at the right time."

"We can't let Luis get away with the dollars, Mario, not now with Lopes breathing down your neck." Harry said.

"We'll meet that problem when it comes." Mario said, "the first priority is to get your daughter to safety."

"Once we all get into this house, what then?" Angelita asked.

"'We', did you say? There's no way that you are..." Harry never finished the sentence.

"Yes, I am!" Angelita said thumping the table hard. "None of you has really thought this whole thing through, have you? At least not from my point of view." She raised her hand to stop any interruption. "Just think of it now – Luis leaves with Laura; Leonid must eventually discover they've gone – that stands to reason, doesn't it? What will he do, eh? He'll either come here himself or send one of his henchmen. Either way – I'm not going to be here when they come. Also, after it's all over, they will be out for our blood. So, I've planned already. When you leave tomorrow to go to Póvoa, then we all leave, and we don't come back."

"What!" Harry exclaimed, "do you mean you're leaving here?"

"Yes, I do mean that and before you go off into one of your long guilt-ridden speeches, let me tell you, Harry Randall, O Pescador, I for one will not be sorry to leave this," she looked around, "this hole! João and I deserve something better. We'll get that boarding-house of ours a little bit earlier, that's all."

She paused and looked sideways at João. "You know I am right. If this hadn't happened, we would have gone on for another couple of years saving a few thousand more escudos to get a better place. And what for? By then, my bones and joints will be rigid, and I won't be able to enjoy it. No! We all leave here tomorrow, and we don't come back. We go to stay with my sister and her husband. Then we get our new place."

Harry and Mario looked at João. He shrugged his shoulders and grunted: "she's right, of course. She usually is!"

"Well then, I suppose what we'll do, assuming all goes well, is to stay at Fonseca's house till evening. I've already deposited extra money in a bank account in Lisbon for you – João and Angelita. I thought it might come in handy sometime in the future. Now it looks as though you could use it a bit earlier."

"Harry…" João began but never finished.

"There's every need, so shut up! As for you, Mario, I hope to repay all you've done, in other ways. I still have important friends in the right places in Portugal. I think you know what I mean. In case things go wrong, I've already written a letter to Sir George Cattermole explaining the situation and your part in it. He'll see things are put right!"

"Harry, I didn't do it for glory. I am doing it because I believe in what we worked for in the old days. I am doing it because Leonid and his group can only cause Portugal great harm. But let's be positive, what will you do if all goes well?"

"Take Laura across the Spanish border, as soon as possible. I've got some spare papers for her, and I'll take the old Volkswagen."

They finished the meal and left Angelita to tidy up. They counted the dollars into 2 bundles of $25,000. Harry slipped elastic bands around each bundle then put them away in his briefcase.

"Of course," João suddenly said, "there is one thing that we were all rather taking for granted."

"What's that?" Mario asked as he finished counting out the last bundle.

"That Leonid and his bunch aren't going to find out about Luis's plan, sooner rather than later!"

"If that happens, my old friend, we'll need all the help that Nossa Senhora da Assunção and the Blue Army of Fatima can muster between them!" Harry said.

CHAPTER 21
LUIS GOES INTO ACTION

Luis hovered near Helga trying to find out whether the usual instruction session was to be held the next day. But nothing anyone said gave him any definite clue. One thing he did notice was the distinct coolness in Leonid's manner towards Helga. He found this both interesting and pleasing. Another thing he observed was that Dos Santos seemed to be avoiding both of them.

Luis rejoiced that all was not running smoothly. Firstly, it allowed him to come to terms more easily with his own rejection. Secondly, it could only help his plans. But try as he might, he could not find out what was happening on Sunday.

He took Laura's evening meal to her room and merely winked and nodded to her. The less she knew, he reasoned, the better it was. He had no idea of the tumult going through her mind.

Returning to the kitchen, he found Catherina on her own and washing up numerous dishes and glasses, once again. In a very untypical gesture, he picked up a drying cloth and set to helping her with the dishes. She smiled at him.

"What's that lot up to?" Luis asked her, indicating the lounge with a nod of his head.

"Planning their course for tomorrow, I think." Luis took a sharp intake of breath with relief, hearing Catherina's words. "Leonid wanted to cancel it, you know. He's so on edge about her upstairs. But that German woman said the real work had to continue. Leonid did not say anything else. You know what I think?" She asked. "I think Leonid is losing his grip on this setup. I think that bitch is trying to take over."

Luis wasn't really listening now to what she said. His relief knowing that the instruction course was still taking place had closed his mind to anything else.

"How many are coming tomorrow, do you know?" He asked.

"I got an order for five extra lunches. Since Eduardo is coming, that means there will be four new members. Not as many as usual."

He felt rather disappointed at such a small number. Frequently they had twice as many. The more people around he thought, the better it would be for him. It would be easier to get Laura away, if there were a lot of people keeping Leonid and the others occupied. They always played to the gallery. However, four was better than none. After the washing up was done, he sat in the corner eating his own meal. Catherina continued chattering away but he wasn't really listening.

He hoped he had thought of everything that he'd need: car, petrol, gun, ammunition, bag for the money. He mentally checked off the list. Then he sat back and relaxed, watching Catherina move gracefully around the room. He admired her long black hair as she shook it away from her face.

With a sudden start, he thought of Laura's blonde hair. He slapped his knees in annoyance at not having considered it before. She'd stand out with hair that colour, amid any Portuguese crowd. The one thing he didn't want was to attract any attention to him and Laura as they walked through the streets. He chewed his lip and pondered the situation.

"Catherina, do you ever wear a headscarf?" He asked.

"Yes, of course, when it is very hot, I always cover my hair. Why?"

"I'm meeting my niece tomorrow," Luis said casually, "I hoped to give her a little present. She wanted a scarf but," he tutted, "I forgot!"

"Luis, that's typical of men! A woman, now, she'd never forget something like that. I suppose what you're really saying is that you'd like to have one of mine to give her, eh?"

"Well," Luis paused, "I would be thankful, and I'll pay for it. I don't want it for nothing."

Catherina smiled and dried her hands on a towel. She pinched Luis's cheek and went out of the kitchen. He sat in the chair waiting for her return. After about five minutes, she came back with two scarves. One was white with blue squares on it; the other was black with small red dots.

"Here," she said, "which one would you like? I've never liked either of them very much, so I won't miss them."

"You're a good girl, one day I may be able to reward you." He picked up the black scarf and put his hand in his pocket to take out some money. She put her hand on his arm and shook her head.

Later as he lay on his bed upstairs, he wondered how easy it would be to persuade Laura to come with him. He worked out how they were to get out of the building. They'd use the enclosed staircase that ran from the landing right down to the top of the cellar. It was dark and steep, but its great advantage was that none of the others ever used it. In fact, he was sure they didn't even know it existed. The only one who might have noticed it was Dos Santos, but he was too fat to have ever forced his bulk inside the doorway. Once outside, Luis had planned exactly how they would make for the lane and reach the car. From then on, it would be easy.

Luis felt a growing sense of excitement and anticipation. He wished that Sunday had already arrived, and he was occupied with action. He swung himself from the bed and went to the door opening it a fraction. He could hear Leonid and Helga talking somewhere downstairs. What fools they'd feel tomorrow, he thought! And he chuckled to himself.

~✣~

Angelita spent the rest of the evening with João and Harry, sorting out the few possessions of worth that they had acquired over the years that they'd lived in the apartment. Most of their wealth had been secreted away in the form of gold chains and coins and kept at a bank in Lisbon, in case they had ever needed to leave in a hurry. Their everyday life had not been luxurious, in fact it was almost spartan. João filled three suitcases and some small crates. Harry looked around at the furniture.

"What about your table and chairs and …?" He asked.

"We leave them. In the ordinary run of events, we might have taken some furniture; but really none of it is worth much." João said. "We'll need to buy new things for the guesthouse and maybe we'll get better stuff than this."

"So, you see, Harry, we will be travelling light." Angelita said.

"The best way to travel. I wish Beth was as frugal. When we married, we inherited generations of clutter from her mother and grandmother. We've never been allowed to get rid of any of it." He turned away for a moment, cleared his throat, then looked back at them. "I don't want to get sentimental, and I know you don't, but I don't know how to thank you both for all that you've done for me. I don't know what I've ever done to deserve your loyalty and friendship."

"You did plenty for us in the past. Besides, Angelita and me we are a couple of old gypsies. We'll enjoy moving on. We are going on to something new, a fresh start for us both. Not often you get that chance, at our age." João said.

Angelita counted the cases and crates, then she piled a box on top of them: "take this lot out to the van tonight, while it's still dark." She nodded in agreement with herself. "Then tomorrow morning, when we leave, it will look as though we're just off for the day."

~✧~

Eduardo was standing in the shadows cast by the houses on the opposite side of the alley. He was puzzled watching Harry and João make three journeys to and from a smallish brown van. But the instructions he'd been given by Leonid, personally, were only to report back if and when Harry left Oporto. He observed that Harry returned to the apartment after a third and final trip. He waited for a full quarter of an hour. There was no more activity. Eduardo shrugged his shoulders and waited for his replacement to take over. He had plans for the evening and did not want them disrupted.

But by midnight, the replacement still hadn't arrived and Eduardo, never noted for his patience, left his position. He reasoned that nothing more would happen until later the next day. Besides, the party to which he had been invited had greater priority than monitoring a deserted street. He glanced back once at the lights in the apartment, then headed away from the Cathedral district.

From one of the rooms into which Eduardo had been trying to peer, Harry observed Eduardo's silhouette leave the doorway. He smiled, nodded, and then returned to his own affairs. He sat and carefully checked the guns and transmitters. He always enjoyed playing about with guns and these new models intrigued him. He reached inside the hidden compartment in his case and drew out an unopened packet; he unwrapped it and took out three silencers. Then he called João and Angelita and demonstrated the way the silencer could be fitted onto their guns.

"I've never used a silencer," Angelita said, "is it important for me to use one now?"

"I hope none of us needs to make use of the guns at all; but if we do, a silencer will be essential. Just think of the panic the sound of a shot would make in a large crowd. With these silencers, the only noise is a very quiet thud. It won't attract anyone's attention." Harry stifled a yawn.

"I think we should all go to bed; we need to be away from here early. Tomorrow, we need our wits about us." Angelita said, ushering João from Harry's room.

When he was alone, Harry collected his things together stuffing them unceremoniously into his case and holdall. He was restless and agitated in a way he had seldom felt in the past before going into action. It was the thought of Laura that had unnerved him. He promised himself that if they got out of this alive, he'd give Sanctum a piece of his mind They had allowed Leonid to develop the new network and have a virtually free run in Northern Portugal. The sudden remembrance of Sir George Cattermole and Sanctum stirred him into action.

Logan's transmitter and codebook were still in his jacket pocket. Harry checked the book, then punched in Logan's personal code number. He signalled a brief message to the effect that things were progressing well. When he'd given the message twice, he tore up the book and burnt it in the ashtray. Then he took the tiny transmitter apart and put it in his case. When Logan's body was eventually found, there would be no reasonable method of giving the exact time of his disappearance and death. Harry didn't want to be involved in any enquiry back home, so this would be the last recorded message from Logan.

CHAPTER 22
SUNDAY MORNING - PÓVOA DE VARZIM THE FEAST OF NOSSA SENHORA DA ASSUNÇÃO

Angelita woke before dawn, on the Sunday morning, the sun's rays had not yet spread across the city. She crept out of bed, not wishing to wake João, and going straight to the kitchen prepared a meal to take with them to eat during the day. She made a sign of the cross in front of the small statue of Our Lady that she kept in the corner by the door. Then, she lit a candle and for some minutes bowed her head in prayer. She didn't hear João come into the room.

"I don't think Nossa Senhora will be of much help today." He said rather scathingly. He had never been a believer and it was the one thing about Angelita that he couldn't understand. "Anyway, what are you asking her to do today?"

"I'm asking for her blessing on us, that's all. I'll feel happier knowing she's watching over us."

"Is Harry up yet?" João asked, as he sat down and poured himself a cup of coffee.

"I haven't seen him, but I heard him walking around the room in the early hours. When you finish your coffee, take this basket of food out to the van. Then come back and we'll have something to eat, then finish our business here."

Harry heard the voices and then João going out, so he went downstairs into the kitchen. Angelita was standing in the doorway holding a box.

"Harry, make yourself useful, take this to your car." She saw him look at it questioningly, "it's food for you and Laura. You'd also better take your case and things now. There is no one about, at this hour, so you won't be seen."

Returning to his room, Harry peered through the curtains. Angelita had been right, there was no one in the alley and no one observing from across the way. He was relieved and yet surprised at the slapdash way that Leonid had organised things. He packed his case and holdall and then took the box of food. As he was halfway along the alley, he saw João on his way back. They laughed when they saw each other.

"She's got us organised, that Angelita!" João said turning to walk along with Harry.

As they were returning to the apartment, they heard the phone ringing. João quickened his pace and then hesitated in front of the phone.

"It could be Mario," Harry said anxiously, "you'd better answer."

"Harry? João?" Mario had started speaking as soon as the receiver was lifted. "It's me Mario, look I haven't got long, say something will you?"

"What's happening? Are we still meeting at the house …?" João's voice sounded anxious.

"I've not got much time – but it's just as I thought, Lopes has put me on duty today. A special request from him! I've arranged to be posted in the square by the church. Unfortunately, I'll be in uniform, so can't come over to you. But if you need help, at any time, make contact. Okay? I must go, I just wish us all good luck."

"It's what he thought might happen, Lopes has put him on duty today." João looked anxiously at Harry. "Fortunately, he's managed to arrange things so that he'll be near the church. Remember, Angelita, if anything goes wrong for us, you're to call Mario on the watch."

Half an hour later, as the pale-yellow rays of early morning sun streaked across the orange rooftops of Oporto, Angelita closed the apartment door for the last time. There was no fuss, no turning round for a last look, just a quiet acceptance that this was the end of one part of their lives. Harry said nothing but admired the way Angelita walked along the alley with her head held high and looking straight ahead.

The three stood by João's old van and arranged to meet at the house in Póvoa. João was to take the route through Matosinhos and the port area of Leixões. Harry would drive through the Via Norte.

João and Angelita set off and Harry watched them go. When they were no longer in sight, he doubled back the way they had come and installed himself in a doorway some distance from the apartment. He glanced at the time and waited.

Half an hour later than the usual schedule, one of Leonid's 'watchers' took up his position, after having looked around for Eduardo's non-existent night replacement. Harry saw him take out a pocket walkie-talkie and call someone. He was relieved to see that the man nodded and smiled then settled down for what would prove to be a long fruitless wait. Harry turned and carefully retraced his steps back to his car.

By noon, they were all installed in the small house near the church in Póvoa. For Harry, João and Angelita the countdown to Laura's ransom had already begun.

~❖~

Despite great attempts at self-control, Leonid found himself becoming increasingly irritated by Helga. What he perceived as her arrogance in front of the four new recruits galled him. He had not been able to sit right through her cliché riddled talk on Marxist philosophy. The turning point in his tolerance came when he heard her say:

"The people is that sole and inexhaustible source of energy that can turn the possible into the necessary and dreams into reality."

He waited for her to acknowledge Maxim Gorky as the originator of the quotation. But she didn't. Instead, he watched in astonishment, as two of the new recruits, obviously assuming the statement to be hers, clapped enthusiastically. Without saying anything, he got up and left the room.

He found Dos Santos in the lounge, checking through the notes for his own talk, which he was to give in the afternoon. "Tell me honestly, Esteban, what do you think of our Comrade Kaufmann?" Leonid looked at him closely, as he asked the question.

"Think about her?" Dos Santos said in a tone of alarm. "What do you mean?"

"Do you think she is a person with great leadership potential?"

"Oh, I suppose you could say that. Not," he added quickly, "that she could approach anywhere near your own tremendous experience and high standards of leadership."

Leonid smiled, wondering what would be said about him to Helga. One thing he knew was that Dos Santos could always be relied on to say exactly what he thought you wanted to hear.

"What are you going to talk about this afternoon?" Leonid asked.

"Helga asked me to discuss the quotation from Lenin: *'only a Socialist Alliance of the working people, of all countries, can remove all grounds for national persecution and strife.'*" He smiled with satisfaction that he remembered it. "I thought that was a good idea. She said that this particular group of new recruits would find it inspiring."

Too late, Dos Santos realised, as he spoke, that he had been stupid to mention that Helga had suggested the title of his talk. He noticed Leonid's brows knit and a look of disgust cross his face.

"Since when has Comrade Kaufmann been the main adviser here, Esteban? If you decide you want a change in the programme, you should always discuss it with me first. I had given you another title." He paused. "Remember she is only a trainee, whatever she may imply. Some of her ideas are dangerously innovative. I don't think that Malyshkin approves." He studied Dos Santos closely. "You don't want to become too closely identified with someone, Esteban, until they've proven themselves. It would be as well to remember that. It could have serious consequences for you!"

The door of the lounge opened, and Helga walked in together with the new recruits. She was laughing and talking loudly, her face flushed with exhilaration.

"We have just finished, Comrade Paustovsky. I wondered whether you wanted to say any more to the group, before lunch?"

"No, I don't think so, thank you, Comrade Kaufmann." Leonid said coldly. "But possibly, the new recruits would like to ask me some questions. I'm certain they would like to know more about the network I have built up here and throughout the Peninsular, during the last few years."

Helga sensed she was being reminded of her junior role in the whole organisation. But she was buoyed up by a mood of confidence in her own ability and a feeling that

Leonid was reaching the end of his period of domination. Throwing caution to the wind, she smirked at the group of four young men.

"I think I covered the interesting historical details sufficiently, didn't I?" They murmured amongst themselves and nodded vigorously in agreement with what she had said.

Leonid laughed and walked over to the little group. He was physically much more imposing than any of them. Whatever else he might or might not have possessed, Leonid knew he could sway the opinions of any group, if he put his mind to it. For the first time since Pedro Batista's death, he felt the challenge to prove himself. He would not allow this upstart German cow to get the better of him!

"The rather inexperienced young lady calls it 'history', comrades, but let me tell you that as Leo Tolstoy said: *'the purpose of history is to know the movement of mankind.'* And, my friends, you and I are in the very process of helping that movement take place."

The small group gathered around him, and Helga found herself removed from the centre, until she was not involved at all. She watched them become engrossed in all that Leonid said. His voice, recently so quiet and dull, had taken on its old vigour. He gesticulated as he illustrated the points he was making. Leonid felt his old powers and enthusiasm returning, as the group responded warmly to him.

Just before they all sat down to lunch, Leonid glanced at Helga and indicated she should sit at the far end of the table, well away from her usual seat. She accepted the suggestion, without demure, although inwardly seething with irritation. It was obvious to her now, she would have to take more active steps to ensure Leonid's plans would go awry. She would no longer allow time to take its own course.

~❖~

Much to Catherina's amusement, Luis fussed around the kitchen like a mother hen. At last, he collected Laura's tray and put the plate of food on it.

"Let me take it up for you, Luis. I know you need to get away to meet your niece, today." Catherina smiled at him.

"No, Catherina, that is kind of you, but you have enough to do today." He picked up the tray.

"Eduardo phoned to say he won't be here till much later. So that will be one less meal to trundle in." Catherina seemed pleased.

"What!" Luis was alarmed to think that Eduardo might arrive just as he was taking Laura away. "How late will he be?"

"I'm not sure, but he said he'll be here in time for the afternoon session. Now get along with you, or you'll miss your niece."

Luis hastened upstairs into Laura's room. He locked the door behind him and handed her the tray. He told her to start eating, then he sat down to think about the situation. If he left now, and the meal hadn't started in the dining room, then someone might still be roaming around the grounds. If, on the other hand, he waited too long he ran the risk of bumping into Eduardo. He rubbed his hand across the stubble on his chin and peered closely at Laura.

"Let me look at you, stand up!" He said rather brusquely.

She stood up, uncertain what he wanted to see. He looked at her for some time, then grunted and put his hand in his pocket. He pulled out from his pocket the black scarf with red dots that Catherina had given him and tossed it over to her.

"Put it on your hair."

"Why?" She asked, as she tied it under her chin.

"Leave the 'whys' to me." He snapped. His heart was pounding, and he felt in a very precarious state. When he saw the way she was tying the scarf, he shook her arm. "No! No! Not like that, behind your ears." He took it from her and tied it gypsy fashion in the way Portuguese country women usually wore their scarves.

He stood back and looked at her again. Her hair, which had gone lank and greasy during her incarceration, was almost covered. But he noticed several strands of blonde hair hung below the scarf.

He stepped forward and pulled the scarf off roughly. Then he took a pair of scissors out of his pocket. He'd had the presence of mind to take Catherina's scissors that morning, thinking he might need them. Laura backed away, as he reached out and pulled her towards him.

"Look, you fool, you want to get out of here, don't you? It's the deadline tomorrow! So today is your last chance. Don't you understand, you've got to do what I say? I need to cut your hair, so it won't show from under the scarf. That's all." He began hacking at her hair. "Anyone would think you didn't want to see your father today."

"What?" Laura gasped and tried to turn her head.

"Keep still, you want your eyes out? I'm taking you to your father. We leave here in just a few minutes, while the others are eating. I've got everything arranged – no trouble – but you must do as you're told, otherwise you'll get us both killed."

When he'd finished chopping her hair, she tied the scarf as he wanted it. She saw that he was shaking. The thought of trusting herself to him horrified her, but she had no other option. She watched as he went to the door, unlock it, and listen. She too could hear the sounds from downstairs.

He beckoned for her to go behind him. Laura crossed the room and followed him through the door. He locked it behind them putting the key in his pocket. They tip-toed quietly along the short distance of corridor that separated the room from the small door inset into the wall. A loose board creaked, and they both froze. Luis felt along the plaster and found the edge of the door. It was so camouflaged by flaking paint and dust Laura would never have noticed it. He took a small key from his pocket and unlocked it. The door opened onto a small landing and a very narrow winding staircase which was in total darkness. Luis pushed her onto the landing, then guided her onto the first step.

"Stand still, while I lock it again." He whispered. "If you move, you'll fall headlong downstairs."

Luis peered out of the door then, grunting to himself, carefully closed it behind him. Once inside and on the landing, he took a torch from his pocket pointing its beams beyond Laura and down the flight of steps. They were almost as steep as a ladder. Laura turned round and began descending backwards, ship style. Luis grunted approval and followed in the same way.

At the bottom of the flight of steps, there was a small level landing with two doors leading off it. Luis squeezed past her and unlocked the door on the right. Instantly, daylight streamed in causing them both to blink. He closed the door until only a thin ray of light came through. Then slowly he opened it wider so their eyes could adjust to the change of light. He put his finger to his lips, urging silence. Then he went out through the door leaving her alone. After a minute or two, he returned, and taking her firmly by the arm led her out into the courtyard backing onto the farmhouse.

"We move fast, eh?" He whispered, she nodded. "We go over there to the vineyard, then cross quickly to the small path. You stop for nothing, okay?" Laura nodded again, feeling a mixture of bewilderment, excitement and fear.

They crossed the courtyard surprisingly quickly and were soon amongst the overgrown untended vines. At least there they were provided with cover from anyone who might look out of the farmhouse windows. Luis looked back and saw Catherina at the kitchen sink, but she did not look up.

They skirted round the vineyard; Luis pointed to the little footpath ahead of them. It was now overgrown with weeds, but at one time it had been a wide path leading to the next vineyard. In the years before the farm had become merely a headquarters for Leonid's activities, the vines had been productive. The grape pickers had crossed from one set of vines to another by the same route making a good path for themselves. Now all that remained was this single track which, unless you knew of its existence, could easily be overlooked.

The sun was rising higher, and the path was steep. It was exhausting making their way to where the car was hidden. At last, Luis pointed proudly ahead of them. Laura peered in the direction in which he pointed and made out a car resembling an old derelict heap. On closer inspection, she saw that there was a heavy layer of sacking which gave the vehicle such a poor appearance.

Luis urged her to hurry, as they tore away the sacking, stuffing it into the car boot. Despite the covers, the inside of the car felt like a furnace. The air was stifling, and the old plastic covered seats were almost too hot to sit on.

Fifteen minutes later, they were on the main road to Póvoa. Luis grasped the steering wheel hard and peered through the windscreen with concentration. They had gone quite some distance and he was beginning to feel easier when as they rounded one of the sharp bends, a van careered wildly towards them in the middle-of-the-road. Luis swung the steering-wheel and swerved to avoid a collision.

The van hurtled along, scraping its wing and doors against the boulders at the side of the road. Luis stopped the car and got out, shaking his fist, just as the van driver turned to look back. It was then that Luis recognised Eduardo.

Visibly shaken by the near miss, Eduardo stopped further along the road, to examine the damage to the van. He then got back in and drove off. It was only later that morning, he remembered it was Luis who had been driving the other vehicle. He had not seen Laura.

"Shit!" Luis shouted, as he speeded up towards the little seaside town. "That was one of Leonid's men. Do you think he saw you?"

"I don't know. I was too scared even to notice him." Laura replied, nervously aware of the implications for them both, if she had been recognised.

"We'll have to hurry. Your father is meeting me outside the church in about two hours' time. I hope he has the money."

"Money? What money?" She looked at him. It had not occurred to her that Luis was doing this for any other reason than that he felt sorry for her.

"My money, Mrs Bayliss. The dollars to pay for your ransom." He grinned and then laughed. "You don't think I would go to all this trouble and risk having my throat cut for love of you and your father?"

CHAPTER 23
THE FARMHOUSE - SUNDAY LUNCH

Eduardo arrived at the farm quite sometime later. The incident had shaken him, and he took the rest of the journey extremely slowly. He parked the van at the side of the farmhouse then glanced at his watch. He saw it was almost an hour later than he had arranged with Leonid. He entered the room, just as they were finishing their meal.

Leonid rose and greeted him warmly, telling him to sit down and wait while he said goodbye to the new recruits. Eduardo sank into an armchair and relaxed. Helga and Dos Santos were both quiet. Eduardo thought Helga looked distinctly sulky.

When he had seen the recruits off, Leonid returned and poured a drink for Eduardo.

"Drink up, we've saved some food for you." He noticed that Eduardo was much paler and quieter than usual. "What's wrong? You don't seem to be yourself."

"Wrong!" Eduardo took a long swig of his wine. "I nearly didn't make it here at all! That old fool, Luis!" Dos Santos looked up. "He damn near killed me just now. Almost ran me off the road."

"What with?" Dos Santos laughed, "that old bike of his? You must have been hallucinating, my friend, Luis is upstairs. Also, he never drives, he hasn't got a car and I never let him use one of ours."

"I tell you," Eduardo said, feeling offended. "I saw Luis driving a battered old car. He was going hell for leather along the road to Póvoa."

"Catherina!" Dos Santos shouted.

Hearing her name, Catherina went quickly into the lounge. She'd already been shouted at by Helga twice that morning, so the thought of further rows made her move faster than usual.

"Catherina, tell Eduardo that Luis is upstairs, will you? Or better still go and fetch him. Maybe it's only the sight of him that will convince him."

She stood there without saying anything for a few moments. She knew quite well that Luis was not upstairs. And although she would have liked to cover for him, she was too afraid of Helga to risk being caught out.

"Luis isn't here at the moment, Mr Dos Santos." She said timidly.

Leonid was irritated by the whole situation. He felt it was time to put an end to it all.

"It looks, Esteban, that if Eduardo says he saw Luis, then I'm sure that he did. What's so strange about that?"

"I've told you; Luis no longer has access to a car." Dos Santos was now curious to know more about Luis' whereabouts. "Where has he gone, Catherina?"

"He was going to take his niece out for the afternoon." She explained.

"His niece!" Dos Santos was surprised. "What niece? His family haven't had anything to do with him for years. So where did this niece suddenly come from?"

"Well," Eduardo paused. "Come to think of it - I seem to recall he did have a woman in the car with him." He suddenly remembered the sight of two heads as the car sped fast up the road. "I thought, at the time, I didn't envy her the trip to town!"

For some reason, he wasn't sure why, Leonid began to feel uneasy. He had always possessed an uncanny knack for sensing trouble before it struck. In the past, it got him out of several nasty incidents. Now, he felt the same sensation.

"Helga, go and fetch the Bayliss woman." He ordered, without looking at her.

"Catherina, do what Comrade Paustovsky said, will you? Fetch the woman down here and …" Helga was interrupted by Leonid roughly seizing her arm and jerking her to her feet.

"I don't think you heard me clearly, Comrade Kaufmann. I said you were to get Mrs Bayliss. Didn't I hear you teaching the recruits today that when an order is given it must be obeyed immediately." He spoke with heavy sarcasm, and she felt humiliated in front of the others.

Helga climbed the stairs, still smarting from the way Leonid had spoken to her. She thought perhaps she had gone too far during the last few weeks in her attempts to outdo him. Now, as she went to fetch Laura, she regretted the rift that had grown between them. She knew that with all the power in his hands, it would not end well for her.

She blamed Laura for the situation and determined to pay her back. Arriving at the door, she looked around for the key. It wasn't in the lock as had been the custom. She went to the top of the stairs and called out: "Catherina, bring me up the key."

"Which key?" Catherina asked.

"The key to this door up here." Helga was irritated by the question. "Hurry up, get on with it."

"I don't have the key. Luis was the last one to go up there, before lunch. He must have left it there."

Leonid, hearing the conversation, didn't wait for anymore. He bounded up the stairs two at a time. Pushing Helga to one side, he banged loudly on the door calling Laura's name. There was no response. He pushed the door and tried to butt it down. The door did not budge. He drew his gun and shot away the lock. The door swung wide open, and he ran in closely followed by Helga.

It was all too apparent that his fears had been justified, the room was empty. For a moment, he stood there quite rigid with anger and frustration. Then he turned Helga and struck her hard with the back of his hand. She was the nearest object on which to vent his frustration.

"You stupid bitch! I told you to look after her, didn't I? It's time you learned to take orders. Once this is over, I shall have you sent back to Moscow for retraining." He pushed her roughly aside and ran downstairs.

"Eduardo, in which direction was Luis was driving?" He asked.

"Towards Póvoa, but he could have been heading directly for Oporto."

"How long ago was this?" Leonid put his hand on Eduardo's shoulder.

"Oh, a good half to three-quarters of an hour ago, I think."

Leonid went over to the window and thought for a while. His mind was racing. He bellowed for Helga and Dos Santos to return to the lounge. They followed anxiously, perturbed by his sudden swing in mood.

"We'll all travel together in the Mercedes. I'll drive." Leonid said, as he checked his gun then crossed over to the cupboard for extra ammunition. "Have you all got guns, silencers and ammunition?" Dos Santos and Helga nodded and were sent to fetch their equipment. "What have you got?" Leonid asked Eduardo.

"My old Colt. It always served me well, so I don't need another one."

Catherina watched; she was anxious that her comment about Luis had caused this sudden flurry of activity. She regretted having said anything. It would certainly not end well.

Eduardo sat in the front of the Mercedes with Leonid, leaving Helga and Dos Santos at the back. For the first few miles, Leonid drove extremely fast. The road was quiet and there was little traffic. However, as they drew nearer to Póvoa, there were not only more cars and donkey carts but coaches as well.

Because the road was winding, it became almost impossible to overtake. Leonid grew impatient and, at one point, pressed his hand on the car's loud horn, then accelerated into the oncoming traffic. In the manoeuvre, the Mercedes overtook several carts and cars causing oncoming vehicles to swerve or stop. Helga and Dos Santos looked at each other in alarm, but Eduardo was evidently enjoying it. Eventually, they reached the outskirts of the town.

"Why the hell is there so much traffic?" Leonid asked in frustration.

"It's the big feast day." Eduardo said. "Don't you remember, it's the Feast of Nossa Senhora da Assunção? Tourists flock here to gather at the little church of the fishermen, as do all the locals and those from surrounding areas. It's quite a day of celebration."

Driving had almost become impossible again. There were endless streams of traffic all heading for the promenade and the route of the procession. The large sleek Mercedes was forced to crawl its way along the dusty streets.

"I'll turn off inland – there's no point in all this!" Leonid said angrily. "It's obvious Luis must have been heading for Oporto to meet Randall." He jammed the car into gear and, despite hooting and shouting from onlookers, reversed along the street.

Suddenly, Eduardo put his hand on Leonid's arm and pointed towards a battered old car, untidily parked halfway up the pavement. Its rear wheel was flat.

"Wait! Stop, Leonid! That's Luis' vehicle." He pointed excitedly towards it. "That's the one Luis was driving, I'm sure. I had a look at it when we both stopped. It's got a large dent in the front panel, see?" He pointed again at the car.

"There must be hundreds of cars like that around here." Leonid said as he pulled in close to the side of the road. He peered at the car, "are you sure, Eduardo?"

"Quite sure."

"All battered cars look the same. They are all dirty and dented." Helga interrupted. "How can you be so certain?"

"I am certain. I know my cars!" Eduardo, who was by now very excited, was adamant.

"Anyway," Helga persisted, "what would he be doing with the Bayliss woman in a place like this?"

Leonid's mind raced through all the possible reasons for Luis to take Laura from the farm. The one thing that kept occurring to him was that he intended to kill her. Perhaps, he had already done so and was now trying to escape. If that were the case, pursuit was pointless. If, on the other hand, she was still alive, then it was vital they track him down immediately.

After some minutes, another thought occurred to him. There was the possibility that Luis was, in fact, doing some sort of a deal with Randall. Leonid tapped his fingers up and down the steering column. None of the others said anything. They waited for him to come to a decision.

"This would be the ideal place for a handover to Randall, wouldn't you agree, Eduardo? Plenty of people, roads jammed full of traffic – a dream of a place for a ransom to take place." He turned and looked at Dos Santos. "Well, Esteban, what about the 'silly old man', now? I have a feeling, and I'm seldom wrong, that the 'silly old man' is about to try to double cross us all."

"Surely …" Helga began but was silenced by Leonid raising his hand to silence her.

"We have no other choice. If Eduardo says that is the car, then that is the car. We search for them among the crowds here. We fan out, Helga you take the beach side of the promenade. Esteban, you take the road that runs parallel to the promenade. Eduardo, you head straight for the market area. Look around amongst the groups of people that will be there."

He opened the car door and peered around. "I will take the opposite side of the promenade, Helga. We will all meet up at the market, in three quarters of an hour. If you see Luis and the woman, then tackle him and bring her straight back to me. I still want her in one piece. If you must shoot, use the silencers on the guns. We cannot afford to attract attention."

Leonid waited until the other three had gone, then he too made his way through the bustling roads. Music blared out from the loudspeakers, and he marvelled at the way a religious occasion turned into nothing more than a grand fairground spectacle. An old woman stopped him and held up a string of medallions of the 'Nossa Senhora' urging him to buy one for good fortune. He pushed her roughly aside, frowning to himself as she cursed him.

As he jostled his way through the throng, he remembered how Pedro Batista had always bought medallions whenever he was stopped in the streets. No amount of lecturing on the evils of superstition would cure him.

Leonid wondered whether Batista had ever really been a committed Marxist or whether it was his love for him that had been the most important factor in his life. He decided that it really didn't matter at all. If Pedro Batista could only walk down the street towards him now, then he wouldn't have cared if he'd been wearing the robes of a priest. Just so long as it was Pedro Batista coming towards him.

CHAPTER 24
DENOUEMENT

About a quarter of a mile from where Leonid was thrusting his way through the crowds, Harry and João were standing inside the little church dedicated to the fishermen of Póvoa. The church itself was packed with people singing a hymn of praise to Nossa Senhora. The air was laden with clouds of sweet-smelling incense. Already, the heavy wooden biers, each with a different Madonna, had been lifted onto the sturdy shoulders of young men and were swaying rhythmically towards the door. The procession was about to begin.

Harry and João stepped outside and watched as the first of the statues came out. It was carried by eight strong men and their gait caused the statue itself to sway precariously in time with their slow march. At least six more statues made their way down towards the tiny square. Interwoven between each statue came groups of singing, chanting children. A rather tinny brass band made up of young men and boys marched ahead of some cadets. Despite the heat, dust, and noise, it was a rather splendid affair. Under normal circumstances, Harry would have enjoyed it. As it was, he was sweating not from the sun's heat but from anxiety.

Mario stood at the far side of the square. He had already established contact with João and Harry. Now he smiled as Angelita, sitting on the low wall near the church, waved to him. She was the only one of the three who did not know who she was looking for. She had seen a photograph of Laura, but she suspected she'd never recognise her from it. Also, it was years since she had last seen Luis and she had no idea what he would look like now. In some ways, hers was the most difficult task, the others at least could be occupied, she just had to wait until something happened, some sign was given - and that could be at any time.

Harry scanned each possible face in the crowd until they all melted into a shapeless unrecognisable mass. He felt for the gun in his shoulder holster and checked the ammunition in his pocket, as if they were worry beads. João was carrying the packets of money.

"He did say he'd bring her here when the procession returned, didn't he?" João asked.

"Yes, he did. But he'll have to get within range of us, long before then. With a crowd this size, he'll need to be in the vicinity before the procession begins to turn the final corner and come along the stretch of promenade. If he hasn't planned for that, then we are all in trouble!"

~❖~

As it happened, Harry need not have worried about Luis' foresight. At that very moment, he was with Laura at the far end of the fish market. Because it was the special Feast Day, the stalls contained souvenirs instead of fish. However, the smell of fish still pervaded the air and made Laura feel sick. Luis was beginning to feel anxious himself. He had anticipated a big crowd but not realised it would be quite so large.

He was forced to push his way roughly through the groups of good-natured people eager to see the statues. Laura was also a drag on him. Days of captivity and poor diet had made her weak and he dreaded the prospect of her fainting. Eventually, he negotiated their way through the throngs around the stalls of drink sellers and ice cream vendors until they reached the square near the church.

Luis immediately spotted Harry and João since they were on the raised level. It was like looking up at a stage. He smiled at his own brilliance and at the way the plan was now working exactly as he had known it would.

"We stay here, Mrs Bayliss, we wait here until the procession returns."

~❖~

Eduardo waited for the others outside the market; one by one they returned looking hot and flustered. There had been no sighting of Luis or the woman.

"If you are going to hand someone over, Eduardo, in all this mass of people, where would you choose?" Leonid asked.

"I remember you gave a talk about this sort of thing when I first joined. You said somewhere where one could slip away easily. On a day like this feast day, I would want to mingle with the crowd. I suppose somewhere where there was a big distraction." Eduardo said.

"Exactly!" Leonid put an arm around Eduardo's shoulders. "It's a pity that your two colleagues here don't have the same degree of insight. When this is all over, my friend, I want you to move to the farm and take over control of the field operations." He looked pointedly at Helga who turned away. "I think we should all move now to just such a place as Eduardo has described – the church of the fishermen."

Leonid walked ahead shoulder to shoulder with Eduardo. Dos Santos waited for Helga to join him, and they walked together. He said nothing, he could see, just by looking at the expression on her face, she would not welcome conversation. Helga was at some stage of tumult that would not take kindly to a word of comfort, he guessed.

They walked in silence a pace or two behind the others. Though Helga said nothing, her mind was actively considering the implications for her future of all that Leonid had said during the last couple of days. It was not to her advantage that he should be successful today.

~✦~

Mario spotted Luis and Laura at exactly the same time as he heard the returning procession and its band. Goose flesh crept up and down his neck, as he recognised them. He pressed the winder on the watch, then the button, and began speaking urgently.

"Hey! It's Luis! Turn to your left, Harry. Don't you look too, João, we don't want to make it obvious." He saw Harry's eyes scanning the crowd without fixing on Luis. "To your left and downwards. He's about five feet from the wall. Can you see him now?"

"Yes!" Harry held his breath. "Yes, I see them, Mario. Come over here by us."

Harry saw Luis struggling through the crowds, as they pressed closer to the church. Each person was seeking a good vantage point. He saw that Laura was pale and listless. He would hardly have recognised her in the heavy black linen dress and drab headscarf. But it was Laura!

"They're here, they're here, João. Look!" He pointed towards Luis. "Give Angelita a call and tell her exactly where to look. I'm going to move nearer the church door. I'll take the packets of money. Give me a little time, then move to the opposite side. Okay?"

João nodded and waited for Harry to move away before he contacted Angelita. When she knew where to look, she turned and peered out into the sea of faces. João had described the headscarf that Laura was wearing. She saw it, and then the figure of Luis beside her. Now that action could only be minutes away, she stood up and followed in the direction that Harry and João were heading.

~❖~

Leonid and Eduardo approached the widest part of the route taken by the returning procession. Bunting and banners flapped everywhere and the noise coming from the band jarred on Leonid's ears. He watched the enormous statues swaying ever closer to him, with each sway there came a creaking noise. At each sway, there was a sharp intake of breath from the eight bearers of the large heavy statues.

He looked up at the smiling faces of the Madonnas with the too perfect babylike features and fixed smiles. These statues represented all that he detested and despised about religion. Their theatricality played on the superstitious fears of the people. Yet, to his mind, it offered them nothing but bondage in this life with a promise of paradise after death. He turned to look at Helga and read from the expression on her face that she was just as bewildered by the whole affair.

In fact, Helga had never experienced anything like it before. Of course, she had read about such processions and seen films of them. But they had been a pale shadow of the reality that now surrounded her. The heat, dust, smell, and the noise served to exaggerate every aspect of the procession and the giant Madonnas added a further dimension of unreality.

A loud cracking sound came from the sky and, as one, the whole crowd looked up. Some children pointed to small plumes of white smoke that showered from where a large firework had recently exploded. Looking out across the bay, Leonid saw a fishing boat with some men on it lighting fireworks at intervals.

~❖~

Luis made his way to the church with Laura close behind him. She didn't recognise her father immediately, he looked like any of the other men standing near the church. His face was unshaven, and his pale linen jacket and faded trousers were so unlike what he wore at home.

Harry looked at her and smiled encouragingly but did not reach out for her at once. Luis released her arm and eagerly grabbed at the small packets being held out to him. Laura crossed to her father and hugged him, sobbing with relief.

It was precisely at the moment when Luis took the packets that Dos Santos caught sight of him. He gave a hoarse shout and ran forward, followed by Eduardo and Leonid. Leonid seized Dos Santos and pulled him back, not understanding why he was rushing suddenly running.

"What is it? Have you seen Luis?" He hissed sharply.

"Yes, yes! There!" He pointed towards Luis and Harry as the exchange took place.

"He's mine! Leave him to me, just give me cover!" Leonid did not wait to see the impact of his instructions. Instead, he surged forward through the crowd.

Eduardo paused not wanting a confrontation on the steps of the church. Instead, he sidestepped to the back and mingled with the crowd. He had decided from the start, that he would wait to see how things turned out, before risking himself too much.

Helga quickened her footsteps and followed in the wake of Dos Santos and Leonid. Her thoughts were not with Luis or Laura or Randall. Her thoughts were fixed on Leonid. She had to see what would happen.

Dos Santos was concerned with just one thing and that was to get even with Luis. He would punish him for having made him look a fool. As for Laura and Randall – they were Leonid's business. As he followed, he stumbled wildly over the wheels of a pushchair being wheeled along by a young mother eager to see the procession.

João caught sight of a stir amongst the crowds. He saw the fat body of Dos Santos as it flayed about wildly in the dust. It was then that he saw the speed with which Leonid was approaching. Instantly, he lunged forward pushing Laura and Harry to the ground.

"Harry, it's Leonid! For God's sake get out of here. He's got a gun."

Laura didn't know who João was, her first thought was that he must be one of Leonid's men. So, when he tried to drag her to one side of the church, she resisted violently.

"Go with him, Laura, he's my friend!" Harry pushed her towards João.

Luis, seeing Laura disappear into the surging crowd with João, drew his gun and pointed it at Harry. Alarm and fear contorted his face. Had he been duped, after all?

"Get going, Luis. Leonid is here! Run, you fool!" Harry shouted as he ducked behind the cover given by the open church door, crouching low.

Harry realised he was trapped. There was no way for him to escape from the area surrounding the church. He glanced towards the square and saw with relief that João had handed Laura to Angelita. The two women were now almost within reach of safety. His own plight seemed inconsequential, now he had achieved what he had set out to do.

The waiting crowd were now in a state of ecstasy as they awaited the arrival of the first Nossa Senhora swaying hypnotically along the beach road and beginning to turn towards the square. Luis, terrified for his life, ran heedlessly into the crowd gripping his precious packages of dollars.

Dos Santos and Helga saw him at the same time and despite herself, Helga gave chase with Dos Santos. She had already lost sight of Leonid amidst the crowd.

Luis turned and saw Dos Santos bearing down on him fast. He hesitated for a moment, before drawing his gun and aiming it at Dos Santos' chest. Seeing the danger, Dos Santos ducked with surprising agility and the bullet tore into Helga's arm. She gasped with pain as blood began oozing through her fingers. She had had enough. She turned away and, with little sign of pain or emotion, walked back towards the road and the Mercedes.

Unlike the others, Luis had no silencer on his gun. Yet, to his surprise, the sound of the shot caused no panic amongst the people. As he fired, yet another firework exploded high in the blue sky above their heads, muffling the gunshot.

Luis began running into the network of small streets that led to the square. He was breathless and terrified. Now he knew that what he could expect was no mere reprimand or beating, it was death. He ran stumbling across the uneven cobbles and turned to see Dos Santos lumbering after him.

There was a doorway nearby, half covered by a large crimson drape hanging from an overhead balcony. Thinking quickly, Luis ducked into the doorway and waited, his finger pressed firmly against the trigger of the gun. He heard Dos Santos panting and lumbering along. He heard him draw closer and saw his feet and legs as they passed the doorway.

Luis stepped out from behind the drape and fired twice. The fat man grunted falling face forwards onto the street. A little girl screamed, and a group of women fled in terror away from the body. Luis turned Dos Santos over and fumbled inside his jacket to find his knife. Then he spotted the hilt above Dos Santos' belt. It was with satisfaction that he drew out the knife and stood there admiring it. Mario watched from across the street, then slowly stepped forward and put his hand on Luis' shoulder.

"I'll have the package and the gun, Luis." He said, as the old man turned to look at him. Part of him felt sorry for Luis. But he did need those fake dollars back.

"I knew it was too good to last. I've never been the lucky one." Luis shrugged his shoulders, as Mario fitted handcuffs on him and led him towards the Police Station. The arrest would annoy Lopes intensely. But that, Mario decided, was his problem. He left Leonid to Harry, once he saw João take Laura away.

"At least you had your own back on that old devil, Dos Santos!" Mario said. "I saw, it was self-defence. We'll see if we can get you a shorter sentence than you really deserve."

"What would I have done with all that money, eh?" Luis said wryly.

~❖~

Leonid had seen Harry pull Laura away from Luis. He saw Dos Santos and Helga pursue Luis into the crowd. Cautiously, he ran around the side of the church. He came closer, under cover of one of the large Madonnas as it was slowly borne towards the church.

Harry and Leonid saw each other at exactly the same moment, over the heads of the crowd. Like two old matadors confronting the last bull, they each waited for the other's next move. Quite suddenly, they were distracted by a group of brightly dressed children singing their way in procession and passing between them.

Harry saw the gun in Leonid's hands and prayed he wouldn't shoot while the children were in the line of fire. Our Lady of Fatima's statue, seemingly suspended above the cotton wool clouds and pink flowers, swayed precariously up the slope leading towards the church door.

For one moment, Leonid took his eyes off Harry, as the statue creaked. Seizing his opportunity, Harry took aim and fired. The bullet grazed Leonid's shoulder, causing him to stagger. Two of the pallbearers of one of the Nossa Senhoras, on the side nearest to him, heard him groan and saw blood spurt from the wound. In shock, they stumbled and lost their footing on the uneven ground. The statue creaked and its full weight was thrown unevenly to one side.

The crowd, standing next to Leonid, watched in horror. Then they hastily retreated, as the Madonna began to tumble in what seemed slow motion. Leonid, usually so alert, was dazed with pain and fury. He looked up and saw the smiling Madonna falling towards him. He tried to shield himself, but his raised arm could not stop the full weight of the statue as it crushed him to the ground.

Harry didn't wait to see any more. His one urge was to be with Laura. He ran from the church, across the square, and to Fonseca's little house where João, Angelita and Laura were waiting.

Eduardo having observed everything that had happened, watched Harry go. Then twirling the keys to the Mercedes, that Leonid had given him when he had parked, he turned away. He walked back along the road. Some half an hour later, in silence, he drove Helga back to the farmhouse. It was empty now save for Catherina.

When they arrived, Helga got Catherina to tend to her arm. After an hour when she had thought carefully what she would do next, she went to Leonid's room. She opened the cupboard and took out his personal radio equipment. Carefully, she tuned in to the Lubyanka wavelength. It took the radio operator in Moscow a short time to call Malyshkin to the control room.

"Comrade Malyshkin ... I have something to report."

EPILOGUE

It was a drizzling, slightly misty morning in early September outside the small chapel at West Norwood Cemetery and Crematorium. The vicar had conducted the service and Logan's coffin had slid through the doors into oblivion.

Sir George Cattermole, Harry Randall and two of Logan's rather distant cousins had been in attendance. Afterwards, there were brief conversations in which the usual things said at cremations were said. Sir George confirmed that all the expenses had been paid. There was no cost to the cousins who could now dispose of Logan's London flat and divide the spoils between them. Then quite satisfied, the cousins went off to the local pub to drink to him. But more likely, Harry thought, to drink to the unexpected windfall from the sale of Logan's nice little flat on the South Bank.

"Come back with me, Harry. The car is waiting over there." Sir George pointed to a large black saloon with darkened glass.

"I don't …" Harry began.

"Not a request, Harry..."

The car was driven smoothly up Brixton Hill, passed The Oval, then across Vauxhall Bridge. As it reached the northern end of the bridge, Sir George tapped on the glass partition and spoke through his intercom to the chauffeur.

"Drop us off here, will you. Then drive back to Sanctum. I'll walk from here." He opened the car door and beckoned to Harry.

The Embankment was quiet, Big Ben rang out three o'clock. The nearby pigeons rose, as one, into the air. Sir George had not spoken to Harry during the entire journey. For his part, Harry was disinclined to have a conversation. He had found Logan's funeral a painful and sad affair.

"So, Randall, what has been the upshot for your family after this Portuguese fiasco?" Sir George asked.

"It's been a difficult time, Sir George, as you can imagine. Laura was quite traumatised by the whole thing. She's in the process of divorcing her husband, asking for custody of the children and is dead set on moving to Devon. God knows why she wants to go there." In fact, he had guessed why, but was not inclined to discuss it with anyone outside the family.

"And you, Harry Randall, what did you have planned for yourself?"

"Nothing more than to go back to the desk job. I think I've …"

"You did, did you! Well, you can bloody well think again!" Sir George both looked and sounded angry. Harry knew better than to comment.

"After the fiasco … and it was a bloody fiasco! You are going back into the field to put things right!"

"But …"

"Shut up, Harry! Leonid Paustovsky is in hospital in Moscow! Malyshkin has put this bloody Kaufmann woman in charge of the Portuguese section of the Peninsular. There's some bloke called Eduardo Monteiro who's her righthand man. She is running rings around our lot! You owe me, Harry! You damned well owe me!"

Harry winced at the prospect. He had seen a delightful winter lying ahead of him. A 9am-5pm job at his desk four days a week and a 9-1pm on a Friday. Then a lovely long weekend.

The idea of being back in Lisbon or Oporto was not appealing. Although … although the temptation of getting even with this Kaufmann woman might just …

"I set things right for that Mario chap of yours." Sir George Cattermole sounded miffed. "Lopes was sent off to front a small station somewhere near Braganza – wherever that is! Mario is now in charge of the Oporto region. Well deserved, from what I read in your report."

"And what about the old ruffian, Luis?" Harry was intrigued to know. Laura had told him how Luis had smuggled her out of the farmhouse.

"Well, it seems that Dos Santos fellow survived, and he is being charged with various things. So, there was no murder charge against this Luis bloke. Your Mario spoke up for him surprisingly. He's just got two years in prison. Since the Kaufmann woman and Eduardo Monteiro were not directly involved in your daughter's kidnap – they seem to have got off Scot free. So, Harry, you bloody owe me!"

They walked towards the Houses of Parliament. The Thames was running high, and its waters lapped at the Embankment wall. Harry went over and leaned against it, peering into the dark murky water. He wondered what João was doing. Had Angelita found their guesthouse? Would João come back for one more push to get Portugal onto an even keel?

"Harry! Once more, this is not a request, old boy! You have no alternative, I'm afraid. You can have between now and January to get yourself organised – but the New Year sees you in Lisbon in charge of the office there. Of course, you'll be going up to Oporto and down to Faro." He didn't look at Harry but stared out across the river towards Lambeth Palace.

Harry wondered what he would tell his wife. Then smiled to himself knowing she would be quite relieved to have the house to herself again.

That evening when everyone had gone to bed. Harry drank a glass of Glenfiddich slowly, savouring the taste. Then he picked up the phone in his study. He hesitated for a second, then dialled.

"*Olá,* João , como vai ..."

Printed in Great Britain
by Amazon

48730152R00155